PRAISE FOR
DEATH, LIES, AND APPLE PIES
AND THE TORI MIRACLE MYSTERY SERIES

"Tori Miracle is a fresh and appealing amateur sleuth who charms you, then pulls you through the dark caves and sinister streets of Lickin Creek. Delighted with her company, you willingly follow along!"
—Sister Carol Anne O'Marie,
author of *Murder in Ordinary Time*

"Malmont does a fine job of creating atmosphere . . . and Tori makes a resourceful heroine."
—*Roanoke Times and World-News*

"HIGHLY ENTERTAINING . . . Tori is an engaging, believable character."
—*I Love a Mystery*

"Likable, eccentric characters, frothy hullabaloo, and humorous situations."
—*Library Journal*

"A CLEVER MYSTERY . . . Loads of eccentric characters provide a pile of suspects in this funny mystery with its share of suspenseful moments."
—*MLB News*

"A BREEZY, WELL-PLOTTED COZY."
—*Publishers Weekly*

"There's something for every cozy reader in this delightful tale—cats, dogs, cooking, romance—and they're tied together with a fine story and engaging characters."
—*Meritorious Mysteries*

DELL BOOKS by Valerie S. Malmont

Death, Lies, and Apple Pies

Death Pays the Rose Rent

A Tori Miracle Mystery

DEATH, LIES, AND APPLE PIES

VALERIE S. MALMONT

A Dell Book

Published by
Dell Publishing
a division of
Bantam Doubleday Dell Publishing Group, Inc.
1540 Broadway
New York, New York 10036

This book is a work of fiction. Names, characters, places, and incidents either are products of the author's imagination or are used fictitiously. Any resemblance to actual events or locales or persons, living or dead, is entirely coincidental.

ISBN: 0-440-22634-1

Reprinted by arrangement with Simon & Schuster

Printed in the United States of America

Published simultaneously in Canada

January 1999

10 9 8 7 6 5 4 3 2
WCD

This book is dedicated with love and gratitude
to my husband, Bruce Malmont,
and to Ruth Harrison,
M. Joan H. Juttner, M.D., and Helen O. Platt.
I couldn't have done it without you.

Chapter 1

Saturday Morning

My day began in New York with such bright promise. From nine to eleven I had a book signing scheduled at Books and More Books, Inc., in midtown Manhattan, and after that I was to fly to the tiny borough of Lickin Creek, Pennsylvania, for a week's vacation.

For breakfast, I cleaned out the avocado-green refrigerator and ate the last slice of cold pizza and drank flat Coke while sitting on the brown sofa with bright orange flowers I'd picked up for a song at the Salvation Army Thrift Store. I looked around me, taking in the grim apartment from the black and gray tiles on the floor of the living room–kitchen combination to the shabby blue velour recliner in front of my TV. As usual, my home-sweet-home was cluttered with books and papers, which were piled up everywhere and anywhere there was a flat surface. I'd been here, in this third-floor walk-up in Hell's Kitchen, for nearly ten years. How had that happened? I'd only planned to be here a couple of years after college—just until I won my first Pulitzer.

It was time, then, to go. I began hauling my stuff

down the dark stairwell. Dark because the landlord had given up replacing the burnt-out lightbulbs since the new ones were stolen immediately. I was out of breath by the end of the second trip, and I still had more to bring down. I vowed, once more, to start my diet tomorrow.

At the door, Sarge, the homeless man who'd been living on the front stoop ever since I could remember, handed me a couple of letters and a catalogue. I handed him a buck in return. He tipped his army camouflage cap and asked, "Where you off to?"

"Right now, I'm going to a bookstore to sign copies of my book. I'd like to drum up a little interest in it before it goes out of print."

"I keep telling you—you ought to write my story. It'd be a best-seller, for sure. I can tell you things about the CIA you never dreamed of. Why in Nam once—"

I interrupted his familiar story. "After that, I'm leaving for Pennsylvania for a week—be sure to give my mail to Murray. Could you flag down a cab for me while I get the rest of my stuff?" Because I planned to leave directly for the airport from the bookstore, I had to take a taxi I could ill afford. Along with my brand-new felt-tipped pen for autographing copies of my book, *The Mark Twain Horror House*, I had with me my new suitcase (new to me, if not the Goodwill store), my cats, Fred and Noel, in hard plastic carrying cases, their litter boxes in a grocery sack, a bag of litter, a larger bag of Tasty Tabby Treats, and that last of the dinosaurs: my portable typewriter.

Displayed in a neat pyramid in the front window of the Midtown bookstore were twenty copies of the *The Mark Twain Horror House*, godawful cover and all, depicting a gorgeous young maiden, scantily clad in a flowing white nightgown, fleeing from a Gothic mansion. What did people think, I wondered, when they read the book and discovered it was about a New York brownstone without a maiden in sight? And there was a large picture of me there, too. Tori Miracle, overweight author with a bad haircut. That'd pull the people in, for sure.

Inside the small store, near the doorway, stood a card table, flanked with potted palms, with more books stacked on it in three uneven piles. On another card table were a glass bowl full of red punch with lime sherbet floating in it and an aluminum tray stacked high with bakery cookies. I smiled at Elisa DeCaprio, the owner of the shop. Life was good!

Elisa suggested I put the cats and their belongings in the storeroom. After I got them settled, I squeezed past the palms, sat on the metal folding chair, and took my new pen from my purse.

"I liked your book," Elisa said. "Sort of a cross between H. P. Lovecraft and Oliver Onions."

I chose to take it as a compliment.

We chatted for the first hour and ate about half the cookies. At last, the little bell over the front door signaled the arrival of the day's first customer. Self-consciously, I touched my hair, trying to smooth it into the short, sleek, sophisticated Liza Minnelli–style hairdo I'd paid for. As usual, it had resisted the best efforts of the stylist and snapped back into a mess of black poodle curls as soon as I'd left his salon. That was yesterday. Today was worse.

False alarm—mailman. Elisa exchanged one pile of envelopes for another, and he left with a cheery wave in my direction. Elisa went behind the counter, where I could hear her ripping open envelopes, unfolding papers, and occasionally groaning. Bills—I recognized her anguish.

I had a cup of punch—not too bad—and balanced my checkbook.

Next in was a kid so young she should have had a truant officer on her tail. She glanced at me with little interest, bought a copy of *The Prophet*, and left.

I ate some more cookies and read three chapters of the summer's number-one best-seller. The sherbet in the punch bowl had turned into a pea-green foam resembling something I'd once seen along the tide line on the Jersey shore, when two women entered and headed directly for the refreshment table. I beamed at them encouragingly. To my surprise, they went in together and bought one book, which I signed, "To Bess and Lorraine, Best Wishes, Tori Miracle."

"It's Lorrayne with a *y*," one of them said. I slipped the book under the table and signed another. What were the chances that I'd ever find another Bess and Lorraine with an *i* to sell that book to?

During the next hour, we sold two more books as well as the best-seller I'd been reading. At eleven, the door tinkled open and my neighbor, Murray Rosenbaum, the "Nearly World Famous Actor/Italian Waiter," entered.

"I borrowed a car to take you to the airport," he said.

"Bless you." Murray was my best friend in New York. The kind of person who's always there when you need a friend, but who doesn't push himself on you when you want to be alone.

I gave Elisa a good-bye hug and assured her that I

didn't feel bad at all about the poor turnout. I hoped my smile wasn't as insincere as my statement.

Murray placed the cat carriers in the backseat of the 1964 Cadillac convertible he'd borrowed from a fellow actor. I dropped my suitcase in the trunk. "Not a real great day, I take it," Murray said with a kind smile, as he attempted to start the car.

I had to struggle to hold back tears. "It's an author's worst nightmare. You hold a book signing and only your mother shows up. Only as you know, in my case, my mother can't go anywhere."

"How's she doing?" The engine finally coughed on.

"No change. I went to D.C. about six weeks ago to see her. Same old thing, tall and thin, blond, patrician, impeccably made up, the consummate diplomat's wife. She thought I was the British ambassador coming for tea."

"I'm sorry. But try to cheer up. Things will get better for you, Tori. You're a good writer. Readers will find you."

"They'd better find me pretty soon, Murray. As usual, I'm down to my last nickel. If it wasn't for that series of articles I'm writing for *American Scenes* magazine, I'd be sharing the front stoop with Sarge."

"You could consider some economizing. Like giving up cable, for one."

"No way. I'd go crazy without old movies to watch. Did you catch *The Hideous Sun Demon* last night? It's the ultimate anti-sunbathing movie."

We had the top down to enjoy the glorious September morning. It was absolutely the best kind of day: sunny, but not too hot; the kind of day that recalled memories of good times gone by and hinted at more to come.

The car was the size of a small yacht, but Murray negotiated the busy streets with surprising skill, considering he hardly ever drove in New York. "So you're going back to that odd little town in Pennsylvania. May I assume the attraction this time is your long-distance boyfriend, that good-looking policeman with the odd name of Garnet?"

I felt the flush creep into my cheeks. I knew I shouldn't have worn a jacket on a hot day like this. "I guess you could say that. He's got the week off, and since we've only had two weekends together since I met him in July, it seemed like a good opportunity to get to know each other better. And, of course, there's Alice-Ann. I haven't seen her since July. Besides," I babbled on, "all that wonderful fresh country air is so good for the cats."

Murray had a funny little smile on his face, one I'd never seen before. "I have an uncomfortable feeling about this, Tori. Like maybe you'll get there and decide to stay. I don't know what living in New York would be like without you."

"Cut it out, friend. I'll only be away for a week. Don't forget to water Charlotte, the spider plant, and make sure the stove from hell isn't leaking gas again. I'll be back before you know it."

I didn't think it necessary to mention I was hesitant about getting into another serious relationship too quickly. Having been dumped twice, I wasn't anxious to repeat the experience.

I hoped that taking a break from the city would recharge my battery; I really needed to get started on the outline for my second book, tentatively titled *The Thomas Edison Horror Machine*, based on this past summer's events in Lickin Creek. And, I had to admit,

I was very eager to spend some real time with Garnet, since we'd only begun to get acquainted. The two occasions he'd been able to leave his one-and-a-half-man police force unattended had been wonderful but all too short. We'd met in July when I'd gone to Lickin Creek to visit my best friend from college, Alice-Ann, and her then-husband, Richard MacKinstrie. While I was there, Richard had been murdered, and during the investigation I'd met the town's sexy, intelligent, well-educated, witty, and sometimes obnoxiously macho police chief, Garnet Gochenauer.

Murray hugged me at JFK as if he really did believe he'd never see me again. I boarded the little commuter plane, took my seat next to the window, and prayed the cats would be okay in the baggage hold. A few minutes later, we were skimming the tops of the skyscrapers. I clutched the armrest nervously, and looked to my seat companion for consolation, but he reclined his seat, and a moment later little, soft, cigar-scented puff-puff-puffs of air erupted rhythmically from his slack lips. I envied him. Flying, to me, is about as pleasant as a trip to the dentist. I could never relax on a plane. Unfortunately, bus service had been discontinued into Garnet's hometown, leaving access only by plane or car.

We were out of the city now. Floating high above the lush gold and green farmlands of central Pennsylvania. The flat fields soon gave way to softly verdant hills that quickly changed into mountains. I held my breath as we crested a peak. I was positive I heard the airplane scrape an evergreen tree. We crossed several mountain ranges before the plane began its circular descent into the secluded valley where Lickin Creek was located. Lickin Creek, Pennsylvania—a little

Brigadoon of a town, nestled in a quiet valley—where nothing ever changed. Where hardly anyone ever visited, and people rarely left. I experienced an odd sensation in the pit of my stomach. What was it? Motion sickness? That same feeling I always got when coming home after a long time away.

A bump, the screech of brakes, and we were on the tarmac of the Lickin Creek Regional Airport. The door was opened, and the few passengers filed out.

A small crowd stood at the foot of the wobbly steps. I spotted Garnet Gochenauer immediately, and my heart skipped a beat. He wore a white cotton shirt with a badge pinned on the pocket and navy blue uniform trousers. An enormous bouquet of red roses was cradled in his arms, and his blue eyes were warm with welcome. I rushed down the steps into his muscular embrace. It felt wonderful to lean against his sturdy body and smell the familiar, spicy scent of his aftershave.

After a few happy minutes, we broke apart, grinned at each other, and went to retrieve my baggage. "All this?" he asked, surveying the pile.

I looked it over. "Seem to be missing the cat food. Oh, there it is."

Loud yowls from the cat carriers proved that Fred and Noel had survived the journey. Garnet took off his hat and scratched his sandy brown hair, which, as usual, was a little too long. "I didn't know you'd be bringing the cats, Tori."

"Is it a problem?" I asked, innocently.

"No, I don't think so. At least, not if they get along with German shepherds."

He led the way to the baby-blue police cruiser with the magnetic sign on the door that said LCPD. Garnet told me once that the department couldn't paint its decal on the car because it was on loan from the local Ford dealer.

We got into the front seat, and he turned and kissed me with a passion that had me tingling all the way down to my toes. "Mmmm, you taste good," he murmured into my ear.

"It's the pepperoni pizza I had for breakfast."

He threw his head back and laughed.

It was good to be with him again!

As we rattled along the brick-paved street toward downtown, I sighed with pleasure as I saw the familiar sights. At the square, Garnet paused at the town's only traffic light, and I took in the courthouse, the library in the old post office building, the Old Lickin Creek National Bank, and the drugstore with the ancient orange-and-blue Rexall sign over the door. All the charming pre–Civil War buildings were painted in soft pastels. Sparkling water sprayed from the fountain in the center of the square. And the fountain's base was surrounded with pots of golden chrysanthemums, courtesy of the Lickin Creek Garden Club, according to the large sign stuck in the grass. I smiled. I really did feel as though I'd come home.

We bumped over the railroad tracks and crossed a single-lane limestone bridge, with badly scarred sides, which arched the Lickin Creek. That was where the town's illustrious founder had fallen in and decided to build a town rather than fix his broken wagon wheel. Heck, if I had a flat tire in the middle of nowhere I'd probably do the same thing. There was supposed to be a historic marker, but all I could see were trees and overgrown underbrush.

The sky was a bright, crisp, azure blue with only a hint of a cloud overhead, and the mountains that rimmed the valley were softened by an amethyst haze. I reached out to touch Garnet's hand. "I'm glad to be here," I said.

"I'm glad you're here." He squeezed my fingers and left his hand where it was.

We seemed to be driving away from town. Before I could ask him where we were going, Garnet turned the car into a long, unpaved driveway, which wound through a pasture full of cows. The drive itself was bordered with three flimsy strands of wire that didn't look as if they could hold in anything, much less a herd of huge black-and-white animals. "Where are we?" I asked, not recognizing any of this.

"Foor's Dairy. The Foors loan their pasture to the borough each year for the Apple Butter Festival. There's someone special waiting for you here."

"Alice-Ann? I wondered why she hadn't met me at the airport."

Garnet grinned. "She's been roped into being in charge of the festival. Couldn't get away, so she asked me to bring you by."

The cows lined up in a row to watch us drive past. "What are they doing?" I asked.

"Just being cows. They're even more curious than cats."

"There's nothing more curious than a cat," I protested.

Garnet parked beside a long, unpainted, concrete-block building. On its corrugated tin roof stood a life-size, plastic black-and-white cow with a sign hanging from its neck that said FOO S DAI Y. We got out, and I inhaled deeply, looking forward to my first breath of fresh country air. "My word," I said, startled. "What's that smell?"

Garnet stuck his nose up in the air and sniffed once or twice as if he hadn't noticed anything amiss. "It's a dairy, Tori. You'll get used to it. Don't let me forget to pick up some ice cream before we leave. Greta asked me to bring some home for dinner tonight."

"Are we going out to her farm?" I tried to hide my disappointment. I'd only met Garnet's widowed sister once and liked her a lot, but I'd thought we'd be alone our first night.

After a telling pause, Garnet said, "I guess I didn't mention it. Greta moved in with me a couple of weeks ago." He smiled apologetically. "Said she'd been lonely out at the farm since Lucky died. Needed to get herself pulled back together. I sure hope it's only temporary. She's practically taken over my house."

My gloom must have showed in my face, for he said, "But it'll be all right. It's a big house, and she's involved with dozens of projects that take her out. We'll have plenty of time to be together."

If he took my silence to mean disapproval, he was right. But for the time being I forgot about Greta, for just then, across the lumpy field, I spotted a tall figure in jeans and a white T-shirt, with streaky blond hair blowing about her face, talking to a small group of people.

"Alice-Ann!" I called, running toward my oldest and dearest friend. We did that silly dance good women friends do when they haven't seen each other in a while. We fluttered our hands, we jumped up and down, and we hugged, which meant my nose was buried deep in her bosom. Alice-Ann stood five-eleven, a good ten inches taller than me. We finally parted and said the usual things: "You look great" and "You haven't changed a bit."

Actually, I thought she had changed. For the better. When I was last in Lickin Creek, she'd been browbeaten by a creep of a husband, and then she'd had to endure sudden widowhood when he was murdered. Now the old sparkle had returned to her eyes.

"I'm so sorry I couldn't meet you at the airport," she said, brushing the ever-present hair away from her golden eyes. "I got roped into being the active chairperson for our Old Fashioned Apple Butter Festival, and it seems everything collapses if I take even a five-minute break."

She suddenly realized the people she'd been talking with were still there. "My manners! Tori, this is the Reverend LeRoi Barkdoll, my right-hand man."

The minister shook my hand heartily. "Nice to meet Alice-Ann's famous friend. These are my boys: Tony, Mike, Alex, and Jared."

The four young men, in torn blue jeans and dirty T-shirts, looked as though they'd be more at home on New York's Avenue C than at an apple butter festival. They shuffled their feet, mumbled a few surly-sounding words, and lit cigarettes rather than shake hands with me.

"We'd best be getting back to work," the cheery minister said. "Come on, fellows, we need to redd out the snack bar."

I grinned at the colloquialism for "cleaning house."

"Nice kids," I said after they'd left.

"Reverend LeRoi has a youth rehabilitation program. Those four boys are his biggest successes," Alice-Ann said.

I shuddered. "I'd hate to see his failures."

Garnet laughed. "I guarantee you'd hate to see them. I hope you never will."

A short, round woman picked her way across the rough field, hailing Alice-Ann as she tottered toward us in ridiculously high heels. Despite the humid afternoon heat, she had a full-length mink coat draped over her shoulders. She was yoo-hooing and calling Alice-Ann's name in an ear-shattering falsetto.

Alice-Ann groaned for my benefit but threw the approaching woman a brilliant smile. "That's Bathsheba Butterbaugh," she said to me under her breath. "The nominal director of the festival. You know, the one who doesn't do any work and gets to make all the speeches." More loudly, "Mrs. Butterbaugh, how nice to see you here. I'd like you to meet my dearest friend from my college days, Tori Miracle."

Bathsheba Butterbaugh squinted at me and extended a hand, heavy with diamond rings. "Just the person I wanted to see," she announced. "When I heard you'uns was coming to town, I talked it over with my sister, Salome, and we decided you should be the Celebrity Apple Recipe Judge for the festival. We always like to get someone sort of famous. Last year it was that . . . who was it?" she asked Alice-Ann.

"The county extension agent," Alice-Ann said, hiding a smile behind her hand.

"What's involved in the judging?" I asked, feeling quite flattered. Me, a Celebrity Judge!

"Not a whole lot. I'll let folks know they can drop their dishes over to Gochenauer's. You just see to it they hand you their five-dollar entry fees and a copy of the recipe wrote so's a body can read it. You decide what tastes the best. Then you make that there recipe yourself, so you know there aren't no mistakes in it. Last year, Mrs. Rathenberger didn't do that, and the recipe we printed up and sold at the Fest called for baking soda instead of baking powder."

I didn't know the difference between the two, but she shuddered as if the memory were too horrible to contemplate. "And, of course, at the final weekend of the Apple Butter Fest, you're the one who awards the trophy to the winner."

"It's very kind of you to ask," I said. "But I won't be able to accept your offer. You see, I'm only going to be in town for one week."

Alice-Ann threw Garnet a strange glance. Something was up. I turned to Garnet and waited for an explanation.

Garnet cleared his throat. "Actually, Tori, I meant to speak to you about this when we got home. My part-timer, Cindy, called in sick this morning with the chicken pox. That means I'm going to have to be on duty after all. I tried to call you, but you'd already left. But she should be back at work next Monday, so if you can stay an extra week we can still have our time together.

"I'm so sorry, but I'm stuck. I promise to make it up to you. Please say you'll stay, Tori." He had an adorable hangdog look on his face that I couldn't resist.

I knew that running a police department with one and a half employees was not exactly a dream job. Besides, I had nothing pressing in New York. I was writing an article for *American Scenes* magazine about the National Hard Crab Derby and Miss Crustacean

Pageant in Crisfield, Maryland, and I also needed to get started on the outline for my second novel, based on the tragic events that had occurred in Lickin Creek when Alice-Ann's husband was murdered. I could work on both here in Lickin Creek.

I took Garnet's hand. "No problem," I said. "I totally understand. And Mrs. Butterbaugh, I shall be honored to be your recipe judge."

"Of course you will" was her reply. "The money we raise from the entry fees will go to the Historical Society, and since you burned it down I figure you should be happy to help us rebuild it."

"I didn't burn it down," I protested. "It was an accident." That, too, had happened during the summer when I tracked down Alice-Ann's husband's murderer through the caves under the borough.

"No need to apologize, dear." The woman left, and I stood there basking in the afternoon sunshine and the warm glow of feeling a part of the local community. At least I basked until Alice-Ann snickered. "I would have warned you if we'd had more time to talk," she said.

"I think it'll be fun," I said, still enjoying the sense of belonging.

Alice-Ann grimaced. "Shall I tell her, or will you?" she asked Garnet.

"What?" My glow was beginning to fade.

"People take the recipe contest very seriously," she said. "Mrs. Harkins, who's famous for being the best cook in town, won for twenty-three years in a row. Then two years ago, an out-of-towner awarded the grand prize to a man. The poor judge was nearly run out of town."

"Oh, great. I was hoping this would be something I could do to get to know people."

"I'll help you. Everything will be all right," Alice-Ann said, patting my shoulder reassuringly. "And speaking of getting to know people, I'm having a few friends over for coffee and dessert tonight to meet you. Mostly people from the festival committee. I've already spoken with Garnet about it. Hope you don't mind."

"Sounds wonderful. Thanks."

Before we could talk any more, a young woman carrying a hammer and saw charged up to us. "Mrs. MacKinstrie, where do you want me to set up the candied-apple booth?"

Alice-Ann let out a prolonged sigh, tempered with a smile. "Come on, Freda. I'll show you. I'll see you later," she said to me. "Right after the town meeting." She led Freda across the field.

Town meeting! Things were getting better all the time. Despite Alice-Ann's warning, I was still quite flattered to be asked to be the apple recipe judge, and now I was going to go to a town meeting. I was becoming an active participant in small-town American life.

Inside the dairy building, a pleasant-faced woman greeted us in typical Lickin Creek fashion: "How're you'uns doing?" As I wondered if the correct response should be "We'uns is doing fine," Garnet answered, "Fine, thanks."

She waited patiently for us to make up our minds. I had trouble making a decision for there were dozens of yummy-looking choices, but at last I selected my favorite, peanut butter chocolate swirl. While she packed it into the cardboard container, I studied her clothes. She belonged to one of the religious denominations the locals call "Plain," which included, but wasn't limited to, the Amish and the Mennonites we've all heard about. She wore a simple, long cotton dress, crisp white apron with no visible buttons, black stockings and shoes, and a starched white cap covering her light-colored hair. Her outfit looked strange and old-fashioned to my New York eyes, but she appeared comfortable.

"How's Mr. Foor doing these days?" Garnet asked as he passed his money over the counter.

"No change, Chief. Don't think he'll ever get any better. But thanks for asking."

As we drove east, back toward town, I asked Garnet what was wrong with Mr. Foor.

"A stroke," Garnet said. "Mrs. Foor takes care of the dairy all by herself. Quite a job."

I felt a pang of sympathy for the Foors. It's lucky we don't know what life has in store for us. Changing the subject, I asked why Lickin Creek had chosen to celebrate apple butter.

"We needed something different. There are way too many regular apple fests around in the fall, like the ones in Arendtsville and Martinsburg. And Winchester does an Apple Blossom Festival in the spring."

He'd been maneuvering the car over the brick-paved downtown streets as he spoke, and we were now on the street of grand mansions known as Lickin Creek's Historical District. Garnet's home was the largest of them, sitting on a low hill, dominating all the others. Like most of the houses in the district, it had started life two hundred years ago as a simple log cabin and then had been added to by succeeding generations until it had become a rambling, attractive blend of Colonial, Federal, Queen Anne, Victorian, and Neo-Classical styles. The immensity of it told of days when people had help.

A porch wrapped all the way around the first floor, recalling a time when people sat out on summer evenings. A row of ten windows on the second floor sparkled in the afternoon sunlight. A gabled roof rose above them, with more windows looking out from the attic. White gingerbread trim dripped like birthday-cake icing from the eaves overhanging the Corinthian columns on the wraparound porch. On each corner of the building, a cylindrical brick tower, topped with an onion-shaped dome, soared high above the slate-shingled fish-scale roof. It was a house for big families, homey despite its grandeur.

Garnet parked under the porte cochere and lifted my suitcase and cat paraphernalia out of the trunk, while I carefully removed the cat carriers from the backseat. The poor dears were too worn out to complain anymore, but they glared at me through the door grates as if threatening some awful kind of cat retribution. I knew they'd sulk for a day or two, then get over it.

The heavy oak double doors were wide open and from deep inside the house came the pulsating voice of a country-western singer. Garnet opened one of the screen doors and yelled, "Greta! We're here!"

He held the door, and I stepped past him into the dim foyer, where the fireplace, faced with pale yellow tile, was the only touch of lightness. The ceiling was dark red, the walls were paneled in brown mahogany, and the floor was covered with a navy blue Oriental carpet. I blinked and squinted and hoped I wouldn't trip over anything. Then Garnet flipped a switch near the door and the hanging Tiffany lamp blazed to life, filling the square entry hall with brilliant swirls of many colors.

To my right was a broad staircase, with railings and balusters of elaborately carved chestnut that rose to the second floor. And flying down the staircase came Greta. She grabbed me by the shoulders and held me at arm's length, studying me carefully.

"Don't you look wonderful!" she gushed. "And so tiny! You mustn't have eaten a thing since last I saw you."

I loved her. Absolutely loved her. No one had ever called me tiny before. Short, squat, shrimp, Munchkin, runt—all those depressing names I'd heard in school. But tiny—never. Tiny was Jane Powell in those wonderful old MGM musicals; tiny implied delicacy and thinness. Tiny Tori. Yes! My diet was working at last!

I grinned at Greta and stared up at her. She was Garnet's height, about five-ten, but where he had a stocky, muscular body, hers was thin and angular. Her deeply tanned face had many planes, all etched with wrinkles. Her long, straight, gray hair was pulled back into a ponytail. A skirt of multicolored Indian gauze twirled around her bare ankles. A black T-shirt was cinched at the waist by a silver concha belt, and multiple strands of wooden and clay beads dangled from her neck. And then there were the scarves—they hung from her like Spanish moss from a southern tree. And—she still wore Earth shoes! Those strange shapeless blobs that made people look like they were always walking uphill. Were they still being made? Or had Greta hoarded some since the sixties?

"Take her suitcase up to the Blue Room, little

brother," Greta ordered. She noticed the cat carriers. "What on earth do you have there?"

"My cats." I opened the carrier doors and Fred and Noel stepped suspiciously onto the rug.

"How charming," she said. I think she was sincere. "Are they used to dogs?"

"Not to my knowledge," I said, bending down to smooth Fred's ruffled orange-and-white fur.

"Come on into the kitchen, Tori. I made a fresh jar of sun tea just for you."

The cats and I trailed Greta as she led the way through an arch under the stairs and down a hallway as dim as the foyer. But when Greta threw open the door at the end of the hall, the kitchen was sun-drenched and twice as large as I remembered it. In fact, it was twice as large as my whole apartment. In every window were old bottles that captured the light and glowed like jewels: sapphire, garnet, amethyst, emerald, aquamarine, and topaz.

In the center of the room stood an old table with a white enamel top and black legs. "Sit down, Tori," Greta ordered. "I'll fetch the tea. Do you use sugar?"

The ringing of the telephone interrupted her. "Hello? Yes, I'm all set. Seven, at the theater. Have you made your calls? We want a good turnout. Yes, I know I don't know you." She chuckled. "See you there."

As she was hanging up, something huge and dark flung itself at the screen door, almost breaking through. "Oh, Bear, come on in." Greta opened the door, and Garnet's German shepherd bounded in, face covered with slobber. The cats let out a unified shriek and shot out of the kitchen, with the dog close behind.

"He's going to kill them!" I screamed.

"Nonsense," Greta said. "They're just getting acquainted."

Garnet entered the kitchen. "He's supposed to be an outside dog; he just doesn't know it."

The dog charged back into the kitchen, from the direction of the dining room, yipping and whining. This time the two cats were in hot pursuit of him. Next thing I knew, all three had disappeared under the kitchen table and were still. I dropped to my knees, prepared to wrestle with the beast, and saw all three curled up in one large, hairy ball, pretending to have been asleep for hours. Fred opened one eye and yawned.

Garnet hauled me to my feet.

Greta smiled. "Isn't it wonderful how fast they've made friends?"

We drank our iced tea out of Waterford goblets, slightly chipped but still bright with Irish fire. They had been purchased at local auctions, I was told, of which Greta and Garnet were devotees. Garnet promised to take me to one soon. Another bit of rural Americana I could look forward to.

"Got to get back to work," he said, as he pushed his chair back from the table. He planted a kiss somewhere between my nose and my right ear. "I'll make this up to you, I promise."

"Will you be at the meeting tonight?" Greta asked him.

"You know damn well I will. And, Greta, let me remind you I'll be there in my official capacity as Police Chief."

He smiled at me. "If it's all right with you, I'll let

Greta take you to the town meeting, and we can go to Alice-Ann's from there. Don't let Greta wear you out with her war stories."

He left the kitchen with Greta close behind him. Bear struggled out from under the table and rested his chin on my lap, and I stroked his soft muzzle while I listened to Greta and Garnet arguing in the front hall.

"Don't try to pull anything tonight," Garnet warned.

"I wouldn't dream of it, little brother. Even *those* people have the right to speak."

"Please remember that *those* people represent the Commonwealth of Pennsylvania, and what they're doing is mandated by law."

A protracted sigh. "I know. I know."

The door slammed.

In a moment another country song came on full blast, and Greta did a solitary line dance back into the kitchen. She sank into a chair and tapped her fingers on the tabletop in time to the beat. "Nothing like the country classics to relax by . . ."

The ringing of the phone interrupted her. After saying hello, Greta covered the mouthpiece with one large hand. "Why don't you get unpacked, Tori? You're in the Blue Room—it used to be our parents' room. Take the right hallway at the top of the stairs. It's the first door on the right."

It was definitely a dismissal. I figured she wanted privacy, so I climbed the stairs, which I noticed continued up to the third floor, went through an ornate archway that led me into another wing, and found my room. I looked around the large bedroom with delight. It was like being in the Lincoln Bedroom at the White House. From the walnut arches of the bed's headboard to the marble-topped washstand and dresser, every bit of the ornately carved furniture came from the Victorian era. There was even the unexpected luxury of a marble fireplace. It was going to be difficult to go back to sleeping on a futon after spending two weeks surrounded by all this splendor.

Garnet had left my suitcase on the bed. As I opened it, I noticed the beautiful colors and fine handwork in the quilt that served as a spread. Anyplace else, I thought, this would be in a museum. I hung my clothes in the old-fashioned wardrobe and wondered a little if I'd done right in agreeing to stay another week. It wasn't the thought of the second week that bothered me, but the first. I liked Garnet's sister, but a week of being entertained by her was not what I'd had in mind when I splurged at Victoria's Secret.

Chapter 2

Saturday Evening

I CHANGED FROM MY TRAVEL-CRUMPLED SHIRT TO A royal-blue silk blouse which I thought looked good with my black slacks, added gold hoop earrings and a gold chain, and sprayed myself with a large quantity of Bellodgia cologne, a carnation scent given to me by the well-known TV psychic Praxythea Evangelista, whom I'd met here in Lickin Creek.

I found Greta in the large dining room that had been converted into an office. She waved at me to have a seat as she continued with her telephone conversation.

"I'm all set," she said. "Don't forget your ammunition."

I stared at her thoughtfully. Ammunition? Maybe Garnet really did mean "war" stories.

The instant she put the receiver down, the phone emitted one ring. Greta waited a moment, and soon paper began to emerge from the fax machine on the beautiful mahogany dining table. She scanned the message, smiled, and ran it through a paper shredder. I felt as though I were in a CIA field office.

"Dinner's ready," she said to me.

I followed her through the butler's pantry into the kitchen, where I was greeted enthusiastically by Garnet's dog and ignored by my own lovely cats.

"Wine?" She opened the refrigerator and pointed to a square box with a little plastic pouring spout.

"Yes, thanks."

She filled a single wineglass.

"None for you?" I asked.

"Just iced tea. I've got a lot to do for tonight's meeting. Sit down and relax, Tori. Everything's ready."

The table was already set with Homer Laughlin Fiesta Ware, a Majolica pitcher shaped like a trout, and iced-tea goblets of pressed glass with a Roman Rosette design. Everything had come from one sale, Greta told me proudly. It had been the highlight of last winter's auctions.

"Sorry I didn't have time to fix much of a dinner tonight," she apologized. She carried the dishes over to the stove where she heaped them with mountains of mashed potatoes and something that she scooped out of a cast-iron skillet.

"There's plenty more since Garnet's not here," she said. She poured iced tea from the trout and invited me to come to the table.

I stared at the plate overflowing with white gravy full of brown lumps.

"Dig in," Greta ordered. "It's frizzled beef. The secret to making it really tasty is to burn the dried beef and flour before you add the milk. Have some pepper relish. Canned it myself last summer."

I took a nibble or two. The predominant seasoning

in the frizzled beef was salt. Not too bad, once I got used to it, but I was glad there was plenty of tea.

"Bet you don't get much good Pennsylvania Dutch cooking in New York," she said.

"Nothing like this," I answered honestly.

While we ate, we talked. It was really the first opportunity I'd had to spend some time alone with the woman, and I found her fascinating. Where Garnet appeared to be solidly establishment, Greta was the last of the Flower Children—still on the road with Jack Kerouac, still quoting the poetry of Larry Ferlinghetti.

After college, and before her marriage, she had spent a year as a volunteer with Operation Brotherhood in Southeast Asia, and once she'd almost drowned trying to save a beached whale. She'd even chained herself to a tree in a Brazilian rain forest before that became a fashionable thing to do, and, predictably, she'd boycotted the tuna industry.

As Greta refilled my wineglass, I asked her, "Wasn't it hard to settle down in Lickin Creek after all that excitement?"

"Not really, Tori. I always knew I'd come back to marry Lucky. He was my rock, my strength. We'd been sweethearts since grade school. He would have gone with me, if he hadn't had the Fine Swine Farm to run. I miss him so much—we should have grown old together."

A tear glistened in one of her bright blue eyes.

I recalled Garnet telling me Lucky had met a gruesome death in an accident with a manure spreader last spring. It was no wonder she didn't want to live on the pig farm anymore.

I tried to lighten up. "Come on, admit it. Life in Lickin Creek has to be a little dull for you."

She poured some more iced tea into her glass, sniffed, then grinned. "Dull? Ha! There's always something going on that needs attention. Right now, right here in Lickin Creek, I'm involved in the most important cause of my life. Let's have dessert," she said, jumping to her feet.

"Something to do with the town meeting tonight, I'll bet."

She nodded, concentrating on scooping the ice cream into crystal bowls.

"What's it all about?"

"Nuclear waste," she snapped, slamming the bowls on the table so hard I feared they'd crack.

"Did I hear correctly? Nuclear waste in Lickin Creek?"

"Actually it's a low-level radioactive waste disposal plant. The company's trying to persuade Lickin Creek to volunteer to be the host community. You'll hear all about it tonight. Go ahead and eat your ice cream, Tori. I have a few things to gather up." She disappeared into the dining room/office, leaving her dessert untouched.

The ice cream Garnet had bought at the dairy was richer and tastier than any I could remember eating. By the time I was through, Greta reappeared in the kitchen and cleaned up with frightening efficiency, refusing my offer of help. She scraped the leftover beef and potato mixture from my plate into Bear's bowl, warning him, "Don't tell Garnet." She rubbed her large, blunt-fingered hands together and looked pleased. "How's that for getting the place redd up in a hurry? Let's get going."

She grabbed two full shopping bags by their string handles and headed toward the door. "Grab my purse and out the lights, will you please?"

I took a second to fill the cats' dishes with Tasty Tabby Treats. To my dismay, Bear had them empty before I left the kitchen.

Greta drove a black pickup truck with a deer rifle suspended in the back window. "Isn't it against the law to carry a gun around town?" I asked.

"Only if it's concealed. Everybody does it." She zipped into a space marked NO PARKING—LOADING ZONE about half a block away from the Art Deco front of the Accident Theater, named to commemorate the founding of Lickin Creek in 1745. Alice-Ann's husband had told me all about the historic moment when his ancestor, George MacKinstrie, heading out west from Philadelphia to seek his fortune, had been sidetracked by a lucky accident. Instead of fixing his wagon, he'd built a town.

"Go on in and grab yourself a seat," she said. "I have some things to do."

As I walked past the small, square box office under the canopy, I saw her heading toward some people who stood in a group, far enough away from the lights of the theater to be only shadows. What on earth was the woman planning? I wondered.

The small overheated lobby was packed with people and smelled of popcorn. I was glad when Garnet appeared at my side with more apologies for having deserted me. I, again, assured him it was all right.

"Where's Greta?" he asked, looking over the crowd.

"Outside, talking to some friends."

"Uh-oh. I smell trouble brewing."

I was beginning to think this town meeting might not be as charming as I'd expected. "Shall I save you a seat?" I asked.

"No thanks. I have to be on the stage." He looked at someone over my shoulder and smiled. "Hey, Doc."

Meredith Jones stepped up. The middle-aged doctor looked much the same as he had during the summer when I first met him. Gray suit, gray eyes, graying hair, and gray-rimmed spectacles. Face pleasant, but boring, with the kind of features you can never quite remember when you're away. "Nice to see you again, Tori," he said.

He was interrupted by Bathsheba Butterbaugh, still in her mink coat, with a hand resting on her left hip. "It's the lumbago. Chiropractic don't do nothing for it. Can't you give me some pills?"

"Mrs. Butterbaugh, the only thing that's going to help you is surgery. When you're ready to go to Hershey, let me know and I'll set it up."

"Humph!" she said, and walked away with a pronounced limp that had not been apparent earlier.

"It never ends," Doc said. "It's both a blessing and a curse being the only doctor in a small town. Everyone expects a free consultation, anytime, anywhere. Come sit with me, Tori." He took my arm and we moved down the center aisle looking for vacant seats.

I recognized a few people. A large hat covered with pink silk roses nodded in my direction. The tiny, venerable woman under it was Miss Effie of the Historical Society. I wondered what she did to fill her days now that the Historical Society itself was history. Seeing her brought back memories of last summer's terrible fire that had destroyed the old building and nearly killed me and Garnet.

Reverend Barkdoll, sitting with one of the rehabilitated juveniles I'd met at the fairground, threw me a jolly wave. Mrs. Foor, from the dairy, was there. She smiled at me. It was a nice sensation—being recognized like this.

As we settled down, I noticed that although the flowered carpet was worn through to the floor in places, the ceiling was decorated with a grand painting reminiscent of the Sistine Chapel, the walls were covered with red silk, and the bas-relief Doric columns sparkled with recently applied gold leaf. Doc caught me looking around. "Had a big fund drive to raise money for remodeling. Unfortunately we ran out of money before we got to the rug."

As if to underline Doc's earlier statement about what was expected from the town's only doctor, an ancient man stood at the end of the aisle and yelled, "Doc! Gotta talk to you!"

Doc sighed. "Hello, Percy."

" 'Scuse me, ladies."

The three women between me and the aisle stood, allowing their seat cushions to snap angrily against the wooden seat backs. They edged their way to the aisle where they tapped their feet and threw impatient glances our way. The elderly gentleman sidled down the row and sat next to me. Doc introduced us: "Tori Miracle—Percy Montrose."

This must be what shaking hands with a mummy feels like, I thought with distaste. The thin skin was cold and dry, transparent and tightly stretched over long, fragile bones. I quickly removed my hand and surreptitiously wiped it on my slacks.

"Doc, I'm still not feeling any better than I was a month ago. Can't you give me something to fix me up?"

"Are you taking the vitamins I gave you, Percy?"

"They ain't helping."

"It's going to take time to get your strength back. Come see me Monday. I'll do another blood test."

"Yo, Montrose, I want to talk to you." A bear of a man, in a white T-shirt with sleeves rolled to show off his muscles, stood at the end of the aisle. Percy's eyes registered something that looked like fear, but it was only a flicker that was gone in a moment.

"Call me at work, Riley."

"You know your secretary won't take my calls, you little creep. I've got the union behind me, Montrose. You can't screw around with the union." He was handsome in a rugged, he-man sort of way. Not my type at all but probably attractive to a lot of women.

Percy laughed. "You and your union are dead, Riley; you just ain't smart enough to lie down."

"We'll see who's dead," the man snarled, turning away. In my opinion, Percy was the clear winner of that skirmish.

"Sorry you had to hear that, young lady," Percy said. "He led a strike last year, and I had to kick the union out and hire all new workers. He won't admit it's all over." He said good-bye and allowed the three women to reclaim their seats.

Doc let out a long, low sigh followed by a short laugh. "Richest man in town, and he hates to pay for an office visit."

A smiling teenage girl came down the aisle, distributing a handful of pamphlets to each row. On the cover was an artist's four-color rendering of an ultramodern group of buildings in a parklike area, surrounded by a ring of mountains that looked just like the ones around Lickin Creek.

"And they say they haven't picked the site yet," Doc scoffed.

"Shhhh . . ." The lady to my right put a warning finger to her lips. "It's time for the meeting to start."

Doc shrugged his shoulders and grinned at me.

The lights blinked several times, and the room filled with people in plaid shirts, Budweiser T-shirts, jeans, cotton housedresses, and pastel polyester pantsuits. After a great deal of noise, at last everyone was either seated or leaning against the side walls.

I directed my attention to the stage, empty except for a row of metal folding chairs, a microphone, and a portable movie screen. But not empty for long, for a small Asian gentleman walked out from the wings and lowered the microphone about two feet. It was the mayor, Prince Somping, a Laotian refugee who'd found his own niche in the land of opportunity.

The mayor held up his hands for silence. "*Sawatdi.* Welcome, my friends. It is good that so many of you have come tonight to hear this presentation. Perhaps it will dispel many of the misconceptions and rumors that have spread through the community."

A low murmur of discontent moved around the room.

"Please, please. Each speaker must be given the opportunity to present his side of the issue. Questions may be asked at the end. Allow me to introduce to you our panel for the evening. First, Raina Jackson, the public relations representative for the Nuclear Waste Disposal Company."

A tall, trim woman, wearing her blond hair in a shining Grace Kelly chignon, stepped out from behind the gold velvet curtains. She acknowledged the smattering of applause with a crisp smile and a nod of her head and took a seat. She smoothed the skirt of her cherry-red business suit and crossed her shapely legs at the ankles.

That's what I'm going to look like in my next life—tall, thin, and blond, I immediately decided.

"Next, our borough manager, Avory Jenkins."

Avory sat next to Raina. He wore a green-and-yellow striped golf shirt, plaid pants, and brown shoes. An unlit pipe jutted from his mouth. He drew thunderous applause and a few whistles.

"Zachariah Mellot, representing the Caven County Commissioners." Zachariah and Avory apparently shopped at the same clothing store. Subdued applause greeted his appearance.

"Our borough solicitor, Buchanan McCleary."

McCleary, skin gleaming in the spotlight like the polished mahogany table in the Gochenauer dining room, walked slowly across the stage. It was hard to judge his height from where I sat, but I guessed he was at least six-four, and his sixties Afro hairstyle added about six inches to that. This time, the applause was sprinkled with a few boos, which brought a wide grin to the solicitor's face.

"And, of course, you all know our chief of police, Garnet Gochenauer."

Garnet bounded down the center aisle, climbed the steps at the side of the stage, and sat next to

Zachariah. The audience greeted him with whistles, foot stomping, and enthusiastic clapping that threatened to go on all night, until the mayor raised his arms and requested silence.

Both the borough manager and the county commissioner spoke for a few minutes, stating why they favored placing a low-level radioactive waste dump in Caven County. I wondered how Garnet felt, but he wasn't asked to speak.

Then the public relations expert from the company stepped up to the microphone. I thought she did an excellent job presenting the company's viewpoint and reminding the audience that both federal and state laws called for setting up regional facilities.

She explained that huge areas of the state were unsuitable for a dump for reasons having to do with geology, wildlife areas, gamelands, watersheds, and so on. "And by means of our screening process, we have identified the areas of the state which we believe are suitable for our needs."

Someone shouted from the audience. "And you're saying Lickin Creek is one of these sites?"

"That's correct, sir. I'm hoping your community will volunteer to supply the site."

"Seems to me it's a done deal!" the man yelled. "Just look at the picture on the cover of that fancy book of theirs. If that doesn't show Old Baldy and Three Hump Hill and Deer Tick Ridge, then I ain't lived in Lickin Creek all my life."

"Purely an artist's conception—" Raina began.

"It's not a conception—it's deception!" cried a woman.

Someone else called out, "I hear you'uns is going

to cart in radioactive stuff from other states. Why does it have to come into Pennsylvania?"

"Pennsylvania generates more than 84 percent of the low-level nuclear waste in the four-state area, sir. It's appropriate that the state that creates the most waste be responsible for its disposal."

"We don't want your dump here," a voice called from the darkness.

Raina's professional smile didn't quite reach her eyes. "The word 'dump' leads to a misconception of our mission." She pressed a button and a picture appeared on the screen showing a traditional landfill, full of society's detritus: old tires, disposable diapers, refrigerators, broken furniture. A bulldozer perched precariously on the edge, shoving a shower of disgusting garbage into the pit.

"Lickin Creek's own landfill," she said. "A traditional 'dump.' "

Another push of the button and the next slide depicted a drawing of a beautiful country scene: gently rolling hills covered with green grass, a small parking lot shaded by mature trees, several unobtrusive office buildings, and rows of rectangular concrete bunkers.

"This is an active low-level nuclear waste disposal site," she explained. "All waste is stored aboveground. This isolates the waste so it cannot come in contact with groundwater."

Click. Same location, only all the concrete bunkers had been replaced by more gentle, rolling hills.

"Same place, thirty years later, only now the modules have been completely sealed and covered with earth. The site will return to its natural state. For five years, our company will closely monitor the site to make sure there is no leakage. After that it will be turned over to the state."

"And how long is the state responsible for monitoring the site?" I recognized Greta's voice, high-pitched from anger.

"After a while, ma'am, the site's radioactive waste will have decayed and there will be no more risk."

"How long?"

"Five hundred years—"

I feared the roars of outrage from the darkened theater would bring down the painted ceiling.

Raina took her seat, smiled patiently at the borough manager, and waited for the uproar to die down. It did eventually.

Avory stepped up to the microphone and tapped it a couple of times. "I think you'uns have gotten so riled up about this that you haven't even thought about all the good this site could bring us. Think about the jobs; God knows we need them. The payroll alone will bring millions of dollars into our community. And the company buys goods and services locally—that's more bucks in our pockets. The taxes they pay will allow us to redevelop our downtown—bring it back to life. And the company's gonna pay us for accepting the waste—with a guaranteed minimum every year. Think on it. That's all I ask. Think on it."

"What about our apple orchards?"

"Some of the land we are considering buying is orchard land, but most of it is wilderness," Raina said.

A rustling noise came from the back of the room as a tall figure stood up. "There are apple orchards all around that land. Orchards that you aren't going to buy." It was Greta, again. "Do you have children, miss?" She didn't wait for Raina's answer. "Would you feed them apples that grew next to a nuclear waste dump? Would you want your children to eat apples that glow in the dark?"

Avory raised his hands, palms out. "This is plain ridiculous—"

Greta raised her voice and drowned him out. "You're not getting away with putting your damn dump in our backyard!" she cried. One of her paper bags crackled as she pulled something from it. She drew her right arm back, and heaved the object with the power and accuracy of a major-league pitcher. A round, glowing object flew over the heads of the crowd and splattered against Raina's white silk blouse. Reddish-yellow pulp oozed across her chest and dripped down the front of the lovely red suit.

Before the audience could do more than breathe "*Oooh!*" a barrage of more round, glowing objects flew toward the stage from every direction.

"CANLICK, CANLICK, CANLICK!" the attackers chanted like cheerleaders at a high school football game, and the audience picked up the cheer.

"What's CANLICK stand for?" I yelled over the noise.

"Citizens Against Nuclear Waste in Lickin Creek!" Doc yelled back.

Like a spectator at Wimbledon, my head swiveled from the attacking army to the dripping victims spotlighted on the stage. I gasped with dismay as Garnet took a direct hit on the forehead. Bloodlike gore dripped slowly from his face onto his spotless white shirt as he leaped off the stage and tried to push his way through the crowd. Over my shoulder, I saw Greta taking off at a run through the double doors.

The next few minutes were bedlam until the theater finally emptied out. "Whew," I breathed to Doc as we stood in the lobby. "That was hardly the Norman Rockwell type of town meeting I was expecting."

Doc grinned. "It was lucky they were tossing tomatoes, not apples. Some of the people on stage could have been hurt instead of merely humiliated."

"Knowing Garnet," I said, "I think he would rather have been knocked unconscious than be embarrassed like that."

"I hate to say it, Tori, but he should have known Greta was up to something. Stopping that dump's all she's been talking about for the past year."

He took my arm. "Let's go over to Alice-Ann's. I'm sure Garnet will join us there as soon as he catches up with that crackpot sister of his. What a night! Lickin Creek's going to be buzzing about this one for a long time."

He was right about that, no doubt about it!

Chapter 3

Later Saturday Evening

DOC TURNED OFF THE MAIN ROAD AND DROVE under a wrought-iron arch with the word SILVERTHORNE worked into the design. We were then on the narrow, gravel driveway, flanked on both sides by tall trees, that led to Alice-Ann's house. After about a quarter of a mile, the drive forked in two directions. One branch led down to Lickin Creek's most famous landmark, Thorne Castle, while the other curved up and around the side of a small hill. It was there that Alice-Ann's house stood—a two-story, gray stone building, of the kind often pictured on Pennsylvania postcards. Originally built by her late husband's ancestors, the MacKinstrie family home looked much as it had for the last two hundred years.

Inside, I knew, the house had been modernized enough to make it comfortable, but not enough to have destroyed its charm. The front door was open, and we walked into the hallway, which extended all the way to the back door and featured a mural painted by an itinerant artist in the 1800s. It showed Alice-Ann's house as it must have looked when it had been first built and also depicted the famous "Scene of the Accident," as the historic moment of the founding of Lickin Creek was called.

Alice-Ann met us there and welcomed me with a warm kiss, then, much to my surprise, welcomed Doc with an even warmer one. "Something you two haven't told me?" I asked when they finally separated.

Their sheepish grins answered my question. "We're keeping it quiet," Alice-Ann said. "It's been only two months since Richard's death."

"Your secret is safe with me," I told her. "I'm so happy for you." She really did deserve a second chance at happiness after having had such a disastrous first marriage.

"Come in and meet my friends," she said, putting an arm around my waist. Doc followed us through an arch into the living room. This was a large, high-ceilinged room with tall, curtainless windows across the back. In the daylight, I remembered, the view through these was spectacular. She'd added more pottery crocks to the decor, I noticed. And now, antique duck decoys dangled from the beams. Gleaming copper bowls, full of fall arrangements, were set about on the various washstands, cobbler's benches, pie safes, and jelly cupboards. Even though it was a comfortably warm evening, a small fire had been built in the stone fireplace. Everything looked cozy and festive.

Several dozen people stood in small groups or were perched on the awkward-looking wooden benches that Alice-Ann felt were the appropriate style of furniture for her Early American house. Personally, I believed that if those early settlers could have had La-Z-Boys, they would have.

Doc handed me a glass of white wine, and Alice-Ann began introducing me. I'd met about half the people there when a group of seven entered from the foyer. I recognized the four men who had been on the stage at the theater. Now they were accompanied by three women. Wives, I assumed.

Mayor Somping's wife was a delicate-boned Asian beauty who looked exactly as a Laotian princess should. Only Garnet and I knew that the mayor's story about being an escaped prince was phony, something dreamed up to impress gullible Americans. It was a harmless secret, and neither of us wanted to break it to the town that its royal mayor had been nothing more than a hardworking shopkeeper back in his own country.

Zachariah Mellot's wife was smiling and middle-aged, with short, fluffy gray hair and a pleasantly plump body. Just what I would have expected the wife of a Caven County commissioner to look like.

But the wife of Avory Jenkins, the borough manager, was a surprise to me. Luvinia Jenkins was a beauty queen–gorgeous blonde, in her late thirties or early forties, I'd guess, and extremely pregnant. She towered over her plain husband by a good six inches, and her simple but expensive maternity dress put his Goodwill golfing outfit to shame.

Towering over the others in the group was Buchanan McCleary, the borough solicitor, who was unaccompanied. We shook hands all around. The men had changed to clean shirts, and only a few tomato seeds lurking in Avory Jenkins's hair were a reminder of what had happened earlier at the theater.

"You all look much better than you did the last time I saw you," I said.

Mrs. Mellot frowned, but the solicitor, Buchanan McCleary, laughed. It was a rich bass sound that rumbled up from the depths of his midsection. "I warned them to expect something like that, but no one ever listens to their lawyer till it's too late, and then they all want to sue someone."

Avory took his pipe out of his mouth and tapped the ashes against his shoe, letting the dottle drop on Alice-Ann's polished wood floor. "Unlike Buchanan, I don't think what happened was funny. Those lunatics need punished in a big way." I noticed that Avory, like many Lickin Creek natives, didn't have the words "to be" in his vocabulary.

"Oh, relax, Avory," Buchanan said. "What happened was funny because we all looked ridiculous with that rotten tomato juice dripping off our faces. But the lunatics, as you call them, aren't criminals. It was only Greta and a few other upstanding citizens trying to protect their community from what they see as a threat. I think the blame should fall directly on us for encouraging the dump people to look at Lickin Creek as a site."

Avory struck a kitchen match on his thumbnail and lit his pipe. While he huffed and puffed at it for a few minutes, Buchanan sighed and rolled his eyes. I had a feeling that this pipe business was Avory's way of gaining time to think of a reply. When we were surrounded by a cloud of disgusting blue smoke, he appeared satisfied and only then answered Buchanan.

"You're paid to represent the borough, Buchanan, not criticize it."

"Right, boss. I stand corrected." He smiled at me. "Catch you later, Tori."

Alice-Ann appeared at my right shoulder. "I need some help in the kitchen," she said. Her lips pruned a little when she noticed the dottle-dappled floor, but she politely refrained from screaming.

At least she refrained until we reached the kitchen, where she slammed a pot holder into the sink and banged the refrigerator door so hard I thought it might split open. "That man is impossible," she muttered. "He wields that damn pipe like a secret weapon. Why I've seen him empty a room in five minutes simply by lighting it."

"How did he ever get such an attractive wife?" I asked, as I took a plate of cold cuts from her.

While Alice-Ann garnished a platter of hors d'oeuvres with fresh parsley, she giggled. "He went to a conference last year at a resort in West Virginia where she was the special-events coordinator. He swept her off her feet, so she says." She caught the look of disbelief on my face. "Maybe he has certain charms we can't see."

"Hidden by those flared-bottom plaid pants, I guess."

We laughed till tears ran down our cheeks. "God, it's good to be here with you," I said, when I was able to compose myself.

"I know what you mean," she said. "There's nobody else I feel so comfortable with."

"Not even Doc?"

She flushed. "I don't laugh with him the way I do with you. But that's okay. He has more of a dry sense of humor. And he just loves Mark."

Mark was her six-year-old son. "Where is Mark?" I asked. "I brought him a *Wizard of Oz* coloring book."

"Don't tell me you're still lost in the Land of Oz,

Tori? When are you going to realize that 'there's no place like home'?"

"Cute saying," I sniffed. "But meaningless, since Dorothy took a long, hard look at the real world, then returned to Oz and stayed there."

"I should have known," she said with a laugh. "Mark's staying over with friends. But he's real anxious to see his 'Aunt Tori.' Maybe tomorrow."

We carried the food into the dining room and stood back as the room quickly filled with guests. Naturally, most of the buzz was about the town meeting and Greta's well-organized protest. I heard angry voices arguing the pros and cons of Lickin Creek becoming a radioactive waste-disposal site. The town seemed to be split down the middle, with its citizens unable to come to an amiable agreement about the question. Unwilling to forcibly shove my way out of the dining room, I found myself wedged between Mrs. Mellot and a younger, very attractive woman whose name I hadn't caught.

They were arguing over my head, as though I didn't even exist, while I looked in vain for an escape route.

"All this is your father-in-law's fault, you know," Mrs. Mellot said. "If Percy wasn't so greedy, none of this would have happened."

Just because he owns the land doesn't make him a villain," the other woman said. "They came to him about selling it, not the other way around."

"Likely story," Mrs. Mellot said with a sniff. "He'd sell his own mother to make a buck. Just look what he did with the strikers. Hired a bunch of scabs to take their jobs. My own brother's been out of work now for more than a year."

"I don't approve of what he did, myself. When my husband takes over the factory, he'll make sure that's straightened out. Everyone will be treated fairly."

"Your husband will be a hundred years old before Percy lets him take over his business. Everybody in town knows what Percy thinks of him."

I spotted an opening in the crowd. "Excuse me," I said to the ladies.

They stared down at me, surprised to find me standing there. "Aren't you the writer of that haunted-house book?" asked the younger woman.

I admitted I was.

"I'm Helen Montrose," she said, extending her hand.

We exchanged how-do-you-dos. "I met your father-in-law tonight at the meeting," I told her.

"Mmmm," she said. Boring, she insinuated.

"I don't want to worry you, but a man at the meeting said some rather frightening things to him. Doc told me the guy was a union leader who'd lost his job after the strike. Do you know who that would be?"

"Had to be Riley Roark. He made threats after he and his men were fired from Montrose Industries. We were somewhat worried at first. My husband even hired a bodyguard to watch Dad for a while, but it turned out Riley wasn't as bad as we thought. Thank God."

"I haven't met your husband yet. Is he here?"

"Mmmm. Business meeting tonight. You know how men are."

I didn't, but I pretended I did by nodding my head and murmuring "Mmmm." I thought I sounded quite wise.

"Something to do with Montrose Industries, I assume."

Helen shook her head. "My husband has his own business, a logging company." She abruptly changed the subject. "Do you ever speak to groups?" she said.

"Of course," I said. It wasn't exactly a fib, because I would, just as soon as I was asked.

"Wonderful. The Lickin Creek Literary Society needs a speaker tomorrow night. Can you make it?"

"Tomorrow night? That's rather soon," I protested.

"Mary Razzlebone was supposed to present a program on Booth Tarkington's *Seventeen*, but she forgot and went to Myrtle Beach instead. I'm really desperate for a speaker. My house. Seven o'clock. Alice-Ann can bring you. So kind of you." She spotted someone she knew in the crowd. " 'Bye now. See you tomorrow."

She left me standing there with my mouth hanging open—still trying to dream up a good reason for not accepting.

Mrs. Mellot turned to me, her usual sweet smile turned upside down. "Did Helen say you wrote about a haunted house?"

"Yes," I began. "My book is based on the true haunting of a town house in Greenwich Village . . ."

"The trash they put in books these days! I'd better not find it in our public library. Devil worshiper! That's what you are! You'll go straight to hell!" She pulled away from me as if I were a leper.

I found myself standing alone as if I really were carrying the loathsome disease. Alice-Ann's friends, who'd been invited here to meet me, were all fighting the battle of the dump or solving the town's problems.

From the snippets of conversation I overheard, I wondered if anything good was happening in Lickin Creek.

"You're one of those people who look lonely in a crowd," Buchanan McCleary, the town's lawyer, said with a warm smile as he handed me a glass of white wine.

"I've always been more of an observer than a participant," I told him. "Probably why I'm a writer." I was grateful for his attention, and it seemed to me that he, as the only African-American at the party, looked rather lonely himself. I couldn't help wondering what it would be like to be a member of a minority group in a small, conservative town like Lickin Creek.

"I overhead Mrs. Mellot's remarks. Don't let her upset you," he said kindly. "She's a good soul, even if she's kind of fundamental about religion."

I gulped my wine and extended my glass for a refill. "I've never been called a devil worshiper before." I wanted to push aside the sobering thought that suddenly came to me: Would I ever fit into Garnet's hometown?

"I've been called worse," he said with a flashing grin. I found myself liking him a lot.

"What's your opinion about all this?" I asked, gesturing at the crowd.

"The dump site? Officially, I support the borough's position that it would be good for the economy of the area."

"And unofficially?"

"It would be an ecological and social disaster."

"You sound like you're caught between that proverbial rock and a hard place."

"I like to consider myself the voice of reason in a borough gone mad with greed."

During the next hour, I had a dozen or more pleasant conversations with strangers who all stated their desire to have Garnet and me over for dinner some night soon. Then the food was gone, the bar was nearly dry, and people were saying their good nights. I was worried about Garnet; he hadn't showed up, and it was past midnight. And I wasn't exactly thrilled by Alice-Ann's laughter when I told her I was to speak to the Library Society tomorrow night.

"Oh, Tori, will you ever learn how to say no?"

"She wouldn't take no for an answer. What could I do?" I asked, hanging my head.

"Cheer up. At least it'll be more interesting than the book review we heard last month. Some horrid thing about the life cycle of the gypsy moth."

"I'll give you a ride home," Doc offered. "Garnet will probably be waiting for you at the house."

We kissed Alice-Ann good night, and I climbed into the front seat of Doc's large, black sport-utility vehicle. "Gave up your Mercedes, I see."

"I needed something more suitable for the bad roads around here. Half my patients live in the mountains and don't have transportation. If I don't bring medical attention to them, they don't get any."

"Sounds like a lot of work," I said, nestling into the soft, luxurious leather seat.

"It's much like practicing medicine in the nineteenth century. But I love it."

The cellular phone under the dashboard rang. Nineteenth century? Hardly.

Doc's face grew serious as he listened. "I'll be right there," he said. He hung up and turned to me.

"I'm sorry, Tori. I need to make a stop before I can take you home. It's an emergency."

"What is it?" I asked, alarmed.

"I'm not sure. Seems Percy Montrose is in trouble. Neighbor found him on his kitchen floor. Hang on, we've got to hurry."

He drove quickly through the twisted streets of the borough and stopped before a white frame Victorian house. All the windows except one on the lower level were dark.

We got out of the car. The flickering white flames of the gas streetlights cast blue-gray shadows on the faces of the people milling about on the brick sidewalk. A black wrought-iron fence surrounding the property kept the spectators from spilling over onto the lawn.

A hysterical, white-haired woman in a blue chenille robe and fuzzy bedroom slippers rushed toward us. "Please hurry!" she screamed through her sobs. "I'm scared he's dead!"

Doc hurriedly introduced her to me. She was Maude Hoffman and she lived next door in the Greek Revival mansion about fifty feet away. She and I trailed behind Doc as he rushed up the walk toward the big, dark house. A weight seemed to lift off Maude's shoulders now that Doc was taking over. Suddenly she was all talk.

"I heard him drive up, a little after nine. You can recognize the sound of his car anywhere—it rattles and screeches shamelessly. Never could understand why with all his money he never got it fixed. Anyway, my rheumatiz was bothering me so I couldn't go to the meeting. I was sitting in my kitchen—that window straight across there—having a cup of cocoa and some butter bread, and I saw a black truck pull into the driveway—just a little while ago. Few minutes later, it drove off, lickety-split with no lights on. I got worried; we've had a regular crime wave around here lately—just last week, someone stole a Kennedy rocker right off of Mrs. Mason's front porch.

"So I got my big flashlight and a butcher knife, just in case there was a burglar there, and went over. The front door was wide open, so I went in and found him lying there. In the kitchen. He tried to tell me something, but it didn't make any sense. Then I got scared that he died."

By the time Mrs. Hoffman had finished her recitation, she was sobbing loudly again, and we had passed through the foyer and into the kitchen. I thought at first it was a child lying on the kitchen floor. Then I saw his wrinkled skin, slightly purple under the old-fashioned fluorescent lights, and the silver hair that was in sharp contrast to the black-and-white ceramic tile floor.

I recognized Percy Montrose, the desiccated old gentleman who had spoken with Doc at the theater. A thin trickle of blood traced its way from his nose to the floor where it formed a dark halo around his head. He wasn't dead, not yet anyway, for his eyelids fluttered open.

Doc dropped to his knees beside him, felt for his pulse, touched his throat, looked into his eyes. Shaking his head in a gesture of helplessness, he got to his feet quickly and ran to the phone on the kitchen wall.

Percy stared up at me from the kitchen floor, blue eyes seeking an answer to the eternal question: Why me? His lips moved. He seemed to want to tell me something.

Thinking to offer some comfort, I knelt beside him, raised his head slightly, and gently lowered it onto my lap. Through dry and cracked lips, he mumbled thickly, "Help me."

"I will," I said, trying to hide the panic in my voice. I glanced up at Doc, who was barking directions to the ambulance dispatcher over the telephone.

"Poison . . . I've . . . been . . . poisoned," Percy mumbled.

"Oh-my-God-oh-my-God-oh-my-God," moaned Mrs. Hoffman. She stood in the doorway between the kitchen and the front hall, wringing her hands and crying.

"Poisoned?" I asked. "What did you take? Tell me."

"Murdered . . ." His hand, already mummified, clutched at my wrist with surprising strength. "Help me . . ."

"I will. Hang on. Doc's calling an ambulance."

His eyes rolled back in his head and stayed there. "No," I think I screamed. "Don't die! Doc, help!" I jostled Percy's head, slapped his face, tried everything I could to bring him back, but my frantic attempts were useless. I touched the inside of his wrist with two fingers and for a brief moment felt a flicker of life; then nothing.

My tears splashed down upon Percy's ashen face as Doc knelt down next to us. "Doc, I think he's . . . he's gone." I had to force the words up through my tight throat.

Mrs. Hoffman moaned.

Doc Jones used his stethoscope to determine officially what I already knew. He freed me from the hand that still gripped my wrist tightly, helped me stand, and held me tight while I sobbed into his chest.

It was the second time I'd had someone die in my arms. A long time ago, I'd held my little brother as he died from the bite of a poisonous snake—an accident that had been my fault. If only I'd been watching him. *If only* . . . the two most heartbreaking words I knew.

The ambulance crew wheeled a gurney through the doorway. "Hospital or Ziffer's Funeral Home?" one of them asked.

"Ziffer's," Doc said soberly. "I'll fill out the death certificate. He's a patient of mine."

The men gently placed Percy's body on a stretcher and covered him with a sheet. Doc followed them as they wheeled him out of the kitchen.

Mrs. Hoffman took hold of the back of my blouse to prevent me from going with them. "Do you think it was Greta, whose truck I seen out front?"

"What?" I was astounded. "Why would Greta have been here?"

"Because she's been coming over and over again, trying to make him change his mind about selling his land to them dump people. I'm almost certain it was her truck I saw in the driveway."

"You've got to tell Garnet."

Mrs. Hoffman shook her head. "All trucks look black in the dark. And ninety percent of the trucks in town are black. It might not have been hers, and if I say something she'll be in more trouble with him." Her hand flew to her mouth. "You don't think she poisoned him, do you? To stop him from selling?"

"I don't think any such thing," I said, hoping I sounded more sure than I actually felt. Greta was famous for her "causes," some of which made her act a little crazy, but I couldn't imagine her getting so carried away that she'd kill someone. However, although

I wanted to think the best of my hostess, inside my head a little voice was saying, "*You don't really know her.*"

Mrs. Hoffman slumped into a chair and groped in her pocket. "My heart pills," she said weakly. "Can you get me some water, dear?"

I went to the sink to get her a glass of water and noticed an aqua-colored mason jar sitting on the butcher-block counter—the kind people used to use for canning, with a zinc lid—and it was filled with crushed leaves and twigs. On the jar was a white stick-on label that said "Agatha's Herbal Cure—Blended Espeshully for P. Montrose."

I carried it over to the table, along with the water that Mrs. Hoffman accepted with a weak smile of thanks. She recovered rapidly once she'd taken her medicine.

"Haggie Aggie strikes again," Mrs. Hoffman said, looking at the mason jar.

"Who's Haggie Aggie?" I asked.

"She's a mountain woman. Lives in a trailer up in the woods near Old Baldy. Some people say she's a witch. She claims to cure sick people with magic potions and herbs. Maybe Percy thought she poisoned him with this concoction." She stopped talking for a moment. "My goodness, maybe it was Aggie's truck I saw here. Maybe she *did* poison him."

"Whatever it is, I'm sure Garnet will want to have this analyzed to see if it contains something harmful."

Doc came back alone. "I'll take you ladies home," he said. "I'm sorry you had to see this, Tori." With one arm around me, he walked Mrs. Hoffman and me out of that awful kitchen and out of the house. He made sure the front door was locked, helped me into his car, shooed the neighbors out of the yard, and walked Mrs. Hoffman up her front steps.

During the short drive to Garnet's house, neither Doc nor I spoke. I was thinking, *Oh, no, not again—I've only been back in Lickin Creek for a few hours, and I'm already involved in another murder mystery.*

In the rear of the house was the old summer kitchen, which had been turned into a den back in the forties when knotty-pine paneling was "in." It was there we found Garnet, sitting on the blue-and-white-checked sofa, with his feet up on the pine-bench coffee table. He looked extremely tired.

He jumped up when we came in and embraced me. "I'm sorry I missed the party," he said. "I've got half a dozen of those tomato-tossing rowdies locked up, and I've spent the last few hours driving all over town looking for Greta." He stopped as he noticed the serious expression on Doc's face. "What's wrong?"

Doc collapsed into an armchair. "Percy Montrose died tonight, Garnet. We've just come from his house."

"What? Percy? I just saw him tonight. What happened?"

"He had aplastic anemia. It was inevitable."

"I thought he'd been looking a little peaked . . ."

"Garnet," I interrupted. "I think Mr. Montrose was murdered."

"What?" The men stared at me. "What makes you say that?" Garnet asked.

"He told me so, right before he . . . he . . ." I couldn't hold back the tears.

Garnet wrapped his arms around me and mumbled some meaningless but soothing phrases into my ear until my sobs stopped. "He said he'd been poisoned, Garnet. There was an old jar in the kitchen, full of evil-looking herbs. Do you think you can get it checked out?"

"I reckon it's only one of Haggie Aggie's harmless concoctions. She makes them up for half the people in town." He saw the look on my face and added, "But I'll take it to the lab first thing in the morning."

Doc sniffed. "That damn old woman's always butting in on my patients—claiming her Pow-Wow magic's better than my medicine. If that toothless, uneducated mountain crone persuaded Percy to take her garbage, then she's practically a murderer. How in God's name am I ever going to convince the people in this town that witch doctors can't help them?"

"Let's all have a drink. I think everyone could use one," Garnet said as he opened the doors of the golden-oak sideboard and brought out a bottle of single-malt Scotch.

"Just a little," I said. I sat on the couch and clutched a throw pillow to my chest. "What is Pow-Wow magic?"

Garnet handed me a crystal goblet containing an inch of amber Scotch. "Pow-Wow medicine is an old Pennsylvania tradition of curing ailments with magic. It's still practiced today, but mostly in rural areas."

"Like right here in Caven County," Doc said, taking his drink from Garnet.

"You're shivering, Tori," Garnet said.

It wasn't the cool air in the room that was causing me to shake, but the shock of everything that had happened tonight.

"I'll light a fire. It'll take the chill off." Garnet reached inside the great walk-in fireplace that dominated the room and swung a long, metal handle from left to right. A clanging noise from above made me jump, "What was that?" I asked.

"I just switched the flue over to the outside chimney. The fireplace was built so smoke from the cookfire could be directed up into a small room where meat was smoked. Very efficient."

"Why not just leave it vented to the outside?" I asked.

"Bats get in."

Bats. Ugh! I shuddered. I hate bats almost as much as I hate snakes. I was glad I didn't have a fireplace in my apartment.

Garnet sat down next to me and rested one arm across my shoulders. Bear, thrilled with the domesticity of the scene, shoved his way in between us and rested his head on my lap. Fred and Noel, delighted by the unaccustomed luxury of a fire, lay nose to nose on the hearth. I admired the flickering flames through the golden liquid in my glass.

"You don't think Percy was murdered, do you?" I asked him. "If you did, you'd be over there right now, right?"

Garnet shared a grin with Doc. "Tori, this isn't New York. We don't have murders on every corner the way you do in the city. That poor old man who died had been sick for months. The only mystery is that he lasted as long as he did."

"Then why would he have told me he was poisoned?"

"How do I know? People say strange things when they're dying. Right, Doc?"

"More than you could imagine," he agreed.

"Mrs. Hoffman said she saw a truck outside his house tonight."

"It's a public street. Anyone can park a truck there. No one was murdered, Tori. Get that idea out of your head."

Doc stood and stretched. "Don't you worry, Tori. Thanks for the drink, Garnet. I've got a busy day tomorrow. I'd better get going."

Garnet walked with him to the front door. When he returned, I asked him, "Are you going to look into Percy's death, or aren't you?"

He sighed. "There was no crime, Tori. So there's no need for an investigation."

He got up to pour himself another drink and I studied the fire and thought about what I should do. Since Garnet didn't believe there had been a crime, he couldn't very well object to my doing some investigating on my own. I had promised the dying old man I'd help him. There had been nothing I could do to save him, but at least I could try to determine if he'd really been poisoned. And if so—then find out by whom.

What better place to start, I thought, than by visiting the mysterious mountain woman who might have been at Percy's house tonight—who might have poisoned him with her herbal concoction.

"May I borrow your truck tomorrow? I think I'd like to meet that woman who left the herb mixture in Percy's kitchen."

He looked doubtful. "Why?"

"I've always been interested in Pennsylvania Dutch folklore."

He snorted.

"Okay. I simply want to ask her if she was there

tonight. See if there's anything she can tell me about his murder. I mean death. Where does she live?"

"In the mountains, near Old Baldy. Place called Burnt Stump Hollow. They don't take kindly to strangers up there, Tori. It can be a dangerous place. Especially for a woman."

He looked into my eyes with such intensity that my toes began to curl. "Look, Tori, you're very special to me. Sticking your nose into places where it doesn't belong can get you into trouble. Promise me you'll be careful."

"I will," I vowed. "After all, I *have* survived in Hell's Kitchen for nearly ten years. Why, I've even been known to take an occasional walk in Central Park on a Sunday afternoon."

The back door slammed, and Greta walked in. "Whew," she sighed. "What a night! How'd you like those glow-in-the-dark tomatoes? Stroke of genius, I'd say."

Garnet's face was nearly purple with rage. "Don't think you're going to get away with this because you're my sister. This time you're going to jail."

She smiled innocently at him. "If you say so, big brother. Put on the shackles. Cart me off to your dungeon in chains." She extended her arms, wrists together.

Garnet groaned. "You're making me the laughingstock of the town."

I left the siblings to continue their battle in privacy and went upstairs. The cats and Bear followed me to my room and jumped onto the bed before I was undressed. I decided not to waste the red satin and lace from Victoria's Secret on them and instead pulled on my most comfortable *Wizard of Oz* nightshirt.

The one that showed the Tin Woodman saying, "If I only had a heart."

With Bear pressed against one hip, Fred sprawled against my other side, and Noel curled in a neat little bundle at my feet, I sighed and thought of old Percy and felt sadness that he would never again enjoy a sweet moment like this.

Tired as I was, sleep did not come instantly. Little creaks of shrinking floorboards, the moans of the house settling on its foundation, soft, almost furtive, unexplained clicking noises from below, all conspired to keep me awake. I lay in the dark and thought about how odd it was that in New York I could sleep undisturbed by sirens, car alarms, and the shrieks of mugging victims, and here, in the peace and quiet of a country town, the slightest sound kept me awake.

Chapter 4

Sunday Morning

The aroma of coffee drifted into my dreams and brought me to consciousness. I peered at the small dial of the pale blue Jasperware clock beside my bed. Seven o'clock. Practically the middle of the night. I quickly dressed in jeans and a pink T-shirt with a ruffle at the neck and followed the wonderful smells into the kitchen, where Garnet was frying bacon. He greeted me with a warm, very warm, kiss.

"I'm sorry about last night," he whispered into my hair. "It's just that I was so upset about Greta's escapade . . ."

"I know," I said, running my fingers through his silky hair. "Don't worry about it. We have plenty of time."

Smoke billowed from the frying pan, and we broke apart so he could rescue the bacon. I filled two mugs with coffee and carried them to the table.

"Are you going to throw her in the slammer? Toss away the key? Feed her bread and water?" I asked.

I was glad to hear Garnet laugh. "I guess not. She'd be bailed out in five minutes, anyway. But she's facing some stiff fines for disturbing the peace. And I'm going to make sure she realizes that what she did was serious."

I tasted the coffee. "Mmmm, good."

"A friend sent it. It's Tarrazú from Costa Rica. Ever been there?"

I shook my head. "Guatemala's the closest I've been." I was thinking about my plans for visiting the mountain herbalist. "Are you sure you don't mind my borrowing your truck?"

Greta answered my question. She'd come in quietly, behind us, as we talked. "His truck's got wheels bigger than you, Tori. Take my car. I prefer to drive my truck, so it just sits out back, and it needs drivin'."

She helped herself to coffee and playfully tousled Garnet's hair. "Still mad at me, little brother?"

"Not mad at all, big sister." He smoothed his hair. "Just show up at the courthouse this morning at ten." He kissed me, jammed his hat on his head, and left by the back door.

Greta and I stared at each other over our coffee mugs. "Where are you planning to go today?" she asked, breaking a long silence.

"I want to visit the herb woman that lives in the mountains, the one called Haggie Aggie. I'm thinking of writing an article about her. Can you tell me where to find her?"

"You take the Deer Tick Ridge Road until you . . ." She grinned at my blank stare. "I'll draw you a map. But be careful up there. The mountain people don't take kindly to strangers."

"Sounds like the buildup to that great horror film *The Hills Have Eyes*," I joked.

"I wouldn't laugh if I were you," she said as

she drew lines on a paper napkin. "You have to go through the village of Grandview." She designated it with an *X* on the napkin. "Don't blink or you'll miss it. Go two-tenths of a mile past the Windmill Restaurant. It might be called something else now. Then turn left where the old Swanson farm used to be, continue up the road until you see . . ."

Her directions were full of turns at barns that had burned down years ago, farms where there were no signs, and distinctive weeping willow trees. I hoped the map would be clearer.

"If you get lost, stop at the church and ask Father Buck for directions. He knows everybody up there. And keep in mind that the Hollow's where the county wants to put the waste dump." Greta drew a large circle in the center of her napkin map. "Right there."

Since we were back on the subject of the dump, I said casually, "That was some riot you organized last night."

"Thank you," she said with a satisfied smile. "Someone's got to show those smarmy little creeps on the borough council that they can't put one over on this community."

"I understand you've been visiting Percy Montrose in the evenings, trying to persuade him not to sell to the dump people."

She laughed. "Damn Lickin Creek Grapevine. It's hard to keep a secret."

"So what do you think will happen now that Percy's dead?"

She spilled coffee down the front of her chenille robe. "Dead? What are you talking about?"

"I'm so sorry. I thought for sure Garnet would have told you last night. He died a little past midnight last night. I was there with Doc. Percy's last words were that he'd been poisoned."

"Poisoned? He said that? Are you sure he said poison?"

"Of course I'm sure. He died in my arms." I shuddered at the memory. "It was awful."

"I've got to find out who's in line to inherit the property, pronto. This is terrible. What if . . ." Her voice faded as she paced the kitchen like an angry tiger.

"Wouldn't that be his son?" I asked, recalling the conversation between the two women at Alice-Ann's party last night. "I overheard Helen Montrose saying something about her husband taking over the business."

"But not the land. I remember something about Percy forming a partnership with some other businessmen. He was the front man. I need to find out who the others are."

"Did you visit Percy last night?" I asked.

She glared at me. "Who said that? Mrs. Nosey Parker Hoffman, I'll bet."

"She said she thought she saw your truck in front of Percy Montrose's house last night, only a few minutes before she found him dying."

"Good old Mrs. Hoffman. A charter member of the Lickin Creek Gossip and Grapevine Society. A woman with a vivid imagination and an overactive mouth." Greta's voice grew shrill. "Well, next time you see Maude tell her to get a life. And you can also tell her it's none of her business what I did or where I went last night. The car keys are on the hook by the back door. Have a nice day." She slammed out of the kitchen and pounded up the stairs.

I thought about our conversation as I fed the cats.

I didn't really think the message about minding her own business was for Mrs. Hoffman, and I felt ashamed of myself for irritating my hostess. But still, I wanted to know where she went last night.

As I turned the key in the ignition of the black 1985 Ford, I made a mental note to pick up a small gift for Greta. something to thank her for the loan of her car and to show her how sorry I was for upsetting her.

A few minutes later, I was downtown. Circling the fountain in the center of the square were ten people dressed in long black robes, wearing skull masks, and carrying signs that read CANLICK and DUMP GO HOME. Part of Greta's group, I assumed.

I'd fallen in love with the early-Victorian village on my first visit to Alice-Ann, more than ten years ago. Main Street with its two- and three-story brick buildings, painted in soft pastel colors, was a photographer's dream. Now, as I waited for the light to change, I noticed ominous signs: paint flaking off some charming old buildings; gingerbread trim that was no longer sparkling white. Small things that suggested downtown Lickin Creek might be going the way of a thousand other dying downtowns. I hoped not.

I drove past the Salvation Army Thrift Store and a tattoo parlor. It saddened me to see that a once lovely gift shop now had a window display of tacky Pennsylvania Dutch souvenirs: cast-iron buggies, plastic Amish dolls, and ceramic skillet-ashtrays with Gettysburg decals. I was beginning to understand why the borough council was desperately searching for a way to boost the local economy.

I stopped at Hoppengartner's Garage for gas. While a teenage boy filled the tank, I wandered into the station with some change in my hand, ostensibly looking for a soda machine, but really hoping I'd bump into Garnet.

"He ain't here," announced the girl behind the government-surplus gray metal desk.

"Do you have any sodas?" I asked coolly, determined not to look like a woman chasing after a man.

"Sure. In the fridge. Help yourself. Leave fifty cents in the dish on top."

"Thanks. Where'd he go?"

She shrugged. "Had a couple of calls this morning, so he could be anywhere." She studied a page torn from a yellow legal pad. "Little Bo Peep and two of her sheep were stolen from the VanCoeurs' front lawn last night—that's out on Still House Road. Bo Peep wore a pink dress, and the sheep had moving eyes."

I looked sharply at the girl to see if she was pulling my leg. She appeared to be serious.

"And there was a drunk-driving report, too—someone was spotted riding a tractor right down the center line of Scalp Level Road."

More of that "crime wave" Mrs. Hoffman had mentioned. I helped myself to a soda and left the garage/police station.

The crime wave would have been funny, if poor Garnet wasn't as overworked as he was. About six years ago, his father, then the chief of police, had been shot and killed by a kid on drugs during a holdup of a convenience store. Garnet had quit his job with a top Philadelphia law firm and come home to take over his father's job. If he hadn't felt such a strong sense of responsibility to the town, by now he could have been one of the top lawyers in Philadelphia, maybe even have entered politics. I wondered if he ever had second thoughts about his lifestyle choice.

Outside, I paid the teenager for the gasoline, glanced once at Greta's map, and took off for Deer Tick Ridge Road, heading northwest, I hoped.

It doesn't take long to drive through Lickin Creek, and I quickly found myself in a new development of brick-and-aluminum split-levels of the "anyhouse-anywhere—USA" school of architecture. Nearby, a new Giant-Bigmart store dwarfed the older strip malls. It was a company with a reputation for driving out small businesses in communities where it opened stores. I wondered if this was one of the reasons for downtown Lickin Creek's decline.

After passing through a depressing mile-long strip of fast-food restaurants, where the air was heavy with grease, the road began to rise to meet the forest. Because of the altitude, the trees here had already begun to change color; touches of gold, orange, olive, and even dark purple were mixed with the leftover greens of summer.

I turned on the radio but found only country-western and gospel music. I quickly pressed the Off button.

When I saw a large apple processing plant, I knew from my map that I'd soon need to make a left turn onto a state road. There was no sign, but I was able to recognize it by the farmer's fruit stand on the corner.

The state road was narrow, a testimonial to Pennsylvania's reputation for being the pothole capital of the country. With almost no shoulders at all, the road zigged and zagged ahead of me all the way to the crest.

On a curve where the road reversed itself at a violent angle, I came much too close to the edge of a "scenic overlook," where there wasn't even a guardrail to offer false security. As I jammed on the brakes, the car skidded sideways and came to a stop with its wheels only inches from the brink of a deep, dark gully. With a shaking hand, I turned off the ignition, stepped on the emergency brake, opened the car door and got out. I could see there was no danger of the car going over, but it had been close—much too close. Right at that moment, I wished I hadn't quit smoking nine years ago. A cigarette would have been soothing.

Below me stretched the entire valley, laid out like an illustration in the Richard Scarry picturebooks I'd loved as a kid. Neat little farms defined by stone walls; silos looking like spaceships waiting for a launch signal; the Borough of Lickin Creek with its dozens of church spires; a soft, green countryside crisscrossed by narrow roads; villages of no more than a dozen or so buildings marking the junctions of the roads. And fading away into a blue haze were more ranges of wooded mountains covered with the smoky mists of autumn.

After several minutes the adrenaline rush subsided and my rubber knees changed back to flesh and bone. I carefully placed the car in reverse and backed onto the road. From then on, it was a sedate twenty to twenty-five miles an hour for me.

When I reached a red barn, decorated with an advertisement for Mail Pouch tobacco, I knew I'd arrived at the village of Grandview. It was one of those places that sprout up at crossroads for no apparent reason. On one corner of the intersection was the Sons of Italy Social Club; across the street was Jeckyl's Grocery Store and Gas Station (one pump); on the third corner was a yellow mobile home with a swing set in the front yard; and on the fourth corner stood a small wooden church, weathered to a soft silver gray.

I had no idea which road to take. "If you get lost, stop at the church and ask Father Buck for directions," Greta had suggested. It was time to take her advice. I pulled into the church's weed-filled gravel parking lot. At best, it couldn't have provided parking for more than ten cars. Perhaps most of the parishioners walked, I thought, then realized that was unlikely in a rural community like this. Not too far away, I saw two farmhouses and a brick barn, and I caught a glimpse of some more trailers tucked away in the woods.

The church was narrow, scarcely more than twenty feet across. Centered directly under its peaked tin roof was a Gothic-style stained-glass window. To the left of the window hung a bulletin board, covered with cracked glass, that read ST. ANNE'S EPISCOPAL CHURCH, SUNDAY SERVICES AT 9, CHOIR PRACTICE WEDNESDAYS AT 7.

To the right of the window was a door in need of paint. A thermometer on a rusted metal backdrop that advertised Jeckyl's Grocery Store was nailed to the door frame.

The door was locked, but I noticed there was a path worn in the grass beside the building. Perhaps I'd find someone out back.

I followed the narrow pathway past three more Gothic windows. What could be the size of the congregation of a church this small? Behind the building was a fence of ornamental wrought iron with dangerous-looking spear points along the top. On the open gate was a sign: KINDLY KEEP GATE CLOSED. I passed through it, into a large cemetery, and carefully shut it behind me.

The cemetery appeared to be even older than the

church, and many of the monuments leaned at crazy angles. Stone angels and tall obelisks, far grander than the plain country church warranted, abounded, and I was delighted to see several Celtic crosses, a reminder that this particular part of Pennsylvania had originally been settled by the Scotch-Irish.

I knelt before the largest to get a closer look at its intricately carved designs—right out of the *Book of Kells*, I'd bet. "In loving memory of our grandmother, Emmy Saylor, 1859–1911" said the engraving on the base. I was deeply touched by the thought of someone's grandchildren putting up such a lovely memorial. I didn't even know where my grandmothers were buried. Another of the joys of growing up as a Foreign Service brat—you didn't know your relatives when they were alive, so you sure didn't know where they were when they were dead.

Someone coughed behind me, a polite cough, the kind one uses to call attention to oneself without startling a person half to death.

I looked over my shoulder and saw a pair of well-worn and, I must say, well-fitted blue jeans. The man wearing them appeared to be about my age: thirty-give-or-take-a-few-years. His smile revealed beautiful, straight white teeth. His nose was aquiline; a novelist of the Victorian period might even have described it as aristocratic. His eyes, under bushy blond eyebrows, were cobalt blue. His unkempt blond hair was nearly shoulder length. He could easily have passed the auditions for a major role on *Baywatch*.

He leaned on his shovel and asked, "May I help you find somebody?" He made a broad, sweeping gesture toward the grave markers with his free arm. His cultured accent was softly southern, bringing to mind thoughts of Thomas Jefferson and the University of Virginia.

"I'm looking for Father Buck."

"I'm Father Buckminister Ashby. What can I do for you?" His smile was dazzling.

"I'm trying to find the woman known as Haggie Aggie. Greta Carbaugh gave me directions, but they kind of petered out. She suggested I stop here and ask you for help if I got lost."

"You're Tori Miracle, aren't you?"

"How did you know?"

"Everybody knows you're staying with Garnet and his sister. Too bad. Here I'd been thanking my lucky stars for finally dropping a beautiful woman into my churchyard, and she turns out to be taken."

I giggled like a silly teenager and, to my chagrin, felt a blush creep up my cheeks. Good-looking guys always do that to me. Someday I hope to outgrow it.

"You have the harried look of someone who's survived the drive up the Deer Tick Ridge Road for the first time. How 'bout relaxing over a cup of coffee?" he asked.

"Sounds nice," I said.

We crossed over to the Sons of Italy Social Club, which was housed in a concrete-block building. Inside it was so dark I stumbled on the doorjamb. The air smelled of last night's beer and cigarettes.

We sat at the bar. The only other customers were two men at the other end. They wore identical plaid shirts and baseball caps that advertised John Deere tractors.

"Hey, Father," one said.

"Hiya," said the other, staring with open curiosity at me.

"Hi, fellas, how's the harvest going?"

"Best we've had in years."

"Did your pickers get here on time?"

The man closest to us nodded. "If you want to check on their living quarters, we patched them up this summer. They don't need paint or nothing. And we got running water in each house, too."

Father Buck smiled. "Glad to hear that. I'll drop by some day this week and say hello."

The men turned their attention to their sandwiches and beer.

"What was that all about?" I asked Father Buck.

"Migrant workers. There are regular ones who come each year for the apple harvest. They follow a circuit and often live under the most deplorable conditions. Since I took over the church two years ago, I've been trying to get the orchardists to fix up the camps. It took a bit of convincing, but things are slowly improving. I've even got Doc Jones coming out once a week to provide free medical treatment."

The cook leaned through the window that opened into his kitchen. "Two coffees?"

Father Buck looked at me and I nodded. When it came, with hot milk on the side, I found it to be rich and delicious. We talked for a few minutes about weather, the Apple Butter Festival, and the depressing state of politics today, while I wondered why a hunk like him was hidden away in this small mountain village. He suddenly surprised me by saying, "I read your book last month. It was very interesting."

"I'm surprised a minister would read a horror novel."

"The Episcopal Church refers to its clergy as priests, not ministers," he corrected. "It was a lot more than a simple horror novel, Tori. You made me believe there really is an evil presence in the Mark Twain house."

"It's fiction."

"But you based it on events that really happened. I know, because I did some research of my own after I read it."

I usually like to talk about myself, especially with good-looking men, but time was escaping and I needed to be on my way. "I appreciate your reaction and would love to talk more, but I really must be going. Do you mind giving me the directions?"

"I was enjoying our conversation so much, I forgot all about why you were here." He gave me detailed instructions on how to find Haggie Aggie. "The road up there is really only wide enough for one car," he told me, "so be careful. Follow it for three miles. You'll see a yellow school bus on the right, turn in there. Park and walk about a quarter of a mile. You'll see a path."

"A school bus?"

"It's Crazy Ralph's place; fairly elegant accommodations for Burnt Stump Hollow."

"Crazy Ralph?" Why, I wondered, was I heading into a place where people have names like Haggie Aggie and Crazy Ralph?

"Ralph McDougal. He's peculiar, but harmless. Leave him alone, and he'll leave you alone."

"Thanks for your help. By the way, what's a nice priest like you doing in a dump like this?"

He grinned. Could teeth really be that white? Caps maybe? "My bishop thought I was too liberal for the southern town I was in. I think I'm supposed to be doing penance, or something." He shrugged. "I fooled him. I like it here." He laid a bill on the counter, and shook his head when I fumbled with the catch of my purse.

"Come again," the cook called through the window.

"I will," Father Buck said.

"Not you. The pretty one."

We were still laughing as we stepped through the door into the brilliant sunlit afternoon. We crossed the street and stood looking across the valley where the apple trees in the orchards were heavy with fruit. "It's so beautiful," I breathed.

"It is now," the priest said. "Too bad it's all going to be gone in a few years."

"Because of the radioactive waste dump?"

He nodded.

"It's a shame," I said, "but, as I mentioned to Greta, the state has to put a disposal site somewhere. Why not here?"

He laughed. "I'll bet you didn't win any points with her. I know it's got to go in someplace, but I'll do everything in my power to keep it from being built here. Let's drop the subject before I have to drag my soapbox out from the basement."

He closed my car door for me and leaned in the window, saying, "Be careful up there, they don't . . ."

"I know—they don't take kindly to strangers, especially women. Don't worry about me, I can take care of myself." I was trying to sound confident. I hoped I sounded cockier than I felt.

Chapter 5

Sunday Afternoon

I'd thought the Deer Tick Ridge Road was bad, but it was a super-highway compared to the road into Burnt Stump Hollow. Gravel sprayed up from the sides of Greta's car like water before the bow of a ship, and low-hanging tree branches stretched bony fingers toward the car and made teeth-grating scratches on its side. I shuddered as something clanked against the undercarriage.

The tortuous road descended into a dense, shadowy forest. Sunlight flashed through the overhead branches like a strobe in some cheap singles bar, making it difficult for me to keep my eyes focused on the winding road. When a deer darted out of the brush and bounded across the road only a few feet away, I nearly lost control of the car.

I kept tapping the brakes, trying to keep the car from going downhill too fast. The two "runaway truck ramps" I'd driven past did nothing to reassure me. These were dirt roads-to-nowhere that went straight up the side of the mountain for about a hundred yards, the idea being if you lost your brakes you could aim your vehicle up one of the ramps until gravity stopped you. That is, if you could reach one before you drove off the side of the cliff.

I met only two vehicles on the road, logging trucks with full loads. The only other signs of human life I saw were a few mobile homes and log cabins, nearly hidden in the woods. From the trash strewn around, I guessed there was no scheduled garbage pickup here on the mountain.

The trees, mostly evergreens with drooping branches, closed in above me. Now, only occasional splashes of sunlight pierced the murky green tunnel through which I drove.

The bright yellow school bus, parked in a clearing about fifty feet from the road, was a cheerful sight in the dark forest. I turned right into the rutted driveway and parked next to an ancient black pickup truck with a flat tire.

Somewhere a dog barked. Otherwise, it was quiet enough to raise some good old-fashioned goose bumps on my arms.

"Hello. Anybody home?" I was still in the car, with the doors locked and the window rolled halfway up. All those warnings I'd ignored for the past two days ran through my head. "Don't go into the mountains alone. It's too dangerous. Especially for a woman. They don't like strangers up there. Especially women."

Darn it, I wasn't going to allow them to scare me off. There was nothing to be afraid of. Nothing had happened. Nothing would happen. Hadn't I, Tori Miracle, made it alone in New York City for ten years? If I could handle New York, I could handle Burnt Stump Hollow, even if I was a woman.

"Hello," I called again. I'd already decided if

there was no answer this time, I'd get out and start my hike to find Haggie Aggie.

The dog barked more frantically. If Crazy Ralph was inside that bus, he probably couldn't hear me.

Pine needles crunched beneath my feet as I stepped out of the car. The barking, I realized, was coming from inside the bus. I walked quickly and purposefully toward the path leading into the woods as though I had every reason for being there in the clearing. A few more feet and I'd be safely hidden in the trees. Just a few more feet . . .

The door popped open, and a man glared down at me from the top step. He was very tall and powerfully built, with a grizzly red-and-white beard and long, gray hair hanging over his shoulders. He wore jeans, a lavender-and-green plaid shirt, and casually dangled a large rifle from his right hand. Next to him stood a big brown poodle with a show clip, staring at me with round golden eyes.

"What d'ya want?" the men said peevishly. "I was trying to take a nap." The dog punctuated this statement with a bark.

"Is that dog dangerous?" I asked.

"Toto? He's a big baby."

"Toto? I'm a big fan of *The Wizard of Oz*. Is that where you got his name?"

"Yeah. Me and Ma went to see the movie when it first showed. I was about thirteen, I guess."

I'd never met anyone who had seen *The Wizard* the first time around. That was way back in 1939.

"Not what you'd expect a mountain man to have, is he?" Ralph said with a jack-o'-lantern smile. He was missing more than half his teeth.

"He's a beauty."

"Found him at the animal shelter. I went to get a regular old hunting dog, but when I saw them eyes, I knew I had to have him. He's been with me five years now. Good friend. Good hunting dog, too." He fondled the dog's silky ears as he spoke.

I began to relax. A man that treated a dog that well had to be okay. The "crazy" nickname had probably been given to him out of affection, not contempt.

"I'm sorry to disturb you," I began. "I'm on my way to see someone, and Father Buck, back in the village, said the best way to go was to park here and walk to her house."

"Must be going to visit Haggie Aggie," he said. "She'll take care of your little problem, no doubt about it."

"I don't know what you mean."

He winked at me. It was not a pleasant sight. "You ain't got nothing to be ashamed about. Aggie'll fix you right up."

Did he think I was going to the herb lady for an abortion? Maybe Haggie Aggie had figured out a way to make her simple Pow-Wow practice more lucrative.

"I'll walk over with you. Make sure you don't get lost or et by bears."

My first instinct was to say no thanks, but the bear reference stopped me cold. There was a mischievous grin on Ralph's face that made me think he was kidding. But—one never knows! "That's very kind of you," I said, accepting his offer.

Without another word, he set off into the dark woods, while Toto danced happily behind him. As I ran to catch up with him, I really wished I'd worn something more appropriate for hiking than faux-Italian sandals.

Father Buck had said to follow the path. What path? "Are you sure you know where you're going?" I yelled.

Ralph grinned at me over his shoulder. "It's my special shortcut. Nobody knows about it except me and Aggie." He seemed to know exactly where he was going. I kept a nervous watch on the ground in front of my feet as evergreen branches slapped at my face and things rustled in the nearby underbrush. This sure looked rattler country to me. Toto bounded on ahead of us, happily barking at chipmunks and chasing squirrels.

Something suddenly wedged itself painfully between two of my toes. "Wait a minute," I called. I leaned my back against a tree, removed my sandal, and shook out the offending pebble. By the time I had buckled the shoe back on, I came to the chilling realization that I was all alone.

I called for Ralph, but the only answer I got was my own voice echoing through the forest. I fought back panic. All I had to do, I thought, was retrace our footsteps and I'd be back at my car. Right. All I had to do was figure out which way we'd come from, and I'd be okay. Trouble was, everything looked the same to me.

I finally decided that the ground over to my right looked somewhat disturbed, as though someone had recently walked through it. That had to be the way back. As I walked, I kept calling Ralph's name, hoping either he or his bouncing dog would come to my rescue. After a good fifteen minutes of shoving my way through vines, branches, and underbrush, I was sure I was going in the wrong direction. Absolutely nothing looked familiar.

Without warning, I stepped out from the shadows of the dark evergreens into an area full of spiky, bright green plants, which towered over my head. I stopped and stared, hardly believing what I was seeing. Something whistled past my left ear, and I heard wood splinter behind me.

Someone was shooting at me! As another shot rang out, I dove for the ground and scrambled on my hands and knees toward the shelter of trees. My back was stiff with fear. Any second now, I could take a shot in the back.

When I realized I was surrounded once more by trees, I leaped to my feet and began to run. Now the forest that had seemed so threatening before was a haven for me. Branches snagged at my clothes and snapped at my face, but I ignored the pain and kept running. Right into Ralph McDougal's arms.

"What happened?" he asked. "I heard shots."

"Marijuana," I gasped. "I stumbled into a field of marijuana. Someone's after me. Let's get moving."

He covered my mouth with his hand. "Shhh," he whispered. "Listen."

There was no sound, not even a cricket or a bird chirped. Even Toto was quiet. "I think you lost them," he said after a few minutes.

I tried to calm my nerves by making a joke. "This place is as dangerous as Central Park."

Ralph didn't crack a smile. "Damn right it is," he said. "Smart thing might be for you to forget you saw it, miss."

"There must have been acres of it." We were moving pretty fast.

"Best to mind your own business."

I was too indignant about having been shot at to

mind my own business. "How can they get away with growing it up here? Wouldn't people see it?"

"Nobody ever comes this far into the forest. They'd be safe enough, at least until the roads go in for the dump construction."

"Dump construction? Is this Percy Montrose's land?"

"Most of it."

"You don't think Percy was growing marijuana, do you?"

Ralph laughed. "Old Percy? Nah! He makes enough money in that factory of his. Besides, no one grows pot on their own land. If you get caught, the government can take the land away, so people look for deserted places on other people's lands or in the state forests. The hills are full of it."

As he talked, we walked away from the illegal crop as fast as we could. My fear subsided somewhat, but I was still furious. As soon as I got back to the borough, I'd tell Garnet about the crop. How dare they shoot at innocent people!

Gradually, my natural curiosity took over as we put distance between ourselves and the marijuana field. "Where, exactly, is the location of the proposed dump site?" I asked Ralph, curious to see if it really would be as much of a disaster as its opponents suggested.

"Couple a minutes from here. I'll show it to you."

His "couple a minutes" stretched into fifteen before we came upon a collapsed stone wall, almost hidden with vines and fallen leaves. Ralph helped me climb over it, and we were in an area that once might have been a clearing. We stood on emerald-green moss, as thick and rich as an expensive wool carpet.

Unlike the unrelenting darkness of the evergreen forest, the woods around us were ablaze with autumn colors. Sunlight danced and sparkled through the leaves.

From not far away, I could hear the musical rippling of water in a brook. "This is the lowest spot in the Hollow," Ralph said in a hushed voice. "And it's the dead center of the five hundred acres they want to take for the dump."

"It would be a crime to destroy such a beautiful spot!"

"Crime's the word for it." He lowered his body onto the mossy ground, propped his back against a tree, and lit a cigarette. "Have a look around. I'll wait here."

Aside from the distant splashes from the brook, the quiet was stunning, but after a few minutes, the forest adjusted to my being there and came alive once more. I walked toward a stand of crimson-leafed maple trees and hadn't gone more than a few feet before I caught my toe on something and took an embarrassing and painful pratfall. I was thankful no one was around to see me.

My left foot was throbbing. Not a broken toe! Please! The dainty straps of my sandal were pulled away from the leather sole of the shoe. All five of my toes appeared to work, but my ankle was already beginning to swell. I couldn't tell whether or not it was broken, but I knew I'd be limping.

Just what had I tripped on, anyway? Something was protruding several inches from the ground. With a stick, I pushed aside some of the grass and debris that nearly hid it and uncovered a small square stone, with something carved on its face.

I rubbed the stone with a handful of dry leaves and could barely make out a few letters: *Wm Smi . . . 54 . . . Mass . . . 1863*. I realized now, of course, that it was a tombstone. Was it a solitary grave or had I literally stumbled into a cemetery?

I probed about with my stick, and sure enough, found some more stones. The largest of them had the easiest engraving to read: *Hypatia Hardcastle, 1790–1853, Father, forgive her.* It appeared to be in the center of the graveyard; the others seemed to be set around it in a circle. I found two more Hardcastle markers, a few Smiths, and several other names. The most recent had died in 1899. I took my notebook out of my purse and copied the inscriptions. I thought it odd that no one at last night's town meeting had mentioned a cemetery.

I stood and brushed the pine needles and dry crumpled leaves from my jeans. "Ralph," I called. "What's up with this old hidden cemetery? Some of these stones date back to Civil War days."

Ralph showed no interest. "I don't know. There's lots of family cemeteries got left behind when the families moved on. We'd better get going if we're going to catch Aggie at home."

I hobbled toward him.

"What's the matter with you?" he asked.

"Stumbled over a gravestone." I was embarrassed to let him know how much it hurt.

"Here, lean on me," Ralph said. I slipped my left arm into the crook of his right elbow, and we slowly made our way back into the gloomy forest.

"Do you know if there's any plans to move the graves before the dump is built?" I asked.

He shrugged. "Don't know, miss. Maybe you should ask someone in town."

After what seemed like hours of hiking over unfamiliar ground, I couldn't keep a whine out of my voice. "Aren't we almost there?" My foot was throbbing, and my nose told me good old Ralph hadn't bathed in a good long while.

"Only been walking five minutes."

I kept remembering the ominous warnings I'd ignored. "It's not safe up there. They don't like strangers. Especially women. Dangerous. Especially for women." In the space of a couple of hours, I'd nearly driven off a cliff, stumbled into a marijuana farm, been shot at, and probably sprained my ankle. They were right. I was wrong. When would I learn to listen?

The herb lady lived in a white trailer with turquoise trim, perched precariously on four crooked columns of concrete blocks. A black pickup, twin to half the trucks in Lickin Creek, was parked to one side. Was *this* the truck Maude Hoffman had seen at Percy Montrose's house last night? I wondered, a twinge of guilt hitting me as I thought of Greta. In the litter-strewn front yard, an enormous blackened kettle hung over a fire fueled by propane gas. The bubbling mixture inside was thick and brown and smelled of cinnamon and cloves.

"Apple butter," Ralph told me. "Me and Aggie go into the orchards after the pickers is through and gather up what's left behind. Aggie makes it into apple butter and puts it up, and we sell it at the Apple Butter Fest."

"That's the biggest kettle I ever saw."

"Holds fifty gallons. It's copper—Aggie says the acid reacts with the apples."

The herb lady was nothing like what I'd expected. The nickname Haggie Aggie had conjured up a vision of an ancient, witchlike creature with stringy gray hair and a wart on the end of her nose. The woman who greeted us warmly at the front door and invited us in was of average height and build, although a little top-heavy, and was about forty, I guessed. Her dyed black hair had faded to an implausible plum color, but was neatly, if stiffly, permed. She was dressed in a pink knit tank top and white slacks over black panty hose, and wore expensive white leather sandals on her dainty feet. Although Doc had called her a "toothless crone," she appeared to be missing only a few teeth in the back—not even noticeable unless she smiled broadly.

Ralph introduced us and said he'd wait outside.

Her name, I learned, was really Agatha Haggard. "So that's where the 'Haggie Aggie' nickname came from," I commented.

"I don't mind it much anymore," she said. "Folks remember it easy. Good for business."

"Set yourself down," she told me, after we had entered her office in a lean-to addition. "That foot looks like it needs a poultice. What'd you do?"

I described my misadventure in the abandoned cemetery, but left out the details about the marijuana. Whoever had shot at me could be looking for me right now, and my safety might depend on them not knowing who I was.

"I'd plumb forgotten about that old cemetery," she said, as she scooped a tablespoon of black powder from a canning jar into a Waring blender. To this she added a small amount of water from the faucet and sprinkled in pinches of this and that from Tupperware containers.

"Maybe you oughta sue someone," she said.

"It's kind of hard to sue someone who's been dead for a hundred years," I pointed out.

She smiled and concentrated on her creation. While she worked, I looked around the small room. Besides the rows of mason jars and plastic boxes full of mystery mixtures, a floor-to-ceiling bookcase was crammed with books. From where I sat, I could see that most were about herbs and plants. One was a guide to collecting wild mushrooms. Another was on the flora and fauna of Pennsylvania. I was surprised to see her library also included a *Merck Manual*, a *Physicians' Desk Reference*, and even a *Gray's Anatomy*.

"I see by your books you're a very up-to-date herbalist," I said to her.

She added a little more water to the compound in the blender and let it whir for a minute. "I want to be good at what I do," she said over the noise. "I got lots of patients who are being killed by doctors. First thing I do is look up their medicines in my *PDR*, to see what they've been taking. Then I start them on proper foods and taking natural medicines—not them poisons Doc Jones prescribes."

With a rubber spatula, she scraped the goo out of the blender onto a white dish and approached me with it. "It's mostly calf bones. I burn 'em and grind 'em into powder. Hold still."

She covered my foot with the greenish-black mixture and wrapped it with a large piece of soft, pink flannel. "That should do the trick," she said with a pleased look on her face. "Try to keep it up as much as possible. You can take the poultice off tomorrow. It'll be all better then."

She led me back into her small living room, which was separated from the even smaller kitchen by a counter, and invited me to rest on the sofa while she made tea. I watched Aggie as she turned on the gas under a stainless-steel tea kettle and spooned something from a jar on the counter into two mugs.

In short time, the kettle whistled, and she poured steaming water into the mugs. A peculiar odor floated toward the living room. She placed the mugs on the maple coffee table before me. "It tastes best with a little honey. Brings out the natural flavors," she said.

I stirred some into my black brew and sipped it. "Nice," I murmured politely.

"My own special blend of rose hips, camomile, and lemon grass."

"Do you grow your own herbs?"

"Some. I collect a lot of stuff in the woods like rose hips and mushrooms. The rest I get mail order."

I took another sip of tea. "I was at Percy Montrose's house last night when he died. I noticed a jar of your herbs on his kitchen counter. What were you treating him for?"

Her eyes narrowed and she looked at me suspiciously. "I know the rumor's going 'round that Percy was poisoned. You trying to blame his death on me?"

"Not at all," I protested. "But Doc was treating him for anemia, and I thought perhaps you were helping him, too."

"Maybe I was, maybe I wasn't. I'm not saying. But I do know there's truth in them rumors."

"Are you saying Percy really was poisoned?"

Her look was cagey. "I'm not saying nothing."

"Aggie, if you know something about Percy's death, you need to tell the police."

"All in good time. Let's say I'm waiting for to hear from someone else first."

"Who? What do you mean?"

"My ma raised me in a shack up here after my dad took off. No water and no electricity. I worked hard to get me this trailer. It's got electricity, phone, a well, even plumbing connected to a sand mound, lots more than Ma ever had. I even got a satellite dish, but the trouble with having TV is you get to see what *real* fancy places is like." Her voice faded, then came back strong. "I've spent my whole life here in this hollow—wanting to get out.

"The company said it'd buy up all property within two miles of the dump site. That meant my place, and for the first time in my life I would have had money. I wanted out of the Hollow—made an offer on a nice brick house in town—two stories—a little garden—a chain-link fence . . .

"But then Percy Montrose changed his mind about selling, 'cause Greta Carbaugh and her CANLICK nuts got to him with their stories about how bad it would be for everyone living nearby. Now if they don't build the dump here, I won't have enough money for the house. Unless, of course, I can come up with some get-rich-quick scheme."

She took our empty mugs into the kitchen to refill them. I pondered over what she'd just said. According to Aggie, but contrary to everything I'd heard at last night's party at Alice-Ann's, Percy was *not* going to sell his land. I'd have to ask around to see if this was true. And, I wondered, was Percy's change of plans, which threatened to end Aggie's dreams of escaping the Hollow, enough of a reason for her to kill him? Or did she know who had?

A loud explosion outside made me jump to my feet. I limped to the door behind Aggie, who opened it and screamed at Ralph.

"Cut that out, you crazy old coot! You're going to bring the law down on us one of these days."

"What happened?" I asked, as I peered around her. I saw a wisp of smoke drifting upward from Ralph's rifle.

"Stupid old man's shooting at planes again."

"Why?" I asked.

"He thinks the government is seeding clouds to keep it from raining," she said.

"Damn right it is—think on it—why else would they put a big airport in the middle of a nowhere place like Lickin Creek?" Upon sharing this inarguable bit of logic, he turned and marched toward the woods with Toto prancing behind him. He paused and turned. "Come on, miss. It's getting dark."

Aggie looked at me and shrugged her shoulders. "Now you know why they call him Crazy Ralph."

My hands shook as I accepted a loaner crutch from Aggie. It was just dawning on me that I'd spent all afternoon alone in the woods with a man who obviously was a certifiable lunatic, and now I had no choice but to walk back to my car with him.

I could smell the spicy apple butter as I hobbled back to Greta's car. It felt like an eon had passed since I'd left Lickin Creek. And what had I accomplished today by my venture into the mountains? Only that I'd discovered I wasn't the only person who thought Percy Montrose had been murdered.

Heading out of the Hollow, as I slowed for a particularly brutal curve, I saw a thin, barefoot child in a gray cotton dress playing in the dirt before a rusty trailer. Dark eyes stared out of her old face. She watched my car with such obvious envy that I felt I was looking at the ghost of Haggie Aggie's childhood. I was beginning to understand Aggie's desperate desire to escape this dismal rural pocket of poverty.

CHAPTER 6

Sunday Evening

THE SKY HAD TURNED TO BLACK VELVET BY THE time I pulled the car into the Gochenauer driveway. Before I had the car door open, Alice-Ann and Greta rushed out of the house.

"Tori, good grief, I've been waiting for an hour. Where have you been? Why is your shirt all torn up? And you've got scratches on your face." Alice-Ann's forehead was creased with concern.

I didn't want to alarm her so I said in a casual way, "I took a drive in the mountains. Had a little accident—nothing major. What's up?"

"The Literary Society meeting. You didn't forget you promised to be the speaker, did you?"

My face must have shown my dismay. I *had* forgotten.

"Oh, no," Alice-Ann wailed.

"Don't panic. I only need fifteen minutes to change. What time am I supposed to be there?"

She glanced at her watch. "Fifteen minutes will be pushing it." She gasped as I retrieved the crutch from the backseat. "What on earth did you do to yourself?"

"It's a long story. I'll tell you all about it later. Is Garnet here?"

"He should be home any minute," Greta said.

I skipped the shower I really needed and sprayed myself with Bellodgia, applied a thick layer of makeup, and brushed most of the dust out of my hair. In my navy blue wool business suit, left over from my newspaper days, I looked pretty darn good, I thought. Except for the hair, but that's hardly ever under control. And the sneakers, of course. But with one foot still wrapped in Aggie's pink poultice I didn't have much choice.

Garnet entered the kitchen from the front hall as I came down the back stairs. He stared at my foot and the crutch. "What . . . ? Are you all right? What happened?" He took my elbow and guided me to a chair. "Should I call Doc?" His forehead was wrinkled from worry.

"I'm okay, Garnet." I was enjoying having somebody make a fuss over me. After so many years of being alone, it was a nice sensation. "I just tripped over a tombstone when I was up in the mountains. No big deal." Before he could rightly remind me about how foolhardy I'd been to go there alone, I added, "By the way, I also tripped over a huge marijuana farm that looked like it covers acres and acres."

I braced myself and told him the worst. "Someone shot at me. I barely got away with my life."

"Dear God," Garnet groaned. He snatched up the telephone and alerted the State Police. He covered the receiver with one hand and asked me, "Can you describe how to find the place?"

"It's somewhere near the proposed radioactive

waste site. Actually, I was lost when I found it, but Ralph McDougal can tell you where it is. Can you keep my name out of this, Garnet? Those guys might come looking for me when they find out who exposed them."

Garnet nodded. "Good idea." He spoke a few more curt sentences into the phone and hung up. "This is the break I've been waiting for," he exclaimed. "There's been so much of the stuff around town this year, I knew there had to be a local source." He kissed me gently on my forehead. "Get some rest," he said. "I'll be back in a couple of hours."

He jammed his hat on his head and was out the door.

"Sounds like a really big deal," I said to Alice-Ann and Greta.

Greta's face was serious as she nodded. "Garnet's been telling me how heavy the drug use seems to be these days. Especially in middle school and the junior high. This may be where it's coming from."

Alice-Ann was practically tap-dancing by the back door. "Come on, Tori, puh-leeze."

"Are you coming with us?" I asked Greta.

"No. I . . . uh . . . I have a meeting to go to."

"Another CANLICK meeting?" I remarked as I walked through the door Alice-Ann held open.

"CANLICK? Of course."

The way she paused for a moment before answering made me wonder where she really was going.

Alice-Ann maneuvered her Volkswagen Beetle with assurance that came from having driven it for more than fifteen years. That little beige Bug had taken us on some wild adventures during our college days.

I couldn't help giggling, and she asked what I was thinking.

"I'm thinking I'm glad this car can't talk."

She hooted. "Remember the time we decided to drive to Mexico City for spring break? Only we didn't realize it would take three days?"

"And we picked up that guy named Raul."

"Or the time . . ."

"Remember when we . . ." We rambled on and on.

"We've sure had some good times together," I said, wiping the laughter tears from my cheeks.

"Sure have. By the way, what are you going to talk about tonight?"

"I'll think of something."

Her mouth dropped open as she turned to stare at me. "You've got guts, if not sense," she said.

Alice-Ann had explained we were to meet at Bathsheba Butterbaugh's instead of Helen Montrose's house. Out of respect for Percy. I said I found it odd the meeting hadn't been postponed. Alice-Ann grinned. "It's not at all surprising. The Literary Society hasn't canceled a monthly meeting in eighty-seven years. Not even when there was a war on. And no one misses a meeting unless they're on their own deathbed. Who knows what the others might say about them."

"Greta's missing it," I commented.

"So she is. She didn't make it last month, either. That's really odd."

The Butterbaugh residence was a large red-brick farmhouse, set far back from the road. The simple architectural style was typical of many I'd seen in the area: two stories high, with tall narrow windows, and a small balcony on the second floor. But the interior was surprisingly elegant and richly furnished. I admired the heavy, carved seating pieces, the sideboard with Wedgwood inserts in the doors, the twelve-foot-high gilded pier mirror, the assorted antique tables, the crystal vases full of fall flowers. The contents of the living room had to be worth a small fortune. I couldn't help comparing the opulence here to the depressing squalor I'd seen in Burnt Stump Hollow. Who said life was fair?

Bathsheba, I was happy to notice, had left off the mink but still sparkled with about a hundred thousand dollars' worth of diamonds. "Have you had any entries yet?" she asked me as soon as I was inside. What on earth was she talking about? I stared blankly at her.

"The apple recipe contest. I've been spreading the word. Have you had many entires?"

I shook my head as Alice-Ann said brightly, "At least a dozen. Remember how pleased you were to get such an enthusiastic response, Tori?"

"Of course." I owed Alice-Ann big for covering up for me.

"Now you be sure and pay special attention to Mrs. Featherstone's apple pie," Mrs. Butterbaugh said with a wag of one bejeweled finger. "She's from one of our first families, you know." Alice-Ann and I exchanged glances as I struggled to keep from giggling.

In the living room, between thirty and forty well-dressed women sat on overstuffed sofas, carrying on earnest conversations as they waited for me. It suddenly occurred to me that it was probably in rooms such as this where the real power lay in Lickin Creek, not in the stuffy rooms at the town hall where the country commissioners met with the borough manager.

Bathsheba's twin sister, Salome, put a cup of coffee in one of my hands and a plate of chocolate cake in the other. Thank goodness Alice-Ann came to my rescue by taking the coffee so I could eat the cake. As I ate, I surveyed the room, looking for familiar faces. I recognized Luvinia Jenkins, who looked uncomfortable in her pregnancy, Mrs. Mellot, and Helen Montrose. "I'm surprised to see her here," I said to Alice-Ann out of the corner of my mouth.

"She and her father-in-law weren't very close," Alice-Ann said. "I think she resented him for not giving her husband more authority in the business."

"I thought her husband had his own business."

"He does, but it's all small-time, small-town stuff. Logging. Apartment rentals. Airport development. Nothing big like Montrose Industries."

The subject of our gossipy exchange approached, and we greeted her with innocent smiles. "I'm so sorry I couldn't have the meeting at my house tonight, Tori," Helen said. "I'm sure you understand."

I said I did and expressed my sympathy for her family's loss.

"Mmmm," she murmured. "It didn't exactly come as a surprise. Perhaps you and Garnet can join us for dinner one night soon."

I figured if even half of the vague dinner invitations I'd received in the past two days came true, Garnet and I wouldn't have to eat at home for six months. I told her I was looking forward to it.

Bathsheba took me by one arm. "We like to start promptly at seven-thirty. And we're already ten minutes late. Alice-Ann, I do hope you'll introduce Victoria."

"Tori," I corrected.

Alice-Ann's introduction was enthusiastic and long. It took her at least five minutes to tell the group about our long-standing friendship. Then she raved so much about how wonderful my book was that anyone who read it would have to be let down. She finished by telling the ladies that today I had bravely and single-handedly discovered a huge marijuana farm in the nearby mountains, which was probably being raided by the state police even as she spoke.

So much for keeping my name out of it!

I received a hero's applause when I stood to speak.

I winged it pretty well, I thought, since like most people, I love to talk about myself. About halfway through my speech, I saw Maude Hoffman slip quietly into the back of the room and perch on the piano bench. I smiled at her and thought she looked almost as nervous as she had last night at Percy's. I continued recounting my experiences as a crime reporter in New York and finished with some amusing anecdotes (mostly made-up) about my glamorous life as an author.

Then came the questions. "How long does it take you to write a book?" "Where do you get your ideas?" "Did you have an agent?" The ladies of the club then returned to the table for more cake and coffee.

Maude Hoffman sidled up to me and asked timidly, "Do you believe in ghosts?" She looked to me as nervous as if she'd just seen one.

I answered cautiously. "I do believe there are evil entities in the world. I'm not sure they're ghosts, though. Why do you ask?"

"I think I saw one tonight," she said. "There was a spooky light moving around in Percy Montrose's house tonight. Just like a ghost. I saw it when I was leaving to come here."

Spooky light, my foot. Someone was snooping

around in Percy's house. Quite possibly his murderer, covering up evidence of the crime, I bet. I reassured Maude that the light was most likely of earthly origin and grabbed Alice-Ann's arm. "We have to go. Now," I added before she could protest.

At my urging, Alice-Ann raced past cornfields back to town, slowing down only slightly when she reached the borough limits. Luckily for us, the streets were deserted.

"You don't really think there was a prowler, do you?" she asked me. "What if he's still there?"

"Oh, I bet someone was there all right. It could have been Percy's murderer. He may be gone by now, but maybe he left something behind that will give him away."

"Or her," Alice-Ann said. "It could be a woman."

"True. I hope we get there before anyone else goes in and messes things up."

"Why are you so interested in Percy's death, Tori?" she asked. "You didn't even know him."

"True, but we shared the most important moment of his life: his death. He asked me for help. He looked into my eyes. Questioning, wondering, pleading with me to save him. It reminded me . . ."

"Reminded you of what?" She made a wide left turn that threatened to overturn the VW.

"I never told you, or anyone else, about this. When I was thirteen, we lived in Thailand. My little brother, Billy, was bitten by a poisonous snake."

"I didn't know you have a brother."

"I don't. He didn't survive."

"I'm so sorry. That must have been horrible for you."

"I haven't told you everything. I was supposed to

have been watching him when he wandered down to the riverbank. Instead, I was lying in a hammock, reading a book. So it was my fault. He died in my arms, after suffering through three days of hell. And there wasn't a damn thing I could do to help him, no matter how much I wanted to."

There's a spot on my upper lip I push on when I want to keep from crying. I put my index finger there and pressed. Hard. "That's not all, either. After that, my mother took up nonstop drinking till she pickled her brain and had to be put in a home, and my father spent all his time chasing girls half his age. Thanks to me, my whole family was destroyed."

Damn, why did I tell her my pitiful story? I feared when she heard what a terrible person I'd been, her opinion of me would change and we'd never be best friends again.

"I thought about Billy when Percy was dying. I couldn't save Percy, either, but maybe—just maybe—I can at least find his murderer."

Alice-Ann stopped the car in front of the dark Montrose house. We could see that the front door was ajar.

"Have you got a gun?" I asked her.

"God, no!"

"How about a tire iron?"

"What's that?"

"I don't know. People always seem to grab them in books."

"I've got a heavy flashlight."

"Good. I can use my crutch as a weapon if I have to."

"Wait a minute," she said, and hugged me tight.

"Dryden wrote, 'Not sharp revenge, nor hell itself can find a fiercer torment than a guilty mind.' Tori, it's okay to forgive yourself." She smiled at me. "Now, 'Lay on, Macduff.' " Alice-Ann had been an English major in college and had a great talent for using appropriate literary quotations.

"Thank you," I said hoarsely, grateful for her thoughtful words. "Let's go in."

"No sign of forced entry," I whispered, examining the front door.

"Either the door wasn't locked, or the key's under the mat," Alice-Ann said.

I lifted the mat with my toe. Sure enough. "Doesn't anybody in Lickin Creek worry about break-ins?"

She shook her head. "It's considered unneighborly to lock doors here."

"Where I live, it would be considered suicidal."

We entered quietly, although I was sure the intruder was long gone. The circle of light from Alice-Ann's flashlight revealed chaos in the kitchen. The floor, where poor Percy had died, was strewn with the contents of the cabinets and drawers.

"What do you think they were looking for?" Alice-Ann gasped.

"Something that would prove Percy was poisoned."

"Like a bottle with a skull and crossbones on the label that says 'Drink me'?"

She had a good point. Whatever it was wouldn't be obvious. What had the killer been looking for? And had he—or she, as Alice-Ann had pointed out—found it? I hoped I still might find something the killer had overlooked. Maybe some sort of Sherlockian clue like a distinguishing footprint or cigarette ash from a rare European brand smoked only by one person in Lickin Creek. Yeah, right.

"I'm going upstairs," I said. "You check the other rooms down here."

Her little squeak of protest followed me as I limped up the winding staircase to the second floor. My way was lit by moonlight filtering through a stained-glass window at the top of the stairs. When I reached the top, I was faced with a bewildering array of doors, all closed except for the one at the end of the hallway.

I walked toward the open doorway, praying that I wouldn't find anyone inside the room. It was an enormous bedroom, which I guessed to be Percy's, and it appeared as if a tornado had ripped through it. Every drawer of the mahogany dresser was open, and clothing and other personal belongings had been hurled onto the blue-and-gold Chinese rug. Even the quilt and sheets had been torn from the four-poster bed.

I stepped into the adjoining bath. It, too, had been thoroughly ransacked. Towels lay in midnight-blue heaps on the white ceramic tile floor, surrounded by the scattered contents of the medicine cabinet. Had the searcher found what he was looking for? And what had it been?

I knelt down to examine the mess, and suddenly I knew I was no longer alone in the room. The hair on the back of my neck bristled as I got a whiff of a man's highly perfumed aftershave. That's when something hard poked me between the shoulder blades. "Put your hands up and turn around. Real slow," a hoarse voice commanded.

I did as ordered. The tall figure in front of me was

an unrecognizable black silhouette in the doorway. He flipped on the lights, and I was momentarily blinded. When I finally could see again, I was staring into the enormous twin holes of a double-barreled shotgun. "You've got twenty seconds to explain," said the voice behind the gun. I briefly considered yelling for Alice-Ann's help, but realized that would most likely get us both shot.

I tried to jump-start my voice, but before I could answer, the gun lowered, and I was able to breathe again.

"I know you," he said. "You're that writer who's living with Garnet Gochenauer. What the hell are you doing here?"

"Me? Who are you, and what are *you* doing here?"

"I'm Chaz Montrose . . . this is my dad's house and I'd appreciate you getting out of his room." He stepped to one side and gestured with the gun for me to come out.

I braced myself, for the second time today, for the shot that could slam into my back any second and preceded him downstairs and into the living room. There, in the dark, Alice-Ann was frantically trying to dial Hoopengartner's garage/police station.

"Chaz Montrose!" she gasped. "Thank God it's you. When I heard voices upstairs, I thought for sure we were dead."

"What on earth? Alice-Ann MacKinstrie? You two ladies better explain why you're trespassing in my father's house. Sit down and start talking."

Alice-Ann and I perched uneasily on a Victorian sofa covered in silk rose brocade, while Chaz Montrose, eyes cold, sat on an armchair facing us. I did some fast talking and felt encouraged when he placed the gun on the floor next to his chair.

Some of my explanation was very confusing, especially when I got to Mrs. Hoffman and her ghost sighting, but in the end he seemed to understand why we were there.

"Do you have any idea what this intruder was looking for?" he asked.

Recalling Alice-Ann's crack about a bottle of poison with a skull and crossbones on the label, I shook my head. "I think he must have left something here that would lead the police to him."

"Interesting. The only thing wrong with your theory is that my father was not murdered. No matter what you think," Chaz said. His fingers moved lightly over a priceless, iridescent gold Quezal vase on the marble-top table next to his chair. Percy, or someone in his family, had possessed exquisite taste and the money to indulge it.

"Dad died from aplastic anemia, which was a side effect of the medicine he had to take for Rocky Mountain spotted fever. He would have died sooner if Doc Jones hadn't pulled him through." He studied his reflection in the silver cigarette lighter he'd lifted off the coffee table. "He was an old man, and the disease took its toll. I'm not at all shocked at his passing."

I still wanted some proof that Percy's death was a natural one. "So you don't think anyone had a reason to kill your father?"

He smiled, and I noticed for the first time that he was the double of that sexy host of *Jeopardy!*, right down to the wavy gray hair and bushy mustache. "I didn't say that. I could start with those poor guys who've been out of work for the last year, all of whom

I'm going to rehire now that I've inherited the business. And I wouldn't put anything past Greta Carbaugh and her nutty CANLICK group."

"I heard your father had decided *not* to sell to the dump company. What are your feelings about it?" I was anxious to see what his reaction would be. From what he had just said about inheriting the business, he seemed to be the main beneficiary of Percy's will.

He shrugged his shoulders. "It's no concern of mine," he said. "That partnership was completely outside of the family interests."

"Partnership? Who else was involved?"

Chaz shrugged again. "I'm not exactly sure. I expressed my disapproval of Dad's buying the property at the beginning. Once it was clear he was going ahead with the project, I stayed out of it." Something near the pink marble fireplace caught his attention, and he got up and walked over to adjust the position of an antique Staffordshire dog on the mantel.

He returned to his chair and appeared to be thinking. "I do recall there was someone from Harrisburg. And Avory Jenkins, of course." He paused as if waiting to see what my reaction would be. I kept my face a blank. "It's all on record at the courthouse if you want to know."

"Thanks for the information. I'll check it out tomorrow," I said.

He looked at his Rolex and said, "It's quite late. I'll give Garnet a call in the morning about the break-in."

We took the hint and said good night.

"Did you see what he was doing?" Alice-Ann asked indignantly, once we were in the car. "He couldn't keep his hands off Percy's things. It was disgusting."

"I know. It was like he was doing an appraisal of

the estate." Perhaps the reason he'd been fondling his father's valuable possessions was because of his fondness for his father. But his manner didn't speak of a man who'd give in to such sentimentality. Nor did he seem particularly broken up about his father's death. It looked like pure covetousness to me. And there was the way his eyes lit up when he spoke of inheriting his father's business. As far as I was concerned, Chaz Montrose was number one on my list of people who had a reason to kill his father.

Alice-Ann didn't waste any time dropping me off. "Baby-sitter probably thinks I've skipped town," she said. "See you tomorrow."

Only Greta's truck was parked in front of the house. She'd thoughtfully left lights on downstairs. I turned off all but one and went upstairs, followed by Fred and Noel. "Poor babies," I consoled them. "You probably thought I ran away from home." Bear, the lazy old thing, chose to stay on the sofa in the den.

As I put my suit in the wardrobe, I noticed my gorgeous red knock-his-socks-off nightie forlornly hanging from a brass hook. Maybe I'd better try it on, I thought. What if it makes me look fat?

The cats were watching quizzically from the bed as I adjusted the little satin bows over the shoulders when I heard a gentle tapping at my bedroom door. I opened it about an inch, peered through the crack, then opened it wide.

Garnet stepped inside and let the door close behind him. "Red is definitely your color," he said.

Chapter 7

Monday Morning

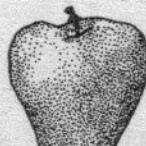

We were not yet destined to spend a whole night together. The ringing of the phone woke us at three in the morning. Garnet's face grew serious as he listened. "I'll be there in ten minutes," he said.

"I'm sorry, Tori. There's a fire downtown. I'll be back as soon as I can." He dressed quickly, gave me a lingering kiss that curled my hair, and left.

When I awoke again, sunlight was streaming through the windows and he hadn't returned. That poor guy. What a miserable job he has, I thought. For his sake, I hoped his sick police officer got back on her feet soon.

Greta smirked knowingly at me when I entered the kitchen. "Sleep well?" she asked, handing me a coffee mug.

"Mmmm," I said vaguely. "Did you have a good meeting last night?"

"Mmmm," she said, equally as vague.

At least my foot didn't hurt anymore. Whether it was thanks to Haggie Aggie's poultice or Garnet's tender care, I didn't know and didn't much care.

"What'll you have?" She gestured with one arm at the countertop. "We've got six kinds of apple coffee cake, three apple pies, two apple strudels, apple bread with and without nuts, apple . . ."

"Right, the contest." The kitchen counters, even the top of the refrigerator, were covered with home-baked goodies. "My word, where did it all come from?"

"People must have been dropping it off all day long."

"But nobody was home. You mean people can just wander in and out as they please?"

"It's the way we like it here, Tori." She handed me two pieces of toasted apple bread on a pretty pink Depression glass plate. "Try it with Mrs. Oberholser's apple jelly. It's nearly as good as mine." She sat across from me. "So, what's up?"

"Last night I had a brief encounter with Chaz Montrose." My tongue still stumbled over the Chaz bit. "He slipped it into the conversation that he has nothing to do with the land being considered for the dump site. Seems his father owned it in partnership with some other people."

"Did he tell you who they are? I need to talk to them right away."

"Hold on a minute. Apparently Percy was the front man and the others were silent partners. Avory Jenkins was one of them."

"Avory? Why that two-faced little sneak! Pretending to be thinking only of the borough's welfare when he stands to make a bundle off the sale of his land. I'd like to get my hands on him and . . ."

And what? I wondered.

"Who else is a partner, Tori?"

"Chaz said he didn't know. But it should be a matter of public record."

"So what's on Nancy Drew's agenda for today?"

"I like to think of myself as more of the Miss Marple type. Mature and observant. I'm going down to the register's office this morning to check the deed book."

"No you're not," she said matter-of-factly. "I just heard on the radio that the courthouse burned down early this morning." She flicked on the radio, ran through several stations, and found one that was broadcasting a description of the fire "live" from the steps of the Lickin Creek National Bank.

"The courthouse! When Garnet mentioned a fire, I was half asleep. I had no idea it was so serious!"

I threw on my clothes and rushed downtown. Perhaps the fire hadn't been as disastrous as the radio announcer had implied. But the Caven County Courthouse, which had narrowly escaped being burned during the Civil War by General McCausland's southern troops, had met its fiery end one hundred and thirty years later.

I parked in the library lot, where the air was heavy with smoke, and walked toward the blackened brick shell. Naturally the street was crowded with spectators as well as dozens of firemen and volunteer fire-police in Day-Glo orange vests. I pushed my way through to the yellow police tape that cordoned off the block. Garnet was inside the barrier, talking with some men. When he noticed me, he waved for me to join them.

"Anybody hurt?" I asked, as I scooted under the tape.

"Fortunately no. The cleaning staff isn't there on Sundays."

Beside him stood Avory Jenkins, his ever-present pipe clenched between his teeth, and the chief of one of Lickin Creek's volunteer fire departments. They picked up on their discussion, and I heard the word "arson" mentioned several times. "It's pretty obvious that a flammable substance was poured in through a broken window," Garnet said to Avory.

"Any witnesses?" I asked.

Avory and the fire chief seemed surprised to see and hear me, but Garnet, who was getting used to me, shook his head. "We've had a firebug in the county for a couple of years. Lost two churches and an elementary school. This is typical of his work."

"Were the firemen able to save any records?"

"The building's a total loss. Birth certificates, marriage licenses, deeds—going back more than two hundred years—all gone."

I was pushing away the nagging thought that the fire might have been set to keep me from looking at the deed book today. That was too impossible to believe. After all, only Chaz Montrose knew I'd planned to do that, and it had been he who suggested it. The fire had to be a coincidence.

"Gotta go." Garnet planted a quick kiss on the top of my head.

"Wait a second," I said. "Did Chaz Montrose tell you that someone looted his father's house last night?"

Garnet sighed deeply. "Yes, he did. He also mentioned he caught you and Alice-Ann rooting around inside the house in the dark. Aren't you carrying your investigation a little too far, Tori?"

"I don't think I am."

"Apparently neither do a lot of townsfolk. Doc had so many calls yesterday from people wanting to know what kind of poison killed Percy that he's ordered an autopsy, complete with toxicology workup, to put an end to all the rumors."

He left with the fire chief. Stymied in the pursuit of my investigation, I looked across the street at the public library. Perhaps Maggie Roy, the friendly librarian I'd met in July, could offer suggestions about what I should do next.

Carved into the marble above the library's double doors were the words POST OFFICE. The hand-lettered sign taped onto one of the doors said LIBRARY CLOSED MONDAYS DUE TO BUDGET CUTS. There were lights on inside, and I could see a woman standing at the circulation desk, so I tapped on the glass.

Maggie unlocked the door and welcomed me warmly, and we were soon sitting in the small, cluttered workroom behind the circulation desk, drinking stale coffee and eating jelly doughnuts. Since we'd first met, she'd added another ten pounds or so to her already generous figure, I noticed, and I made a mental note to restart my diet tomorrow.

We had some catching up to do to cover the past few months. "I'm so glad you stopped by," she said when there was a pause in the conversation. "I heard about you finding that pot in the Hollow. Maybe it'll open the eyes of some of our leading citizens who insist we don't have a drug problem in this town. It's getting really bad. Especially among the young people."

"How did you hear about it?"

"The Lickin Creek Grapevine. How else?" She chuckled. "And it's been on the radio all morning."

I cringed inwardly. Now I could only hope the State Police caught the perpetrators before they came after me.

She didn't notice my distress. "The police estimate the crop to be worth millions of dollars. Good work, Tori. I'm proud of you. But I do wish you wouldn't go wandering around in the Hollow. Didn't anyone tell you it's very dangerous to go up there alone?"

"A few people did mention it," I told her, refusing her offer of more coffee. I did accept one more doughnut and told her about my investigation of Percy's death and why I'd now come to a dead end in attempting to learn who the owners of the controversial mountain land were. Talking about the land reminded me of the gravestone inscriptions I'd copied. I showed Maggie my notebook and asked if she was familiar with any of the names. Especially the one on the oldest and largest stone: Hypatia Hardcastle. The name intrigued me, and I wanted to know more about her and the family members buried around her.

She studied the list for a few minutes, then shook her head. "None of the names are familiar. And I don't recall anyone mentioning a cemetery on the dump site. Seems to me it should be illegal to move graves unless the descendants give permission."

"Perhaps there are no plans to move them, Maggie. I've heard chilling stories about cemeteries having simply been covered up without the public's knowledge. Just recently some Revolutionary War graves were found under a building in New York when it was being renovated."

"That gives me the creeps, Tori. I've heard rumors about a paupers' graveyard being covered by a parking lot in downtown Martinsburg. How can anyone stoop so low as to desecrate a graveyard?"

She looked at my scribbles again. "Look at these

dates, Tori. There's quite a few from the Civil War time period. Maybe you ought to run these names past an expert."

"Any ideas of whom?"

She nodded. "Sure do. My fiancé's a reenactor. If he can't help, he can tell you who can."

Maggie told me that a huge reenactment camp was set up in the field behind the Holiday Inn. "It's one of the largest we've ever had in the area. They're going to reenact the Battle of Lickin Creek for the Apple Butter Festival this weekend."

"That sounds like something I'd like to see."

She gave me directions, told me how to recognize her fiancé, Bill Cromwell—the most handsome general in uniform—and we hugged good-bye with promises to meet again soon.

I had no trouble locating the Civil War reenactors' camp, since the Holiday Inn was one of Lickin Creek's chief landmarks. I left my car in front of the motel and walked around the sprawling building to the back. There, past the swimming pool and a row of sky-blue portable toilets, hundreds of little white tents dotted the plowed fields.

A woman in a long, full skirt smiled at me as I entered the encampment. She was dishing something out of a kettle into a blue enamelware bowl. "Would you like a sample?" she asked me.

It smelled wonderful. "What have you got? Something made from an authentic Civil War Recipe?"

"Actually it's chili. The Holiday Inn sent it out to us."

"I think I'll pass," I said. "But thanks. Do you know where I can find Bill Cromwell?"

Following her directions, I traipsed through the

field to the largest of the tents. Maggie's fiancé was sitting on his haunches in front of a campfire. He looked just like Martin Sheen playing General Lee in *Gettysburg*, except he wore a Union Army uniform. Even though I knew he was an accountant in real life, I thought he looked very noble and romantic.

He stood, removed his plumed hat, and bowed low. "A pleasure to meet you, ma'am. Any friend of Miss Maggie's is a friend of mine." Lucky Maggie, I thought. Her fiancé was adorable.

He showed me around the interior of his little tent. Everything in it was actually from the Civil War era, right down to the straight-edge razor he used for shaving.

After the tour, we sat on low stools before his campfire. I told him about the long-lost graveyard I'd found and showed him my notebook, full of names, numbers, and abbreviations.

He studied it and could hardly restrain his excitement. "See this one," he pointed out. "G.A.R. was the Grand Army of the Republic. U.S.C.T. stood for the United States Colored Troops, established in 1863.

"This cemetery is a historical treasury. The 14th Regiment—that was the Rhode Island Heavy Artillery. The 51st Mass., the 29th Connecticut, the 41st—that was a Pennsylvania regiment. The 54th Mass. . . ."

"I didn't realize there had been such a large black participation in the Civil War."

"Over 186,000 men—more than 135 regiments. It's only recently that they've started to receive some of the recognition that's due them."

He was beginning to sound like a professor I'd had in college. "The only black regiment I'd heard of was the one in the movie *Glory*," I said. "I thought it was the only one."

"Correcting popular misconceptions like that is one reason we reenactors feel so strongly about what we do. No cemetery should be left to go to ruin, but it is especially appalling when one remembers that these brave men gave their lives for this country. They deserve to be treated with respect. One of the goals of my brigade is to locate and clean up the old cemeteries where these veterans are buried."

"You sound as if the hills are full of lost graveyards," I said with a smile.

"They are," he said, sounding serious—and so young. "There are hundreds of abandoned farms and old ghost towns in Pennsylvania. Most of them sprang up in the nineteenth century to support quick-hit mines and the lumber industry. When the coal and the trees ran out, the people moved on, leaving everything behind, including their dead. With the vegetation that's grown up over the past hundred years or so, it's almost impossible to find any traces of them now."

"That's the way this place is," I told him. "Most of the stones have fallen over, and it's completely overgrown. Unless you're clumsy enough to trip over a stone like I did, you wouldn't even know it's there. But now that I've found it, it seems to me that efforts should be made to locate the family and have the graves moved before the land is covered by the waste dump."

I thought of Buchanan McCleary, the borough solicitor. "I know a lawyer," I said. "I'll ask him if there isn't some law protecting old cemeteries."

"Good idea. And I'll check with a state archaeologist friend of mine in Harrisburg."

We agreed to meet again in a few days and share what we learned. I said good-bye and left him chewing out a soldier in an authentically pungent wool uniform, who'd shown poor judgment in drinking Diet Pepsi from a can.

I made the logical mistake of looking for Buchanan McCleary's office in the town hall, several blocks from Main Street but not far from the courthouse. The woman who sold dog licenses in the front office directed me to the town hall annex in the next block.

The annex was a building with a red-tile roof left over from its original incarnation as a Pizza Hut. Sharing the parking lot was another building that looked a lot like it had started life as a gas station. The sign above its door said CHURCH OF GOD, WHERE DO YOU WANT TO SPEND ETERNITY? I thought both attempts to recycle buildings were ingenious.

I pushed the door open and entered a large room. Buchanan McCleary sat with his back to the door, his feet on his desk, talking on the telephone. His smile lit his face as he swiveled to face me.

"What a nice surprise. Can I get you some tea?"

"As long as it isn't herbal," I said, remembering Haggie Aggie's strange-flavored brew.

"Earl Grey. I always stop for a cuppa around this time. It's a habit I picked up in England when I was a Rhodes Scholar."

I liked the way he worked that bit of information in right at the beginning of our conversation. Letting me know he was no local-yokel.

He unfolded all of his six feet eight inches and stepped across the room to where there was a kettle on a single-burner hot plate. "Milk or sugar?"

"Both." He handed me a blue-and-white Spode mug filled with aromatic tea. "Lovely," I said, admiring the china. "Did you bring this with you from England?"

"Certainly did. No point in letting down one's standards here in the colonies. Now, what can I do for you?"

I briefly told him of my suspicions that Percy had been murdered. He knew all about it, of course.

"So you want to know who Percy's silent partners were? Any particular reason?" he asked me.

"It seems the logical place to start. If they wanted to sell the land and Percy wouldn't go along with the sale, it was to their advantage for him to die. And there's something about a silent, secret partnership that challenges the reporter in me. I keep thinking that innocent people don't have anything to hide."

"There are a number of reasons—all perfectly legal—for not wanting a partnership to be a matter of public record. I happen to know who one of the partners is because he was visiting Percy one day last year, and Percy introduced him to me at the VFW."

"VFW? What's that?"

"Veterans of Foreign Wars—it's the social center of town for the over-forty crowd. We were all having dinner one night. He had a name you can't forget: Aldine Schlotterbeck. From down in Harrisburg, I think."

I jotted down the name in my notebook. "That's two, then. Chaz Montrose told me Avory Jenkins is a partner."

He made a little tent with his fingers and rested his chin on it. "Interesting! I can't assist you officially, Tori, but I'll do a little digging and see what I can come up with. Now that you've told me about Avory, I'm beginning to wonder who else stands to gain from the sale of that land to the dump company. As borough solicitor I'm supposed to remain neutral, but off the record I'd like to see that dump go elsewhere."

"There's one other matter I need to ask you about," I said as I pulled my list of tombstone inscriptions from my purse.

Buchanan studied it.

"Do you recognize any of the names?" I asked. "I want to find out if any of their descendants are living."

"Actually, I'm not really local. My family came from Mercersburg, as you might have guessed."

I didn't have the foggiest notion what he was talking about and said so.

"My name. President Buchanan was from Mercersburg."

"How could I not have known that?"

His grin split his face. "He might be a forgotten president to most Americans, but not to the folks in my hometown. Suppose you tell me why you're trying to identify these people."

I described finding the cemetery and what Bill Cromwell had told me about the African-American veterans who were buried there. "I understand there're many deserted graveyards in the hills, and I want to know if there's a law protecting them."

"It's a legal, moral, and ethical dilemma. The descendants of these people should be notified—at least a good-faith effort made—before construction starts. Then a decision needs to be made whether to move the bodies to another cemetery or if the site should be sealed off as a shrine to heroic African-Americans of the slave era." He opened the top drawer of his desk and pulled out the Lickin Creek telephone book. "No Hardcastles listed. Got a page and a half of Smiths, though. This won't be easy."

He studied the list again. "You say Hypatia Hardcastle had the largest stone?"

"Yes. It was definitely the most important one there."

He leaned back in his chair. "Here's my suggestion, Tori. Go see P. J. Mullins at the *Chronicle* and ask her to run an article about the graveyard saying a search is being conducted for the descendants of Hypatia Hardcastle. Get the public interested. I can't get involved because of my official position with the borough, but you can. Who knows, maybe Hypatia can accomplish from the grave what Greta and her CAN-LICK people have been trying to do for months."

"Do you mean this could stop the dump from being built in the Hollow?"

"At least it might slow things down. Maybe the company will get fed up and look elsewhere."

I swallowed the last of my tea. "Thanks, Buchanan. I'll go see P.J. right away."

His expression turned serious. "Be careful, Tori. You might find people won't appreciate what you're trying to do."

Chapter 8

Monday Afternoon

Standing in the parking lot shared by the town hall annex and the Church of God, I could still smell the smoke from the courthouse fire. I glanced up at the clock on the town hall tower and was surprised to discover it was only a little past noon. The newspaper office was just a few blocks away, on the other side of Main Street. Since it was such a warm, beautifully bright day, I left the car where it was and walked.

The borough's weekly newspaper, the *Chronicle*, was housed in a narrow brick building, built in 1846 according to the words engraved on the tarnished brass plaque next to the front door. The red vinyl furniture with metal arms in the waiting room dated back to the forties when the present publisher's grandfather had still been in charge. Dusty daisies in a pink plastic vase sat on a maple coffee table next to an overflowing ashtray. I couldn't see that anything in the room had changed since my last visit.

From the next room came a protracted, hacking cough. P. J. Mullins, the editor/publisher of Lickin Creek's only paper, was sitting at her rolltop oak desk when I walked into her inner sanctum. A trail of blue smoke drifted up from the cigarette dangling from the corner of her mouth. I was glad she smashed the butt in the full ashtray before hugging me.

P.J.'s usual style was to dress like Katharine Hepburn in pleated men's-style slacks and a white cotton shirt over a turtleneck jersey. Today, a red silk scarf at the neck added a jaunty touch. Her steely-gray hair was short, and she wore little half-moon glasses perched low on her nose.

"About time you came by to see me," she scolded pleasantly. Her accent was Hepburn's, too. Clipped and raspy. In fact, a lot raspier than I remembered.

She waved me to have a seat, sat at her desk, lit another cigarette, coughed maniacally for about five minutes, and said, "I'm putting out a special edition tomorrow. First time in years I've had enough news to warrant it. First you find that marijuana farm in the mountains, then the courthouse burns down. This is great stuff!"

One of the reasons I'd been glad to get out of the reporting business was it was hard for me to think of tragedies as great stuff. But I refrained from saying so. Instead, I asked P.J. if she had any space left in tomorrow's special edition.

She lit a cigarette with the one that was nearly finished and asked me why I wanted to know.

I told her about the sad little graveyard, standing forgotten in the woods of the Hollow. About the graves, so overgrown with vegetation that they were invisible. About Hypatia Hardcastle, surrounded by the Civil War veterans.

"What's your interest?" she asked me.

"I started out just being curious. Then someone

told me about the African-American involvement in the war, and I began to think there might be a book in that graveyard."

She stared at me over the top of her glasses. "Did you know that's the land the dump company's looking at buying?"

"Someone did mention that," I said innocently.

Her laugh, which rumbled moistly up from her lungs, made my skin crawl. "Your little cemetery could generate a lot of controversy. I love it." She coughed. "I'll squeeze something in, and do a longer follow-up story in the regular Saturday edition."

She changed the subject abruptly. "Have you had any experience editing a newspaper?"

"I don't think I . . ."

"It would be temporary. Three months—six, tops."

She clasped a tissue over her mouth and coughed for a minute or more. "I need to have a little operation. I'll be off for a few months, recuperating. Nobody in town knows beans about running a newspaper. Hoped you could help me."

My mistake was in not immediately saying no, but trying to excuse my way out. I voiced several reasons why I couldn't. No place to stay? No problem—P.J. had a college professor friend who was going on sabbatical and needed a house sitter. Book to finish? Paper's a weekly—"You'll have plenty of time to write," she assured me. Whatever the objection, she had the solution.

I couldn't escape until I promised I'd think about it. By the time I reached the car, I'd half convinced myself it would be a good move. Cheap apartments in New York were easy to sublet, even in a rotten neighborhood like mine. The job would take care of my money problems for a while, I'd be able to finish my book, and I'd have time to find out if Garnet and I were really meant to be a couple. I was eager to talk it over with him.

As I drove through the square, I noticed the pots of chrysanthemums had been removed from the base of the fountain, replaced with baskets of red and gold apples. The fire trucks were gone, and only a few firemen were to be seen. It was a peaceful picture, if one ignored the blackened courthouse walls.

I stopped at the State Liquor Store and bought a bottle of German wine as a small gift for Greta. It had an attractive label, not one that I recognized, but I figured it would probably be better than that boxed wine she kept in the refrigerator.

Greta was standing at the kitchen counter, busily chopping vegetables and singing along with some country-western singer on the radio. The cats lay sprawled on the kitchen table, and Bear sat alertly at Greta's feet, barking at three-second intervals, waiting for something, anything, to drop.

"Thank goodness you're home!" she yelled over the din. "Just look at all this food. We have to start taste-testing, or we'll be run out of house and home by all this stuff."

I handed her the wine bottle. "For you."

"Thanks, Tori. This looks lovely. I'll pop it in the fridge to cool."

So I set aside my investigation for the time being and joined Greta at the table, where we methodically took small bites of about fifty apple creations and wrote our comments on the accompanying recipe cards.

I sampled a salad consisting of apples, tomatoes, onions, and garlic, flavored with mint. "No way!" I felt the same about the sliced beets and apples in lemon Jell-O. But something called a schnitz pie, made from dried apples, had a really good chance of being the grand-prize winner.

Greta suddenly glanced at her watch and jumped to her feet. "I gotta go. Will you redd up, please?"

I was a little surprised at the abruptness of her departure but glad of an excuse to end the tasting session. I'd already reached the point where I was offering silent thanks to the inventor of the elastic waistband.

To "redd up," as Greta said, I emptied the plates into the sink and shoved the scraps down the drain. When I flipped the switch I assumed would turn on the garbage disposal, a light came on overhead instead. To my dismay, there was no disposal. I had to spend the next five minutes scooping the mess out of the drain by hand. Then, overly full and sapped of energy, I flipped through *TV Guide* to see if there was a horror movie on to relax to. There wasn't, so I settled for Oprah.

When the phone rang, I was delighted to hear Garnet's voice. He whispered a few things about last night's rendezvous that made my cheeks burn pleasantly. Then he said, "Why don't you call Alice-Ann and invite her and Doc to go out to dinner with us tonight?"

"Can you get away?" I asked. "I know how busy you are."

"I need a break. The town's quiet; Luscious ought to be able to handle things by himself for a few hours."

I called Alice-Ann and arranged to meet her and Doc at seven at the Log Cabin Restaurant on the east edge of town.

When we arrived, the parking lot was already full of trucks, so Garnet had to leave his parked on the shoulder of the road. The restaurant really was constructed of logs, big black ones with white plaster filling in the chinks between them.

The huge, brightly lit dining room was packed with men in jeans and plaid flannel shirts and women in rather plain cotton dresses. Heads turned to watch as the four of us entered, then voices greeted Garnet and Doc with "Hey, boy" and "Yo, man."

We sat at a table for four, where the place mats were white paper, printed with advertisements for local businesses. Our waitress, in peasant blouse and dirndl skirt that maximized her hips, placed plastic-covered menus in front of us. "Tonight's special is chicken-corn soup," she said. "If we got any left. You'uns should know you can't come late if you want good eats."

I was still full from the afternoon tasting session, so I ordered a chef's salad to go with my soup. Alice-Ann congratulated me on sticking to my diet as she tackled a platter of overdone roast beef and french-fried potatoes, smothered with gravy.

Garnet finished off a giant-sized serving of fried chicken, leaned back, and patted his middle with a happy sigh. "Haven't had a meal like this since Greta moved in. She thinks eating out's a waste of good money—especially when, as she says it, she can cook better than any restaurant."

Over dessert (yes, I had a tiny piece of cheesecake), we chatted, and when it was my turn I told them about my attempt to identify the inhabitants of the secret graveyard, including my visits to the library, the Civil War reenactors' camp, Buchanan McCleary's office, and the *Chronicle*.

Alice-Ann got very excited. "Do you think there's a chance this could hold up the construction of the dump?"

"Probably not. But it might slow things down so much that they'll decide it's easier to look for another site."

Garnet just shook his head.

"I hope so," Alice-Ann said. "Wouldn't that be great, Merry?"

Doc shrugged noncommittally. He and Garnet exchanged superior "guy looks."

"Have you found out any more about Percy's murder?" Alice-Ann asked.

"It wasn't murder," Garnet interjected.

"If Tori says it's murder, then it's murder. She was the best crime reporter in New York, you know. And you know as well as I do that without Tori, we never would've solved the mystery of my husband's murder."

Good old Alice-Ann, I thought, always my best and most loyal friend.

Garnet groaned and refilled his coffee cup from a white plastic thermos jug.

"I learned the name of one of Percy's partners," I said. "Someone down in Harrisburg. I'll give you his name if you like, Garnet. Maybe you want to check him out."

Garnet's only response was another groan.

"Okay, I'll do it myself. But first, I want to visit Haggie Aggie again. I have the feeling she knows more than she's saying."

Garnet rolled his eyes, while Doc grinned. "Look, Tori," Garnet began. "You're meddling in local affairs that don't concern you. Why don't you just drop all this?"

"But why? You've already said you didn't think Percy's death was murder."

"It's not your investigation of Percy's nonmurder I'm worried about. What does worry me is the drug gang whose cash crop you've ruined—those guys are bound to be out for your hide. I don't want you to get hurt. Try cooling it until we catch them, okay?"

There was no point in arguing. It would only upset him. But I did intend to return the crutch Aggie loaned me. And ask a few questions. I was sure if I moved with caution, I'd be all right.

Somehow the subject then changed to fishing and the size of the natural brown trout in the Lickin Creek. Even I had to agree it was more appropriate for dinner conversation than murder.

I couldn't remember when I'd enjoyed an evening as much as this one. It was like being back in college, double-dating with Alice-Ann and two great guys. The thought occurred to me that if things worked out with Garnet and me, evenings like this could become a regular part of my life.

Yes, the more I thought about it, the more I liked the idea of staying on for a few months as acting editor of the *Chronicle*. I couldn't wait until Garnet and I were alone to tell him about the offer. What, I wondered, would be his reaction to having me around full-time?

As if he were thinking along the same lines, Garnet took my hand and squeezed it. He leaned close, clear blue eyes looking deep into mine, and began,

"Tori, there's something I've been wanting to talk to you about . . ."

His right front pocket beeped. "Damn," he said and went to find a phone. He was back in a few minutes. "Bunch of kids having an apple fight in the square. I warned the Garden Club not to put those fruit baskets around the fountain.

"I'm sorry, Tori, but this is a typical evening in our little town. I have to go. It's turning out to be a hell of a vacation for you. But I promise I'll make it up to you next week."

The moment was gone. Whatever he'd planned to tell me would have to wait.

CHAPTER 9

Tuesday Morning

"HAS GARNET ALREADY LEFT?" GRETA ASKED.

My cheeks heated up. "How should I know?" I said, taking a gulp of coffee that burned my tongue.

She grinned.

I nibbled a piece of the spicy applesauce-marshmallow cake that had appeared on the kitchen table sometime during the night and shooed Fred off the newspaper that lay folded in front of my plate.

My picture nearly filled the front page of the *Chronicle*, under the headline "SPOOK WRITER SMOKES OUT POT." I don't know where it came from, but it made me look as though I had three chins. But what chilled me to the bone was that someone had used a wide-tipped marking pen to draw a red circle around my photo, then had neatly bisected my face with a slash that cut diagonally through my left eye to the right side of my mouth.

The fright I felt must have shown in my face, for Greta came to look over my shoulder. "Good Lord," she gasped.

"Where was the paper when you came downstairs?" I asked her as I stared at the picture. Someone was trying to scare me away. Who?

"On the porch, where it's always left. I brought it in but got busy making breakfast and didn't even look at it."

I shivered. Not only did someone use our own paper to send me an ominous warning, but it also occurred to me that my face was on every breakfast table in Lickin Creek. Even the most mentally challenged illegal drug runner would recognize me instantly. I hated to admit it, even to myself, but Garnet apparently was right. I'd been meddling in places where I had no business to be, and I was in danger.

I sipped my coffee and let my eyes skim the rest of the front page. An article about the courthouse fire took up most of the space. In a box in the lower-right-hand corner was a smaller, less lurid lead, "THE SEARCH FOR HYPATIA HARDCASTLE." My name was featured prominently in the write-up.

I skimmed the rest of the paper to see what I'd be expected to cover if I took over. Besides the two-column obituary for Percy Montrose, there were a list of winning lottery numbers, a photo of the grand champion steer at the Caven Country 4-H Beef Club's Annual Roundup, and an article about this being the time to store hay for winter. Classified ads filled the remaining space. At least it wouldn't be difficult to maintain P.J.'s standards, I told myself. That is, if I wasn't wiped out by a vengeful drug gang. Why hadn't I kept my mouth shut?

Last night, after Garnet dropped me off before heading downtown to put an end to the apple fight, I had found a note on the table saying Maggie had called. It was too late then to call her back, but I figured by now she'd be at the library. When I called, she urged me to hurry down, saying she had some information to share with me. Infuriatingly, she wouldn't give me a hint of what it was.

Since I planned to visit Aggie Haggard after stopping at the library, I grabbed her crutch from the drip pan of the oak hall tree next to the back door.

"Better take an umbrella," Greta suggested. "Looks like we're going to get some weather."

Downtown, the black-robed protesters were still circling the fountain carrying CANLICK signs. It had already begun to rain, and they looked miserable but determined. Inside the library, I stepped around a group of preschoolers enjoying story hour and found Maggie shelving books in the history section. She wiped the book dust off her hands and led me into her office. Her desk was covered with yellowed newspaper clippings and tattered folders.

"I spent most of yesterday afternoon going through the pamphlet files and our historical collection," she told me. "I've found a couple of mentions about your Hypatia."

I accepted a mug of coffee and settled down in Maggie's chair. "I'll leave you with this," she said. "I promised to tell the kids a Johnny Appleseed story. Then I've got to type about a zillion catalogue cards. I can't keep up with everything here. I sure hope Alice-Ann's considering my offer."

"Alice-Ann's thinking about coming back to work? I didn't know that." I was surprised and a little hurt my best friend hadn't shared this with me. Of course, I hadn't yet told her about my taking a job with the *Chronicle*, so I supposed we were even.

Maggie shrugged. "We've just talked about it once or twice. Seems Richard's estate is a real mess. By the time she settles with all his creditors, she thinks she'll need to work. She probably didn't tell you because she didn't want to worry you. There's more coffee in the pot. Help yourself. I'll be back in an hour."

The newspaper clippings were from a paper that preceded the *Chronicle*. The first mention I found of Hypatia Hardcastle described a property she'd purchased in town in 1833 from John and Mary Saylor for $450 in cash. According to the article she was a single farm-woman from Burnt Stump Hollow, in her forties, who had three children.

One clipping from the historical file folder was a brief announcement that the Hardcastle land in the Hollow had been sold to some local businessmen by Ann Smith in 1906. The article went on to say that Miss Smith retained the right to move the family cemetery sometime in the future.

When Maggie came in and perched her ample rump on the desk corner, I was leaning back in the chair thinking about Hypatia. Although the references I'd read were not very descriptive, I found myself imagining a middle-aged woman in a patched cotton dress, her hair hidden by a kerchief, walking with head held high into the courthouse to buy her land. With her were three young children, dressed in clean, carefully mended clothes.

"What was it like for her?" I wondered out loud. I assumed she was a black woman because of the other graves around her. Had she once been a slave, or was she born free? How had she managed to save $450? That must have been quite a sum in those days. Had she and her children lived all that time in the Hollow? How proud she must have felt when she was able to buy property in town. Most of all, I wondered about the inscription on her tombstone: *Father, forgive her.* There simply had to be an interesting story there. "I think I'd like to write a book about her."

Maggie terminated my soliloquy. "Sorry, Tori, I need my desk back."

I vacated the chair. "Seems to me it won't be too hard to find people who were related to her."

Maggie smiled a lopsided grin. "It'll be hard if they don't want to be found."

"Why wouldn't they . . . ?"

"Think on it. What if her descendants don't want to be publicly identified?"

"Because she was black? In this day and age? It's impossible for me to believe that someone would be ashamed or embarrassed about coming from mixed lineage."

She smiled at my indignation. "I don't think people are quite as liberal in Lickin Creek as they are in New York."

"I'm an optimist," I said. "I'll bet the article in today's paper turns up someone."

Maggie looked up at me with a quizzical look on her face. "Don't count on it."

According to the clock on the wall, it was already noon. If I was going to talk to Haggie Aggie, I'd have to be on my way. "I don't know how to thank you for doing all this research for me," I began.

She brushed my thanks away with a wave of her hand. "It was my pleasure. Really. Every now and then I like doing things like this to remind me why I went to library school."

I left Maggie thumbing through a *Library Journal*, retrieved the car, and drove out of town.

The road up the mountainside was even more treacherous than usual. The rain had stopped, but now mist swirled up from the valley below, creating cloud pockets that drifted across the road and that would, without warning, suddenly surround the car in a soft, white cocoon. At first, I thought mine was the only car on the road, but several times when I glanced in my rearview mirror I noticed a black car fading in and out of the wispy fog bank behind me. Otherwise, except for a couple of logging trucks barreling down the mountain, I was alone.

Ralph's school bus home was a yellow ray of sunshine in the gloomy forest. Reluctantly, I parked and got out of the car, hoping I could make it into the woods before Ralph saw me. Somewhere off in the distance I heard a barking dog. I was sure it was Toto. Luck was with me, and I reached the trail without being seen.

I had a few doubts about finding my way to Aggie's. What if I stumbled into another marijuana field? Worse yet, what if whoever owned the field wanted to seek revenge on me for exposing them? What if Ralph saw me, shot first, and asked questions later? Fortunately, my good luck held.

I followed the path through the woods instead of Ralph's infamous "shortcut," and after about fifteen minutes I stepped into the clearing, where a fragrant batch of apple butter was bubbling away in the copper kettle.

I climbed the concrete block steps, knocked on the door several times, and waited. Knocked again.

No answer. The door, I noticed, was slightly ajar. It creaked as I opened it wider. I stuck my head through the opening, and called, "Aggie, you home?" I stepped inside, worried now that something had happened to the herb woman.

From the rear of the trailer came the sound of a toilet flushing. Aggie walked into the living room, tucking her blue-and-white-striped T-shirt into the waistband of her white slacks. I'd never heard anybody actually scream "EEEK!" before.

She eventually accepted my apology for having barged in uninvited and offered me a mug of her newest herbal blend. While she bustled about in the kitchen area, I snooped around the living room hoping to get a better picture in my mind of Haggie Aggie, Pow-Wow doctor, herbalist, and probable abortionist.

Lying open on an end table was her *Physicians' Desk Reference*. I picked it up, curious to see what Aggie had been researching. I only had time to notice a passage that had been highlighted in yellow when Aggie took the book from my hands and slammed it shut.

"Honey?" she asked.

"Please."

We sat across from each other on brown-velour-covered recliners and sipped our tea.

"Hear you're looking for relatives of the people in that graveyard you found," she said.

For a moment I thought the Lickin Creek Grapevine was doing extra duty, but then I noticed the *Chronicle* lying on the floor beside her chair. I nodded. "Have you ever been there?"

"Once or twice, I guess. Don't care much for that dead-body smell you get there."

I ignored her rude remark. "Have any idea who, in town, might be related to the people in the cemetery?"

She laughed. "Hardcastle? Nobody around by that name . . . now."

"How about in the past? Any you can think of?"

Her eyes narrowed. "So what if I can? You sure got a lot of questions. What is it you want from me?" she asked, her voice and eyes cold. "I know you didn't come all the way up here just to return my crutch."

I shuffled my feet in the orange shag carpeting and decided the best way to deal with her outrage would be to speak frankly. "I want you to tell me what you know about Percy Montrose's death," I said. "You said something last time I was here. Made me think you know more than you're saying."

The anger left her eyes and was replaced by something even less attractive, something sly and sneaky. I sat down and waited. Sometimes the best way to get someone to start talking is not to say a word.

"I was there, you know, the night he died. I went there that night to warn him that someone was trying to kill him, but I was too late. He fell on the floor and there wasn't nothing I could do to help him. So I took the poison and left."

"So it was your truck Maude Hoffman saw, wasn't it? How could you have left him there, knowing he was dying?" Righteous indignation sometimes overcomes my good judgment and makes me speak out recklessly.

"I already told you there wasn't nothing I could do to save him."

"You said you went there to warn him. How did you know someone was trying to kill him?"

Her mouth clamped tightly shut.

"How did you know he'd been poisoned?"

"I got proof."

"What is it?"

"I ain't telling you. I told you I gotta get off this mountain," she said. "I'll do whatever it takes."

"Are you planning to use what you know to get money out of someone? Blackmail's illegal, you know. And dangerous. You're not going to get anything out of this but trouble."

A puff of derision burst through her lips. "I'll take my chances. I don't have much to lose." She gestured with one arm at the tiny, cheaply furnished room.

"I don't believe a word you've said," I taunted her. "I think you're making all this up. If Percy really was murdered, the killer had to be quite crafty because his death appeared to be a natural one. I guess it would take a much more clever person than you and me to figure out how it was done."

As I hoped, this taunt jolted her ego. "I know how it was done. I told him . . ."

"Told him what, Aggie? What do you know? If you've really got proof that Percy was murdered, tell me what it is and where it is."

The sly look was there again. "If I tell you, Miss Smarty-Pants, how do you think I can get what I need?"

"If you don't, how can we ever be sure that the murderer gets the punishment he deserves?"

"Maybe I'll get what I want, then tell."

Charming lady. Not only a blackmailer, but a double-crossing one as well.

I made one more attempt to squeeze information out of her. "Why don't you tell me where you're keeping this proof you mentioned?—sort of as insurance that nothing bad happens to you. You don't even have to tell me what it is."

She burst out laughing. The woman was smarter than she looked. It was time to get out of there, or I might be tempted to do something that could be construed as illegal. Like strangling her till she told the truth.

I moved quickly to the door, my shoulders tense with the fear that she might come after me. I still wasn't a hundred percent sure she hadn't killed Percy herself. After all, she'd just described Percy's death to me and admitted she'd been there the night he died. The rest of what she'd told me about blackmail could have been an attempt to misdirect me.

As I reached the edge of the clearing, she called after me, "Ain't you afraid someone's going to get you?"

I turned to face her. She was in the doorway and smiling wickedly. "Who?" I asked. "Who's going to get me?"

"Maybe whoever murdered Percy. Maybe those drug farmers you put out of business."

"I'm not scared," I said with a bravado I didn't feel.

"You should be," she replied. She laughed and slammed the door with a bang that rattled the aluminum on the side of her trailer.

I made it safely to the car. As I opened the door, I heard the sharp retort of gunfire coming from the woods. "Sonsabitchingcloudseeders," Ralph yelled, not far from me. I jumped in, locked the doors, and drove as fast as I could out of charming Burnt Stump Hollow.

In the village of Grandview, I stopped at the crossroads where the Episcopal church stood and spotted Father Buck raking leaves among the sculpted angels and Celtic crosses in the churchyard. On an impulse, I pulled into the parking lot. He smiled broadly when he saw me.

"Hope I'm not interrupting anything," I said.

"Nope. Just getting ready to wash up. I read about you in this morning's paper. You're quite the heroine!"

I smirked.

"Damn fool thing to do, though, prowling around the mountains like that."

My smirk faded.

"Won't you step inside my humble abode?" We'd been walking beside the church as we talked, and now stood next to a lean-to shack attached to the back of the building.

"Ah, the vicarage. I've wanted to visit one ever since I read my first Christie novel." I stepped inside.

The solitary room was lit by one lightbulb, hanging from a cord over our heads, and simply furnished. But what was in there was all top-quality, from the walnut desk on my right to the comfortable leather armchair in a corner with a halogen reading lamp standing beside it. Overflowing bookshelves completed the picture of a single, literate man who spent quiet evenings alone. The single brass bed was unmade, and Buck turned red, mumbled something about "the butler's day off," and drew a handmade quilt over the rumpled sheets.

"Excuse me, I'll be right back." He stepped through a door, which was open just long enough for me to see it led into a small bathroom.

I heard the sound of running water and splashing. A few minutes later, when he came back, he wore a fresh shirt and was clean-shaven. The little patch of toilet tissue stuck to his cheek was a winsome touch.

He asked me how my investigation into Percy's murder was coming along. I was glad to hear him say "murder." At least someone believed me. I filled him in on what I'd been doing since we'd first met: the discovery of the Hardcastle graveyard, learning that Percy's house had been searched, the Civil War Reenactment Camp, what I'd discovered about Hypatia Hardcastle at the library, and my visit an hour earlier to Haggie Aggie's trailer.

"Whew," he breathed, brushing a stray lock of hair off his forehead. "Not only beautiful, but brainy."

I looked around to see where the inane giggle had come from. Certainly not *moi*!

He glanced at his watch. "Let's get lunch."

While we waited for our food at the Sons of Italy Social Club, we talked a little about murder and graveyards. "What I'm most interested in is that cemetery," he said. "Genealogical research has always been an interest of mine. Tracing births and deaths through courthouse records is the easiest way, but that's obviously closed to us. But often the most useful material is what's found in old family heirlooms: Bibles, diaries, pictures, stuff like that. There's bound to be items scattered around town that can help us. I happen to get together with some fellow ministers from town every Tuesday night. I'll ask them to spread the word in their churches."

We ate hot Italian sausage sandwiches and laughed a lot. When we walked outside, the trees were casting purple shadows on the parking lot. Where had the time gone?

Father Buck took one of my hands between both of his. "If I may be serious for a moment," he said. "I'm concerned about you. Investigating murder is not a game."

"I know that," I said, trying not to show my indignation.

"I want you to know that I'll do everything within my power to help you. Whatever happens, Tori, you know you can count on me."

I watched him in the rearview mirror until he was no more than ant-sized.

Funny, I thought. In New York, a city of seven million people, I never seem to meet an attractive, intelligent man. And yet, here in bucolic Lickin Creek, I'd met several. Too bad about Father Buck. Under other circumstances, meaning no Garnet in my life, I'd have really been interested in him. I chalked it up to that wise old adage "Them that have get."

Mists were again swirling up from the pavement as I began my slow journey down the Deer Tick Ridge Road. Turning on my lights didn't help at all. Most of the time I could barely see the white line down the center of the road. I could only imagine the sheer drop, on my right, to the valley below.

Once I nearly ran into the back of an Amish buggy. Luckily the bright orange triangle on its back warned me off just in time. I passed it and saw several children waving at me through the tiny windows.

A black car pulled in close behind me. Damn tailgater, I muttered. I tapped my brakes a couple of times as a warning to the driver to drop back a little. He ignored my signal. In fact, when I checked the rearview mirror, the car appeared to have moved even closer.

It had been a mistake to take my eyes off the road.

It veered to the left at a violent angle, and I very nearly went straight off the edge. I jammed the brakes, jerked the wheel, skidded onto the narrow shoulder, then returned to the road. I was shivering, shaking, and sweating all at the same time. And the damn black car was still only inches from my rear bumper.

I heard the screech of metal against metal before I felt the car shudder under the impact of the collision. The idiot had rammed me from behind! I struggled with the wheel and kept the car on the road.

I looked into my mirror to see if the car behind me was okay. What I saw sent a stab of fear through my heart. The car was bearing down on me, again. Fast. I caught a quick glimpse of the driver's face. He was laughing!

I grabbed hold of the wheel and tensed my shoulders a split second before I was hit again. This time the shock of the impact was so great my hands were ripped from the wheel. There was no way I could get control of the car. It spun in a dizzying circle and shot off the side of the road.

CHAPTER 10

Tuesday Afternoon

THE CAR PLUNGED DOWN THE INCLINE, SHAKING me half to death as it plowed through underbrush and bounced off boulders on the steep slope. Glass shattered as a tree limb broke through, and all I could do was cover my eyes and hope for the best. I sensed the car was slowing down, but my relief was short-lived, for the car groaned as if alive and slowly rolled over. My head hit something—the roof?—and suddenly all was still.

I unhooked my seat belt, thanked God I'd remembered to fasten it, and fell halfway through the hole where once there'd been a door. All I could think of was I should get away from the car before it blew up, the way they always did in movies.

That's when the pain in my right arm shot into my brain, and I passed out. Lucky for me, the car didn't explode.

Angels awoke me. Beautiful, rosy-cheeked angels with smooth golden hair and pale green eyes were staring down at me through a haze of clouds. One of them giggled and began to suck its thumb. Thumb sucking, giggling angels? Where was I?

I struggled to sit up and knew immediately from the pain in my arm that I was still alive. I blinked half a dozen times, and the clouds cleared. I could see now that my angels were children, four girls wearing pink cotton dresses with black pinafores and a small boy in a blue shirt and black pants held up by suspenders. He wore a flat-brimmed straw hat, and took his thumb out of his mouth long enough to say, "You English?"

"American," I croaked, wondering why he'd asked such an odd question.

"Children, children, move back. Allow the woman to breathe."

A woman in a long purple dress and black apron leaned over the boy, concern showing in her green eyes. "Do not worry," she said. "We will get you out." Her voice, with its strong Pennsylvania Dutch accent, was soothing. Somehow I knew everything was going to be all right.

The two oldest girls and the woman freed me from the front seat of the car, a procedure so painful that I wished I would lose consciousness again. "I am Lydia Stoltzfus," the woman said, as she ran her hands over my legs. "Can you stand?"

With help, I could. She pulled off her black apron and fashioned a sling for my arm. "It is broke," she announced. "We must get you to the doctor. Come girls, help the woman climb the hill. Reuben, you will carry her purse."

"I can't do it," I moaned, looking up. But somehow I was tugged, pulled, and pushed up the steep hillside by Lydia and her daughters, while little Reuben, still giggling, followed behind.

We finally reached the summit, and I shuddered

when I saw the skid marks where I'd gone over. I couldn't imagine how I'd survived the crash.

A handsome brown horse attached to a gray covered buggy stood waiting for us. Once I was settled in the backseat, the children sort of packed themselves in around me. "I will hurry," Lydia said. "Will you be all right?"

I nodded, in too much agony to speak.

As the horse clip-clopped down the road, I was glad for the children's presence; they kept me from toppling over. Lydia turned slightly sideways, so she could keep an eye on me and still watch the road. "I saw the car hit you," she said indignantly. "It did not even stop."

My head hurt, and I couldn't remember anything about my accident except the roller coaster–like ride down the slope. "Try to sleep," she said in a kind voice. "Time will pass more quickly."

When I awoke, Reuben was waving a piece of paper under my nose. "I colored it for you," he said.

"Leave the woman alone," Lydia said. "You can see she is not well."

I peeked out through the louvered side window and saw we were driving through Lickin Creek. "Fast trip," I murmured.

"You slept," Lydia replied with a little smile. "Here is the clinic. Reuben, you will go inside to get help."

Fifteen minutes later, I was lying on a hard cot in the emergency room of the Lickin Creek Medical Clinic, wearing only a hospital gown made transparent by thousands of launderings.

"Is there a federal law that requires emergency

rooms to be freezing?" I asked the nurse as she readied a hypodermic needle. "And why does a person with a broken arm have to get naked?" I tend to babble when I'm scared.

Doc Jones placed a reassuring hand on my shoulder. "You'll feel better in a minute," he said. "Roll over on your side." I felt a prick as the needle went in. In a short while I seemed to be floating far above the pain-wracked body on the cot.

Soon my right arm was immobilized in a heavy cast from palm to elbow. I wiggled my fingertips and was relieved to find they still worked.

Alice-Ann flung open the emergency room door and rushed to my side. "Tori, ohmygod, ohmygod, oh . . ." Tears streamed down her face.

"I'm okay," I said. I tried to smile, but my face muscles had gone numb. "Need a nap," I managed to say.

Doc patted my shoulder with detached, professional sympathy, muttered something unintelligible, and left the room with his arm around Alice-Ann's waist. The next time I opened my eyes, I was staring up at identical twins in blue police uniforms.

"Funny, I didn't know you had a brother, Garnet."

They both waved their hands in front of my face and spoke in one voice. "How many fingers am I holding up?"

"Oh, no. Not the double-vision thing!"

Two Doc Joneses pushed the two Garnets aside. They examined my eyes, tapped my knees, tickled the bottoms of my feet, and proclaimed it was only a mild reaction to the painkiller. By the time the examination was finished, I found I could alleviate the problem by closing one eye and squinting.

"You look mah-vel-ous," I told Garnet. He did, too. His leftover summer tan looked even darker than usual in contrast to the sparkling white of his shirt. And those eyes! Why had I never noticed they were the warm blue of a tropical sky? His two front teeth overlapped a little, just enough to make his smile more engaging than perfect. Lucky me, I thought.

He kissed me gently on the forehead, and smoothed my hair away from my forehead.

"I must look a mess," I said.

"You look wonderful. Lydia Stoltzfus is waiting outside," he said. "Thank God she saw the whole thing from her buggy; otherwise you'd still be lying down there at the bottom of the cliff."

"Bless her and all her little Stoltzfuses, too," I said. "Please ask her to come in. I'd like to say thank you."

Lydia entered, surrounded by her children. They were followed by a nurse who clucked disapprovingly but didn't chase them out.

"Thank you," I said.

"I am glad to have helped." She smiled shyly, not looking at all like the capable woman who had rescued me.

"Here is your picture," little Reuben said, waving his drawing at me. "I did it for you."

"Reuben, behave yourself," Lydia said sharply.

"It is the bad car, Mama. The one that pushed the English woman off the road. I drew a picture of it for her."

Garnet grabbed the paper out of the little boy's hand and stared at it. "Unbelievable," he blurted out.

"His teacher says he is very good at drawing," Lydia said.

"Better than good. Tori, he's drawn a black car. And he's got a number written down. The kid's got the license number of the hit-and-run driver!"

"He has recently learned to write numbers," said Reuben's proud mother.

"Let me see," I said. Garnet handed me the drawing. I squinted until it came into focus. It was really very well done; little Reuben had talent. I stared at it intently, trying to recall the accident. For a fleeting second, I remembered seeing a face in my rearview mirror, a laughing face, the face of . . . But it wouldn't come into focus.

"Stay right where you are," Garnet ordered, as if I had a choice. "I'm going to the office to run a check on this license number."

Chapter 11

Wednesday Afternoon

I WAS STRETCHED OUT ON THE VICTORIAN SOFA in the front parlor, covered with a granny-square afghan, crocheted by Greta, of course. Splashes of color moved like a kaleidoscope across the floor as the late afternoon sunlight filtered through the stained-glass window.

Fred was stretched across my lap, and Noel was curled up at my feet.

"Poor guys," I said, stroking Fred. "Mommy's been ignoring you."

Alice-Ann, who was sitting on the floor helping her son, Mark, choose the right crayons for his *Wizard of Oz* coloring book, snorted. "Mommy! Tori, you and Garnet ought to start a real family."

"All in good time, my friend. By the way, Dorothy's shoes were silver in the book, not red."

"I like green," Mark said.

It was a cozy scene. Greta had lit a fire before leaving for Percy Montrose's funeral service. According to her, the family was furious at Doc and Garnet for not releasing his body earlier. Doc had put his foot down when I said I planned to go to the service.

"Absolutely not," he'd said. "You had a mild concussion, and you must stay down and quiet for twenty-four hours."

He was right, I knew, but I was frustrated at not being able to scrutinize the people who attended. Instead I had to settle for asking Greta to observe everyone there carefully for signs of guilt and report back to me.

The pain in my broken arm had receded to a dull ache, thanks to the potent painkillers Doc had sent home with me. But I still couldn't seem to think clearly. "I think that concussion has put a cloud cover over my brain," I mused out loud.

"What's wrong? Should I call Merry?"

"I didn't mean to alarm you. It's only that I believe I was deliberately run off the road. I keep thinking it has something to do with Percy's murder, but I don't know why. Unless . . . unless someone thinks I know too much. Even though I don't know what I'm supposed to know. Oh, dear, none of this makes sense."

Alice-Ann clasped her hands over her mouth and gasped. "You mean someone's trying to murder you? Ohmygod, ohmygod!"

"Could I have another one of those nice pills, please?" I asked. "It's nearly time for my next dose."

She brought me a pill, a glass of ice water, and a slice of one of the latest apple pies to appear in the kitchen. After swallowing the pill, I took a small taste of the pie. It's important to keep up one's strength after an accident. "Pretty good," I said.

Alice-Ann sampled hers. "Not as good as mine. Maybe I'll enter the contest. Has Garnet identified the license plate number yet?"

"I don't know. He didn't come home last night."

We heard the roar of an engine and the crunch of dried leaves as a car approached the front of the house. "Maybe that's him now," I said. It was.

His uniform was crumpled, and his face was etched with lines I'd never seen before. "How are you feeling?" he asked, kissing me gently.

"I think I probably feel better than you do, Garnet. You need to get some sleep."

He collapsed in an armchair. "Sleep? What's that?"

Alice-Ann hurried into the kitchen and returned in a minute with a glass of wine. He smiled his thanks and drank half of it in one swallow. Then he grinned at me. "Got him," he said.

I squirmed into a slightly more upright position. "Tell me," I said eagerly.

"Car's registered to Janice Nicewander of Kennedy Street. I went directly there after leaving the hospital. She wasn't home, but I found her teenage son trying to bury her smashed-up bumper out back in the woodpile. Guess he thought he could hide the evidence. Front of the car's all crumpled up. The little Amish kid got the license number dead-right.

"Of course, he tried to lie his way out of it. Said he'd had a fender-bender yesterday morning and hadn't gotten around to reporting it. I reminded him that he turned eighteen last month . . . that he's going to be treated as a grown-up by the court . . . no more scoldings from the judge and a few months of sleeping in a wigwam at a wilderness camp. Told him I had enough evidence of attempted murder to send him up for twenty years. Suggested if he came clean I'd put in a good word for him in court.

"That's when he began to sing like Pavarotti. It

all had to do with the marijuana farm, I'm afraid. The punk thought of himself as a real tough 'wise guy,' but when it came to saving his neck, he couldn't wait to name names."

"He tried to kill me because of the marijuana farm I found?"

"Right," Garnet said. "They wanted to get even with you. Do you realize how huge this is? By finding the farm and exposing it, you cost them hundreds of thousands of dollars."

"Stop keeping me in suspense. Do you know who they are?" I asked.

"I could only act on the names Jared gave me. I've been out with the State Police all night, rounding them up." He looked sideways at Alice-Ann and grimaced. "I hate to tell you this, Alice-Ann, but one of them is your friend Reverend LeRoi, and the guys who did the actual farming were four of his so-called rehabilitated kids."

"The man who's been helping Alice-Ann with the Apple Fest preparations?" I asked. "I met him at the fairground. And a boy named Jared, too," I recalled. Garnet nodded.

"I don't believe it," Alice-Ann said. "Not for a minute. The man's a saint." Alice-Ann's face was flushed, and her eyes were filled with tears. "Why, he does so much for juveniles in this town . . . his recreation center . . . the dances . . . the activities . . ." Her voice trailed away.

"Right," Garnet said. "And he was in a position to get to know the worst of the kids, like our friend Jared, and recruit them to grow and sell drugs."

"I've got to go," Alice-Ann announced. "I cannot believe this." While she helped Mark gather up his crayons, she kept shaking her head and muttering, "Can't depend on anyone. Not anyone. This whole thing is awful. Tori, I'll call you tomorrow." She practically pushed Mark out the door.

"Poor Alice-Ann," I said. "She's too kindhearted for her own good. Even in college, she never thought ill of anyone. I suppose that's how she got duped into marrying that scumbag husband when everyone told her he was no good. Once, I . . ."

"Planet Earth to Tori, come back."

I was chagrined. "Sorry."

He stood up. "Think I'll get another glass of wine. Want some?"

I shook my head. "I'm still on medication."

When he returned and was settled comfortably in his chair, I said, "I was really off the track—I thought the guy forced me off the road because of my asking questions about Percy's murder."

"Look, Tori, there's something you need to know. The pathologist called me from the Harrisburg lab today."

"And?"

"And Percy did die from aplastic anemia . . . just as Doc said. No doubt about it. There were no traces of any kind of poison in Percy's system. There's no way he could have been murdered."

I struggled to a sitting position, dropping the afghan and the cats to the floor, and told him about Haggie Aggie.

When I was finished, he was very quiet. "You say she told you she *knows* Percy was poisoned? And how it was done?"

"That's right. And she hinted that she was blackmailing his murderer."

His mouth twisted into a crooked smile. "Sounds like she's got as active an imagination as you do. Next thing I know, she'll be writing books, too."

"Damn it, Garnet. Murder isn't funny."

He threw his hands up. "I surrender. Next time I'm up in the mountains I'll drop in on her and ask a few questions. But, I assure you, it's not very high on my list of things to do. Not much point in investigating a crime that didn't take place."

He finished his wine while I steamed. Doubts were running in and out of my mind. As a reporter, I'd always done my best work when I relied on gut instincts, and they were telling me that Percy's death was murder, all evidence to the contrary.

The back door slammed and Greta appeared in the archway, splendid in her funeral garb of black broomstick skirt and velvet Navajo shirt. She posed there, one hand pressed to her forehead, the other clutching a purple tie-dyed scarf to her breast.

"I have never—ever—ever seen anything like it!" she announced dramatically.

"The funeral? What happened?" I asked eagerly.

She sank into a bentwood rocker. "It was a fine funeral. One of the nicest I've been to this year. At least, until . . ."

"Can I get you a glass of wine?" Garnet asked.

"No, thanks."

I was bursting with curiosity. "Tell me, please. What on earth happened?"

"First of all, Chaz Montrose did not show up. Can you imagine? The man did not come to his own father's funeral. Even with all their disagreements over the years, you'd think he'd have the decency . . . As you can imagine, poor Helen Montrose was the picture of restrained fury. Then, at the cemetery, at the very moment the minister was reciting the ashes-to-ashes-dust-to-dust bit, Mrs. Foor, that nice Plain lady from the dairy, got up from her chair, walked over to the edge of the grave, and . . . right in front of everybody . . . well, I still can't believe it."

"What did she do?" Garnet and I yelled together.

"She spit on Percy's coffin!"

CHAPTER 12

Friday Morning

THE HOUSE WAS TOO QUIET FOR MY LIKING. Funny how rural tranquillity takes getting used to after ten years of city living. Even the cats and Bear seemed to be tiptoeing around me, as though they'd been warned not to disturb the invalid. I'd even have welcomed some of Greta's country music to break the silence, but Greta had left early "to stir things up downtown," she said, trailing behind her a banner that said NO NUKES IS GOOD NUKES. The last time I'd seen Garnet for more than a minute at a time was on Wednesday when he'd come home to tell me about arresting Jared and the Reverend LeRoi Barkdoll.

Thanks to Doc's powerful painkillers plus the shock of my accident setting in, I'd slept through Thursday. I must have needed the rest because I had awakened this morning feeling halfway human again and decided to skip the pills. When Maggie called to invite me to watch her fiancé participate in the first annual reenactment of the Battle of Lickin Creek, I accepted eagerly.

I had an hour to kill before she was due to pick me

up, so I took a yellow legal pad from the stack on the dining room table, helped myself to a second slice of apple pizza, and began to make a list that I headed PERCY MONTROSE MURDER: SUSPECTS. Putting problems in writing helps me focus. Several times in the past, the solution I'd been looking for jumped right off the page at me after I'd recorded all the known details.

The leading suspect on my list was Chaz Montrose. I printed his name next to the numeral one. I couldn't forget the way he'd fondled his father's valuable possessions. There are some people who can never get enough. His motive, as far as I could see, had nothing to do with the advent of the nuclear waste dump, but everything to do with greed.

Number two. Haggie Aggie. The herbalist's story about knowing who murdered Percy could have been made up to throw me off her trail. She must have realized it was only a matter of time until someone remembered seeing her truck outside Percy's house the night he died, and she'd prepared a story to explain her presence there. Motive? She told me she'd do anything to get out of the Hollow. And if the dump company bought her mountain property she'd have the money she needed to move to town. Maybe she killed Percy when she learned he'd changed his mind about selling his land to the dump company.

Three. Avory Jenkins. He'd said publicly he supported bringing the dump into the community because it would provide economic relief for the financially depressed valley. What he hadn't said publicly was that as a part-owner of the land, he'd make a huge profit if it were sold to the dump company. I made a note in the margin reminding myself to find out what his financial position was. Did he need money desperately enough to kill his partner?

That brought me to number four. The partner from Harrisburg with the strange name, Aldine Schlotterbeck. Who was he, and what was his story? I definitely needed to check him out. Why not now? I reached for the phone and dialed Information.

I reached Mrs. Aldine Schlotterbeck, who told me her husband was recovering from a heart bypass operation.

I told her a tiny white lie about being a journalist doing a story on the proposed low-level radioactive waste disposal plant. "I understand the company is considering the purchase of some land your husband owns."

"Really?" she said. "Aldine never talked about it with me. He doesn't think women should be concerned with business."

A real twentieth-century guy, this Aldine.

"If you'd like to talk to him about it, visiting hours are one to three and six to eight." She told me his room number. "Why don't you drop in on him? I know he'd enjoy the company."

I thanked her and said I'd call on him soon. Greta had accepted my apology for wrecking her car a hundred times over and had assured me she didn't mind—that the only thing that mattered was that I was okay. Her insurance company had promised to provide a rental car until her late husband's car was repaired, and she'd said I could use it since she preferred to drive her truck. As soon as it arrived, I'd interview Aldine Schlotterbeck in the hospital.

Back to my list. After the number five I wrote "Partners," followed by a question mark. Were there other partners I didn't know about? From what Chaz Montrose had said to me, I thought there must be others. But for the moment, I had to leave this space blank.

The phone rang. I answered, hoping to hear Garnet's voice, but the caller was a beautician who'd seen my picture in the *Chronicle* and offered me a free makeover. I told her I thought I looked fine the way I was and hung up. Talk about nervy people!

Six. Riley Roark. The man who'd led the strike at Montrose Industries and been fired. I'd heard him threaten Percy at the town meeting on Saturday night. His menacing remark, "We'll see who's dead," had proved to be ominously true.

Seven, Mrs. Foor, the pleasant Plain lady who'd spit on Percy's grave. One doesn't spit on a grave without good reason. What was hers?

The phone interrupted me again. I snatched up the receiver and said a curt "Hello."

"Did you do it?" a voice asked.

"What are you talking about?"

"Greta?"

"No, this is Tori Miracle, a houseguest . . ."

The person hung up.

Very mysterious, I thought. Did she do what? My mind leaped immediately to a conspiracy theory. Reluctantly, I wrote down the eighth name. Greta. I was ashamed of myself for even thinking of her as a suspect. After all she was my hostess, my friend, and the only sister of the man with whom I seemed to be falling in love. But a black truck just like hers had been spotted in Percy's driveway. And she did go to extremes in sticking up for what she believed was right. Not to mention that I'd heard her say she'd do *anything* to keep the dump from coming in. I had her word only that Percy had come around to her side and decided not to sell. She could have lied about that to make me believe she had no motive for killing him.

A horn honking out front interrupted my thoughts. Maggie was here already.

We found an empty spot on the side of the hill overlooking a cornfield that had been sacrificed for a battlefield. Maggie spread out a blanket for us to sit on and opened her cooler, filled with sandwiches, sodas, and homemade brownies. "Thought you'd need to keep your strength up," she said. When I passed on the brownie, she ate it herself.

"Ooooh, look. Isn't he handsome?" Maggie had spotted her fiancé riding horseback toward the field from the tent encampment. Behind him rode a dozen men in the uniforms of the Union Army. Next came the flag bearers and drummer boys, and after them marched the infantry, hundreds of men, some hardly more than boys, bearing rifles. They were singing a rousing marching song: "Bring the good old bugle, boys, we'll sing another song; Sing it with a spirit that will start the world along . . ."

"That really brings the goose bumps up," I whispered to Maggie.

"Hmmph," she muttered. "They shouldn't be singing that."

"What's the matter?" I asked. "They sounded terrific."

"Sherman's March to the Sea took place in the fall of 1864, nearly six months *after* the Battle of Lickin Creek. It's an anachronism to be singing 'Marching Through Georgia' when the event hasn't yet taken place."

Since all I knew about the Civil War came from seeing *Gone With the Wind*, I was able to relax and enjoy what I was watching without being critical. "Seems strange to be sitting on a hillside having a picnic lunch while men are preparing to kill each other," I said. "Even if it *is* only a reenactment."

"Strange, yes. But very authentic. During the war, local residents really did come out to watch battles."

Over the crest of a hill, across the field, came the gray-uniformed Confederate army. Naturally, they were singing: "I wish I was in the land of cotton . . ."

A young boy stepped between the two armies and played a stirring call on his bugle that was the signal for the battle to begin. The two sides charged at each other with their rifles blasting. On the edge of the field, several large cannons were fired. The air became so thick with black smoke that it was impossible to see what was happening on the field below, but I could hear screams, more rifle shots, the clanking of sabers, the whinnying of horses.

Then, as quickly as it had begun, the skirmish was over. The bugler's call sounded retreat, and the soldiers, alive and dead, withdrew to the sidelines.

"Is that it?" I asked, disappointed.

"Hardly. It'll go on like that all afternoon." She'd barely finished her statement before the men rushed back into the field. My eyes smarted from the acrid rifle smoke.

Someone behind me laid a hand on my shoulder. "Careful," I snapped. My arm's broken." The hand didn't move.

I turned my head and found myself nose to nose with Chaz Montrose. "You're hurting me," I said.

He smiled unpleasantly but removed his hand.

"What do you want?" My mouth was so dry I was speaking in a falsetto voice. I doubted he could understand me.

"I'm warning you right now, Miss Hot-Shot New Yorker, my family's getting tired of you asking questions about my father's death. Lay off, or be prepared to suffer some unpleasant consequences."

To show him how unimpressed I was by his pomposity, I turned my back on him and pretended the reenactment below had my complete attention. I was tensed, almost afraid a blow would fall on me, but nothing happened. He just laughed nastily and walked away.

"Good grief," Maggie gasped. "To hear him talk you'd think he cared about his father. Why, did you know he didn't even come to the funeral?"

"You were there?" I asked, determined not to let Chaz Montrose's offensive demeanor ruin my day.

"Of course. Percy Montrose was one of the library's most generous benefactors. The library board let me close for two hours so the entire staff could go."

"I wish I could have been there . . . but Doc insisted I stay in bed. Greta told me that something shocking occurred. Did you see what happened?"

"I'll say. Most all the mourners were dropping flowers into the grave onto Percy's coffin. All of a sudden, Mrs. Foor stepped forward and spit in there. Can't say I blame her, but it's always a surprise when a Plain person acts weird. One expects them to behave better than your average sinner. Want a soda?" She opened the cooler and pulled out two Diet Cokes.

I took one and placed the cold can against my forehead. It felt good. "What do you mean . . . about not blaming her?"

"It was ten years ago—no, maybe fifteen—anyway, the Foors' little girl was hit by a car and killed instantly as she crossed the highway on her way to school. When her father heard about it, he had a stroke and hasn't spoken since."

I sensed what was coming. "And Percy Montrose was the driver?"

Maggie nodded. "He never went to trial. It was labeled an unfortunate accident, and that was the end of it. Or almost the end. I heard rumors that Percy paid big-time guilt money to the Foors to ease his conscience. That's how they were able to buy the dairy. Lots of people thought it was hushed up because of him being so rich and powerful."

Despite the warm autumn sunshine, I felt cold inside. "Percy destroyed her whole family. How she must have hated him."

"It really was an accident," Maggie said. "I remember my mother telling me several people saw the little girl run right out in front of the car without looking. Percy tried to stop, but couldn't."

It was beginning to look as though everyone I'd met in Lickin Creek had a secret, and I was discovering them one by one. Uncovering the tragedies in people's lives was not something I enjoyed doing. Some things were better left hidden.

But, I reminded myself, I had a job to do, and if that required me to rummage through people's pasts, then that's what I was going to do. And I'd better get started.

"Maggie, can I borrow your car?"

Her face showed concern as she handed me the keys. "Are you still taking medication?" she asked.

"Haven't had any for the past twelve hours. I'll be

all right." I pointed at the field where both armies were singing "The Battle Hymn of the Republic." "Isn't that your Bill with the saber? My, he's quite the swordsman."

I took advantage of her distraction to leave quietly.

I decided to start by questioning Avory Jenkins, so I drove downtown, headed for the town hall. But I couldn't get through the square. The CANLICK protesters had swelled to a large crowd, and Greta was standing on the rim of the fountain yelling at them through a bullhorn while they waved banners and cheered her on. Garnet's going to love this, I thought, as I detoured down a side street.

At the town hall, the dog license lady in the front room told me Avory Jenkins was out emptying parking meters. "Could be anywhere. Don't know when he'll be back."

I saw by the clock on the wall that it was nearly noon. "Does he ever go home for lunch?" I asked.

She shrugged and turned back to the woman she'd been waiting on when I came in. "It'll be two dollars if Jay Jay's been neutered," she said.

"Have you got a phone book?" I asked.

"The Jenkinses live in the last house on the Stillhouse Road," she said without looking up.

So Avory's position as borough manager wasn't exactly a glamour job. As I drove, I tried to imagine New York's mayor out collecting money from the parking meters—and decided it would be a terrific way to make him really earn his pay.

A temporary roadblock prevented me from going in the direction I thought I should take. I asked the volunteer fireman directing traffic what was going on.

"Someone's put soap powder and red dye in the fountain," he said. "The square's full of pink bubbles."

I felt sorry for Greta, knowing what she'd have to face tonight when Garnet came home.

I turned down one of the borough's many one-way streets, where commercial properties mixed with narrow brick and stone town houses. At the first intersection, a half dozen men carrying picket signs walked in a slow-moving circle in front of a driveway where a sign read MONTROSE INDUSTRIES. Two more men sat on lawn chairs under a beach umbrella sharing a boxed pizza. They raised their hands in greeting and yelled, "Yo."

"Yo," I answered with a wave. It occurred to me this would be a good opportunity to talk to Riley Roark. I pulled over and asked if he was there.

One of the two seated men put down his pizza slice and snickered. "Riley? He's gone home for a few hours. Taking a long break."

The other men grinned knowingly. "Yeah, real long. Getting his Friday afternoon dee-lite." They all laughed.

Whether or not Riley Roark went home for a nooner was of no interest to me. All I wanted to do was ask him a few questions. At my request, the first man gave me directions to Roark's house on Tapeworm Road while the others continued to laugh.

Tapeworm Road lived up to its charming name; it was narrow and winding. There were only a few small houses in sight, and they all looked as if they'd been put together by weekend carpenters. The Roark house was set back from the road, nearly invisible behind a stand of tall pines.

I noticed there were two vehicles parked in the

long gravel driveway. One was what I expected Riley Roark to drive, a big old blue truck with spotlights on the roof. The other, though, was a surprise, a shiny black Lexus, far superior to the truck in age, style, and price.

I left Maggie's car at the bottom of the drive and walked toward the house. There was no doorbell, so I knocked and waited. When nothing happened, I knocked again. Still no answer, so I stepped off the porch and walked around to the back door, which I found ajar.

I stuck my head through the opening and called out, "Anybody home?" My words echoed in the empty kitchen. From another room down the hall I could see beyond an archway came the sound of someone cursing. "Hang on," a man's voice yelled.

Riley Roark walked into the kitchen, bare-chested and zipping his jeans. "Who the hell are you?"

"Sorry to bother you, Mr. Roark. I was wondering if you'd take a few minutes to answer some questions."

The scowl on his face was enough to frighten King Kong. "I already have a credit card; I don't want to buy any brooms, lightbulbs, or brushes; and my roof doesn't need fixed, so get the hell out of here."

I did. But not before I saw, through the archway, a naked woman step through a doorway into the hall. The look of surprise on her face when she saw me was laughable. The woman was Helen Montrose. Embarrassed, I hightailed it out of there.

Very interesting, I mused, once I felt I was safely locked in my car. Helen Montrose was having an affair. And not with just anyone, but the man who'd led the strike against her father-in-law's company. Another person with a secret. I wondered if Percy had known about them.

Maybe he had found out, and *they* had plotted together to kill him to keep him quiet. Riley Roark had just become number one on my list, and Helen Montrose was up there with him.

I decided to continue on to the Jenkinses' house on Stillhouse Road. The street name didn't exactly conjure up images of Park Avenue, and I had the dismal houses on Tapeworm Road fresh in my mind, so I was quite surprised to find that the Jenkinses' was a huge multilevel, nearly all glass, with a million-dollar view of the mountains. Two swans, one black and one white, cruised smoothly on the silvery surface of a small pond, set about by graceful weeping willows. It was a spot of breathtaking beauty.

I pushed the doorbell, and a woman's voice came out of the wall. "Who is it?"

"Tori Miracle. We met at Alice-Ann's."

I heard the door unlock. It opened. Electronic wizardry. There was no one in sight.

"In the den—to your right," Luvinia Jenkins's voice called out. I followed her directions and found myself in a two-story room, the kind called a "great room" in the decorating magazines. Luvinia lay on a white leather sofa with a lap robe stretched tightly across her bulging abdomen. She was the most pregnant woman I'd ever seen.

"Please have a seat. I'm sorry, but I can't get up. I've got a ghastly backache. If you'd like some tea or coffee I can ring for Maddie."

"Please don't bother," I said, choosing a French country–style armchair, upholstered in real silk. The painting over the stone fireplace was a beautiful reproduction of . . . I looked again. It was no reproduction. I'd been in several homes belonging to wealthy people in the past few days, but this one was the big money winner.

"I'm delighted you stopped by," Luvinia began. I found her southern accent delightful to listen to. "I was telling Avory only last night that I wanted to have you and Garnet over for dinner, soon." She winced a little as she shifted her position. "But as you can see, we will have to wait a bit.

"What brings you here today?" she asked.

"The editor of the *Chronicle* asked me to do a series of articles for the paper—as you might have heard, I used to be a reporter. They'll be personality profiles—sort of 'getting to know the human side' of your elected officials. I'd like to start with your husband. Is he here?"

She shook her head. "You just missed him. But I can give you some information if you like."

We chatted for a few minutes. I felt an immediate rapport with her, as though we'd been friends for years. I kept marveling at how this beautiful woman could have married someone as average as Avory Jenkins, and I felt I was being generous by rating him as high as average. I had to find out why.

I took out my notebook and pretended I was starting the interview. "I understand you and Avory met at a convention?"

She smiled. "Yes. Daddy had just bought the resort in West Virginia, and I was coordinating the special events until he could find someone permanent.

"Avory was there for at town managers' meeting. The airline lost his luggage, and he didn't have any clothes. Not even a toothbrush. So I loaned him some of Daddy's things. He looked so cute in them, I just couldn't say no when he asked me to have dinner with him. We fell head over heels in love. And were engaged within three days."

I was taking mental note of what she was saying. "Daddy" owned a resort. That meant he was rich. Avory had looked "cute" in Daddy's clothes, meaning Luvinia hadn't seen him in his bell-bottom trousers.

"I was a Miss Virginia, and a third runner-up in the Miss America pageant, Tori. I met lots of men, but they were either interested in me as a trophy wife, or they were after my money. I can't tell you what a relief it was to finally find a genuinely nice man. I get down on my knees every morning and thank the good Lord for . . . oooh."

"What's wrong, Luvinia?"

"Owww!"

"Is it the baby?"

"Aargh." She was doubled up, trying to clutch her back and hug her stomach all at the same time.

I shouted for the maid, who took one look at the situation and ran for the telephone. She explained to someone on the other end what was happening, then turned to me, a worried frown on her face. "Can you drive her to the clinic, miss? Doctor Jones says to hurry."

I drove as fast as I dared with only one arm, sharing Luvinia's agony as the car bounced over ruts and potholes. It seemed to take forever, but suddenly we were in front of the emergency entrance, where two strong men were gently lifting Luvinia onto a stretcher. As soon as she was inside, a security guard yelled at me to move the car. I parked in the closest free space, the one that said PASTOR PARKING ONLY, and ran to the emergency room.

A young nurse sat at the reception desk reading a paperback book with a semi-naked Indian and a redheaded woman locked in a passionate embrace on the cover. She marked her place with a tongue depressor. "You Tori?"

I wanted to answer, "Me Jane." But this was definitely not the time for foolishness, so I nodded.

"Doctor Jones says you can go right in." She gestured at the double doors with a sign over them saying NO ADMITTANCE. I went in and found Doc in a conversation with a nurse. Both were dressed in long green gowns and paper hats.

"Tori," Doc greeted me warmly. "Thanks a million for getting Luvinia here so soon. She's being prepped for surgery right now."

"Surgery? What's wrong?"

"Nothing, I hope. I had already planned to do a C-section, but not till next week. She'll be a proud mother in about ten more minutes." He stopped and took a long hard look at me. "You should be in bed, young lady."

"I'm all right," I said. But suddenly I didn't feel real great. I ached from my banged-up head to my bruised foot, and my broken arm throbbed painfully with every beat of my pulse.

"You really should go home, Tori."

"Well, I'm not going home. I'm going to rest here a few minutes, then I'm driving to Harrisburg to talk to one of Percy Montrose's partners."

"Against your doctor's orders," Doc said to me. "Sit down, I'll get you something. Can you take aspirin?"

I flopped into a vinyl-covered armchair and nodded. He left the room and returned a moment later with an aspirin bottle. "Take two now and the other two in three hours," he ordered.

"Typical doctor advice: 'Take two aspirins and call me in the morning,'" I joked. He glared at me. "Guess you've heard that one before."

Doc disappeared through the door to the operating room, only to pop right back out. "Luvinia wants you to stay till the baby's born."

"No problem." I put my head back and closed my eyes. I knew I'd be okay after the adrenaline rush, generated by our wild ride to the clinic, had subsided.

The double doors burst open, and Avory rushed in. "Where is she? Is she okay? I should have been with her. Has the baby come yet? Why did I ever leave her alone?"

"Doc says she's fine, Avory. Come sit down."

Avory refused to sit. He paced the floor, chomping on the stem of his pipe, which, thankfully, was not lit, and wringing his hands. Every few seconds an exclamation of worry or a short prayer would burst from his lips. I did what I could to calm him and assure him Luvinia would be just fine.

After about ten minutes had passed, Doc entered the room and smiled. "Congratulations, Avory, you've got a little girl. She's waiting to meet you in the recovery room." He held the door open and gestured for Avory to enter. "You, too, Tori. Luvinia wants to see you. She's convinced she'd never have had the baby if it hadn't been for you."

Avory's face was pale, and his hands were shaking as he approached his wife's side. Luvinia, with her baby cradled in her arms, beamed at him. "Isn't she beautiful, Avory?"

Avory bent over and touched his daughter's tiny

fingers, then stroked the fuzzy blond down on her little pink head. There was awe in his voice as he said, "She's the most beautiful creature I've ever seen, except for you." He burst into tears.

I felt a little embarrassed to be there with them at this special moment, but Luvinia turned her big lavender-blue eyes to me and thanked me over and over for having helped her. "I don't know what I'd have done if you hadn't been there," she said.

I modestly brushed off her praise. "Maddie would have called an ambulance. Everything would have worked out just fine."

But she clutched my hand and continued to thank me profusely. There were still questions I needed to ask Avory, but not now. Not while the couple was enjoying its first blissful hour of parenthood. I figured I'd talk to Aldine Schlotterbeck first and catch Avory another time.

When I left the clinic, I was emotionally and physically drained and knew I should follow Doc's advice and go home, but I had it in my mind that I needed to visit Aldine Schlotterbeck and didn't want to put it off. I got directions to Harrisburg from the nurse, threw away the nasty note some irate minister had stuck under my windshield wiper, and drove east toward the Pennsylvania Turnpike.

CHAPTER 13

Friday Afternoon

THE TURNPIKE WASN'T TOO BAD TO DRIVE ON, despite being pocked with potholes like most of Pennsylvania's roads, and it led me to the interstate going north.

The road was beautiful, winding through heavy forests, shedding summer greens for the dramatic colors of autumn, and through rich, rolling farmlands. As I crossed over numerous small streams, every curve in the road brought a spectacular new vista into view. Once I'd actually thought Pennsylvania was all coal mines, steel mills, and soot-stained manufacturing cities. How wrong I'd been.

I crossed the wide Susquehanna, drove past lovely old mansions on Front Street, now mostly converted to businesses, and pulled into the Polyclinic parking lot. A volunteer at the information desk directed me to Mr. Schlotterbeck's room. But to my dismay, the room was empty, and the sheets had been stripped off the bed. My stomach was doing nervous flip-flops as I approached the nurses' station.

"I'm sorry, Mr. Schlotterbeck passed away about an hour ago," I was told. "Are you family, dear?"

"Yes." I winced at the fib. "What did Uncle Al die from?"

"Postsurgical complications."

"But my aunt said he was doing fine."

The nurse signaled I was dismissed by picking up a patient's chart. "These things happen, dear. I'm sorry."

I was suddenly fearful that he, too, had been murdered. "Did he have any visitors today?" I asked.

The nurse shook her head. "None. Not even his wife."

As I drove back on the turnpike, I suddenly felt exhausted. I could barely focus on the road. Doc was right. I should have been in bed instead of gallivanting all over the countryside. I blinked to clear my eyes, only they didn't want to reopen. The car swerved, my eyes popped open, and I overreacted by jerking the wheel sharply to the right.

An eighteen-wheeler thundered past me. The driver blew his horn and waved his arms at me, warning me to get off the road. "Good idea, buddy. Thanks," I muttered. I pulled onto the shoulder, as far from the road as I could get, turned the engine off, and sank into a deep, dreamless sleep.

A flashing light woke me up. That and someone pounding on the driver's-side window. I was slumped over on the front seat, and it was a considerable struggle to sit back up. When I did, I saw a man's face pressed against the glass. "Are you all right, miss?" he yelled.

I saw now he was wearing one of those Smokey Bear state trooper hats. I rolled the window down an inch. "I got sleepy," I told him through the crack.

"I'll have to ask you to step outside, miss." He sounded very young and very official.

I asked to see his badge first, then opened the door and got out. The night air had turned frigid, and I stomped my feet trying to get warm.

"Please touch the tip of your nose with your finger."

My God, the man thought I was drunk! I finally convinced him that I really was sober but too tired to drive home.

At his suggestion, I locked Maggie's car and got into the police car. While he chauffeured me back to Lickin Creek, I resumed my interrupted nap.

He shook me gently to awaken me when we arrived at Garnet's house and walked with me up the porch steps. "I don't think it's a good idea to be driving so soon after a serious accident," he said.

"Next time I'll be more careful." I opened the door, noting that, as usual, it wasn't locked. "Many thanks, my friend. You probably saved my life tonight."

I think he blushed a little, but it was hard to tell because of the yellow glow cast by the bug bulb in the porch light.

The house was very, very quiet. "Kitties, Mommy's home. Where are you?"

From the dark living room came Greta's voice. "They're in here with me, Tori."

I entered the room and groped for the light switch. I was momentarily blinded when the lights came on. Then I saw Greta sitting on the sofa, holding Fred on her lap. "Hi. What's the idea of sitting in the dark?" I asked.

She stared at me with cold, steel-blue eyes.

"Greta, what's wrong?"

She reached for something next to her on the sofa

and held it up. "I found this on the kitchen table, Tori." Her expression sent chills down my spine.

What she was showing me was the yellow legal pad on which, this morning, I'd written my list of murder suspects. And, as I recalled all too well, the last name on that list was Greta's.

We talked far into the night. Or rather, I talked. She listened. I assured her I had meant nothing. That I was simply jotting down names at random. That I truly appreciated the kindness she had shown me. That of course I didn't think of her as a murder suspect.

She was quiet through all of my apologizing, but I felt she was coming around to believing me. She put an end to it by standing and stretching. "That's enough, Tori. I understand—sort of—and although I'm hurt, I'm willing to try to forget the whole thing. Just promise me that from now on you'll leave me out of your so-called investigation. By the way, I do have an alibi—which I do not care to share with you or anybody else."

I promised with all my heart and went upstairs. Between my feelings of guilt at having offended Greta and the long nap I'd taken in the state trooper's car, sleep was a long time coming.

CHAPTER 14

Saturday Morning

FATE HAD GRANTED LICKIN CREEK NEAR-perfect end-of-summer weather for the opening day of the Apple Butter Fest. As I stood with Garnet near the wooden cider barrel stage where the official Apple Butter festivities were taking place, I could hear the laughter and cries of children mingling with the nostalgic music of the calliope on the antique merry-go-round. There was a Ray Bradburyesque, old-fashioned ambiance to the quaint country festival.

Earlier, Garnet had come to the bedroom and announced, "Good news, my part-timer's back at work, and I get the day off. Let's go to the Apple Butter Festival."

On the way to the fairground, I told him what I'd done to upset Greta. He patted my hand. "Greta's an understanding person. She'll get over it. What I don't get is why you suspect her of murder. Especially of a murder that didn't take place."

I ignored his dig and said, "She was very low on my list, Garnet. I don't really believe she'd murder anyone, but she does get kind of fanatical about her causes."

Garnet chortled. "Fanatical is putting it mildly."

"And it seems as though every time something strange happens, she's unavailable. She was missing when Percy died; she stayed home from the Literary Society the night his house was burglarized; she was out yesterday . . ."

"What happened yesterday?"

"I drove to Harrisburg to interview Percy's partner, Aldine Schlotterbeck, and—"

"You drove to Harrisburg? In your condition? Are you crazy?"

I continued as if I hadn't been interrupted. "—and found he'd just died. Another natural death, Garnet—surgical complications, the nurse said. But I've never believed much in coincidence. By the way, I nearly fell asleep driving home and had to leave Maggie's car on the turnpike."

"I'll drive you out to pick it up later," he said with a sigh. He didn't have much to say after that, but I could tell by the set of his jaw that he was letting it all sink in.

Along with about two hundred people, we cheered for the new Apple Butter Princess. She was a lovely teenager in a strapless white gown, who cried a little when Bathsheba Butterbaugh placed a rhinestone tiara on her blond head.

The princess gave a touching, if tearful, acceptance speech thanking her parents, her teachers, and her sponsor, the Lickin Creek Volunteer Fire Company Number Three. After that, she handed a first-place trophy to the winner of the Apple Baby contest, a two-year-old boy wearing miniature overalls, plaid shirt, and a fringed straw hat, who bawled through the whole presentation.

Garnet took my arm, and we strolled down a line of display booths, named Candied Apple Lane, looking at the exhibits: huge piles of red, green, and yellow apples; scarecrow art; old cars; quilt displays; puppeteers; and even a lumber-sawing demonstration.

Garnet received numerous enthusiastic greetings from bearded men, yelling "Yo!" and "Way to go, man!" When I remarked I hadn't noticed so many beards before, Garnet said the men were preparing for the hunting season. "They think their beards will keep them warm when they're out in the woods."

I was pleasantly surprised several times when people came up to me, shook my hand, and congratulated me on breaking up the drug ring. Perhaps I was, at last, overcoming my terribly unfair reputation as the "woman that burned down the Historical Society." Last summer when I'd confronted the murderer of Alice-Ann's husband in the basement of that old building, a kerosene lantern had tipped over, igniting the great piles of newspapers stored there. Some townspeople still had trouble understanding it was an accident.

We turned down Golden Delicious Drive and stopped before a display of antique farm engines. "Here's what I wanted to show you," Garnet said. I heard a noise that sounded like a bulldozer with hiccups coming from a large red machine with metal-rimmed wheels that was belching huge clouds of black smoke into the air.

"What does it do?"

"Nothing anymore," he said. "It's a one-cylinder, five-horsepower 1917 New Holland. I've been working on it all year. It belonged to my grandfather." I could hear the pride in his voice.

"Garnet, it won a blue ribbon! Congratulations!"

He beamed.

We stopped at a small shack, its sides covered with peeling sheets of asphalt brick, that was the Daughters of the American Revolution snack bar. Garnet ordered two apple sausages on potato rolls and two cups of cider.

We carried our food to the Johnny Appleseed Stage, where two men were clog dancing to some lively fiddle music, and sat on a hay bale to watch. I was unfamiliar with Appalachian dancing, but it brought to mind Irish folk dance, reminding me once more of Pennsylvania's Scotch-Irish heritage. The music was so infectious, my feet couldn't keep still. I'd have clapped hands like the rest of the audience if I'd been able.

Despite the prickly hay poking through my jeans, it felt good to relax with Garnet by my side. Now, I thought, would be a good time to tell him about P. J. Mullins's asking me to be the temporary editor of the Lickin Creek *Chronicle*. "She's having surgery next week. I have to tell her right away whether or not I can do it."

He nodded when I was finished. "Do you want to?" he asked.

"Yes," and as I answered I realized I really did. "Very much."

"Then go for it," he said.

"It's going to be wonderful being right here in town with you and Alice-Ann," I said.

"There's something I need to tell you, Tori. This isn't easy." Garnet pressed his hands together until his fingers turned white. "But I'd better get it over with."

I smelled it coming. I'd been through it often enough; he'd spoken the traditional words men use when they're getting ready to end a relationship. "Go ahead," I said coolly. I could take it. It wasn't the first time and probably wouldn't be the last.

"I'm not sure anymore that being a small-town police chief is what I want to do the rest of my life, Tori. A friend from law school has been after me for a couple of months to take a job with his government agency. I've decided to accept his offer. I'm taking a year's leave of absence from the Lickin Creek police force and going to Costa Rica as a police adviser."

He exhaled, a long, slow whistle. "I'm glad I got that out."

I sat, stunned. I'd not only been brushed off, but the guy was leaving the country!

Before I could say anything, he added, "I was hoping you'd come with me, Tori. I know you have your book to finish, but you can write there just as well as in New York."

He wasn't dumping me after all. My heart soared with happiness. Until I remembered P.J.

"Oh, Garnet, I'm so happy for you! And I'd love to go with you. Maybe in six months. Or even in less time, if P.J. gets back on her feet quickly."

He took my hand and squeezed it. "I have to take three months of language training in D.C. before I go, so the timing will probably work out well. And once I get down there, maybe you can come for a visit."

"Just try to keep me away," I said. My heart was pounding. I'd just made a couple of major life-changing commitments. It would take some time for me to adjust.

He put his hands on either side of my face and kissed me tenderly. It lasted until the people around us started snickering. Reluctantly, I pulled away. "Let's see if we can find Alice-Ann," I suggested.

We paused at the Kid Land Arena to watch the bobbing-for-apples contest followed by the apple pie–eating competition. Everyone seemed to be having a fantastic time. Garnet and I held hands like high school sweethearts. Everything about the day was a throwback to a sweeter, more innocent time.

"Tori—over here." Alice-Ann was standing next to a sign that said YE OLDE STRAWE MAZE. "Want to try it out?" she asked when we joined her.

"I don't like mazes very much," I said. "I got lost in one once in England. Took me hours to find my way out. Scared the hell out of me." Alice-Ann and her former assistant, Reverend LeRoi, had stacked the bales of straw up to create walls eight or nine feet high. I stepped through the entrance, found myself in a claustrophobic dark tunnel with only a tiny patch of blue sky showing overhead, and backed up. "Maybe another time," I said.

"Did you get my apple pie?" Alice-Ann asked me. "I dropped it off in your kitchen this morning."

I shook my head. "We left in such a hurry, I never went in there. I'll look for it when we go home."

"You'll love it. What makes mine special is I add candied orange peel, golden raisins, and ricotta cheese. And I put sherry in the crust."

"My, that does sound different!" I hoped I wasn't going to get into trouble with my best friend over this contest.

A teenage girl, wearing a white T-shirt that said

"Apple Butter Official," came running across the field hollering Alice-Ann's name. "Come quick and bring the first-aid kit. Mr. Gettel stuck a chisel in his thumb at the shingle-making booth."

Alice-Ann grabbed a Red Cross box. "See you guys later," she said, and took off behind the girl.

Over the loudspeaker system came an announcement. "A demonstration of apple-butter making is now taking place in the show ring on Granny Smith Street."

We joined a circle of spectators surrounding a large copper kettle, just like the one I'd seen bubbling away in front of Haggie Aggie's trailer. A pretty red-headed girl in a long calico gown stirred the mixture with a long wood paddle, while she explained how to make apple butter.

"Let's go," Garnet said, "unless you want to stand here and watch it bubble for the rest of the day."

"As exciting as that sounds, I think I'll pass." I ducked as a swarm of bees went by, attracted by the sweet-smelling apples. A booth selling jars of apple butter caught my eye. Maybe a small gift for Greta would defuse some of her anger toward me. I'd better pick something up for Maggie, too, to apologize for abandoning her car.

The man in overalls and a straw hat, standing behind the counter, was Ralph McDougal. The sign above his head said "Agatha Haggard's Speshul Home-Made Country Apple Butter." Since I'd seen the medical textbooks and pharmaceutical guides in her trailer and knew Aggie was literate, I assumed the spelling was intentionally creative.

Toto recognized me first and bounded around the

side of the booth to greet me like a long-lost rich relative. Ralph's eyes brightened, and he said, "You're that young lady what I walked over to Aggie's." He looked right and left, bent forward so only I could hear, and asked, "Did she take care of your problem?"

I bit my tongue between my teeth. "Everything's fine, thanks. Where is Aggie today? I'm surprised she isn't here with you."

"Making more apple butter. What I brought is nearly all."

"All what?" I asked.

" 'All' means 'gone' in Pennsylvanian," Garnet explained.

"I wonder if I'll ever learn your language."

I selected two jars of apple butter, which Ralph gift-wrapped for me with brown paper and twine. "You ought to come back up and visit me and Aggie," he said. "It's been nice and quiet up there the past few days since them cloud-seeding planes stopped flying over."

My antenna for news had always served me well. It was tingling now. "When did the flights stop?" I asked.

He scratched an ear. "Nearly a week ago . . . seems to me I haven't seen more than one or two planes go by since last Sunday. And they were them big passenger planes—not the little ones they use for cloud-seeding."

I grabbed Garnet's arm. "Sunday was the day I reported the marijuana farm to the State Police. Call me crazy, but I'm thinking that might have something to do with the absence of small planes."

Garnet clamped down on his jaw so hard I feared he'd break a tooth. "The airport . . . of course. It's way out on the edge of town. Nobody goes there unless they're meeting a commuter flight, and that's only once a day. What better way to get the stuff out of Lickin Creek!"

Garnet placed a hand under my elbow and steered me through the crowd. "I'll take you home first, then I'll check it out."

CHAPTER 15

Saturday Afternoon

"WHAT SHOULD WE DO ABOUT MAGGIE'S CAR?" I asked, when Garnet stopped in front of his house.

"Give me the keys. I'll send someone from Hoopengartner's out to fetch it." He reached across my chest and opened the car door. "I'm sorry to leave you like this . . ."

"Don't worry about me. Go catch some bad guys. I'll be fine."

We kissed good-bye, and I went inside the house. All was quiet. It seemed like the perfect atmosphere for a nap. The Apple Fest had worn me out more than I liked to admit. I climbed the stairs to my room, where I found Fred nestled on the antique quilt and Noel curled up in a ball on the marble-topped dresser. I took off my dusty clothes and put on a comfortable nightshirt, the one with the picture of the Cowardly Lion of Oz and the slogan "Courage," and climbed into bed with Fred.

Fred stretched out on his back and allowed me to rub his soft white tummy. I stroked him rather absent-mindedly, for I was actually thinking about Garnet. If he couldn't even get away from work for more than a couple of hours on his day off, how could he ever expect to take a year's leave of absence?

It occurred to me that Garnet and I had switched positions. I was the one who'd grown up wandering the world with a Foreign Service family, and I was the one who'd suffered culture shock upon returning to the United States to live. Then, when at last I met a man I thought I loved and began to consider putting down roots, Garnet, the man with roots seven generations deep in Lickin Creek, decided to take a government job abroad. And from the little he'd told me about becoming a police adviser, I feared he was going to be a Spook, my least favorite type of government worker. I'd seen the Agency at work in most of the countries I'd lived in, and I was not one of its admirers.

A bloodcurdling scream woke me. I sat up, startled, hoping I'd had a bad dream. Another scream. This was definitely not a dream!

"Stay here," I warned the cats and opened the door a crack. No one was in the hall, so I tiptoed to the top of the stairs and waited.

"Greta?" I called. "What's wrong?"

"Tori! Help me! He's dead!"

I tore down the stairway and followed her cries into the kitchen. She was crouching over something on the floor with her back to me when I burst into the room.

"Bear!" I cried when I saw the big German shepherd lying perfectly still on the floor, his head resting in a pool of foul-smelling, yellow-green liquid.

"He's dead, isn't he?" Greta sobbed.

I got on my knees and placed my hand on the dog's chest, where I could feel a faint flutter.

"Not yet," I told her. "Have you called a vet?"

"No, I just walked in and found him." She jumped to her feet, grabbed the phone, and punched some numbers. After an interminable wait, she said, "Jennifer? I think Bear's dying." Pause. "We'll be there in five minutes."

I ran back up to my bedroom, jerked on my jeans and shoes, and rushed back downstairs.

Greta had Bear wrapped in a blanket and was waiting for me to help carry him out to her truck.

"Look at this. It was on the floor under the table." She showed me a partly eaten pie.

Bear had eaten most of the crust and about half of the curdled-white filling. He'd left the raisins, I noticed. I sniffed, noting it smelled of oranges, cinnamon, and cloves. "We'd better take it with us. See if the vet can identify what he ate."

We half-carried, half-dragged the unconscious dog outside, and hoisted him into the truckbed. I ran back in for the pie, while Greta warmed up the engine.

"I don't understand why he ate it," she muttered as she drove wildly through the downtown streets. "He never touched any of the other things people left this week."

"Maybe one of the ingredients was kibbled." It was a weak joke, but I was trying to distract her.

Jennifer Seilhammer, the veterinarian, was waiting for us in the doorway of her office. She and Greta carried Bear into the examining room and laid him on a stainless-steel table while I stood by helplessly, clutching the pie.

"Looks like he might have been poisoned," Jennifer said. "Do you have any idea what he might have gotten into?"

"This." I showed her the pie. "We don't know what's in it."

"I'll have it analyzed. Right now, we have to concentrate on saving poor Bear. It would be best if you two waited outside."

I knew Greta didn't want to leave, but I took her arm and led her through the waiting room into Jennifer's small, cluttered office. In there, I found a coffeepot, paper filters, and a can of Maxwell House.

"Greta, do you know how to use this thing?" I asked. "I only do instant."

Fixing coffee took her mind off the dog for a few minutes. While she was occupied, I used the phone to call Garnet's office. He hadn't returned from the airport, but the woman who answered promised she'd get a message to him right away.

We carried our mugs into the waiting room and sat down to wait. Despite Greta having said she was willing to forgive me for including her name on my list of murder suspects, there was considerable tension between us. I was sure of one thing: Greta hadn't poisoned the pie. She would never take a chance on hurting Bear.

"Do you know what I think?" I said, trying to break the uncomfortable silence.

"What?" Greta didn't sound very interested.

"Everyone in town knows I'm taste-testing apple recipes. Someone was trying to poison me with that pie."

I'd gotten her attention. "You mean the drug growers? Because you found their field?"

I shook my head. "I don't think so, Greta. Death by poison seems too subtle for the type of people that ran me off the road. No, I think this has something to do with Percy's death. I've been asking questions, and the killer must think I'm getting too close. First he tried to scare me off by marking up my photo in the newspaper, and when that didn't work he decided to do me in with poison. Now my theory is this: The killer is someone well known to your family because he wasn't frightened of the dog. Remember the Sherlock Holmes story about the dog that didn't bark in the night?"

Greta smiled for the first time. "Bear wouldn't bark at Jack the Ripper. He thinks everybody is his best friend. Everybody in town knows that."

So much for that theory!

"How's my dog?" Garnet was standing in the doorway with distress showing on his face.

I jumped up and hugged him. "We think he's been poisoned. The vet's still working on him."

"Poisoned?" He looked at Greta. "Do you think the Oberholsers are putting rat poison out again?"

I answered for her. "We're pretty sure it was in an apple pie. He ate nearly half of it before he got sick." I quickly told him my theory that the poison was intended for me.

He put an arm around me and held me as close as my cast would allow. "I hope you're wrong," he said.

Jennifer picked that moment to walk into the room, wearing a pink operating smock. "I think Bear's going to be fine. But I want to keep him here under observation for a few days. I'll send a sample of his stomach contents along with that pie to the lab. It does appear to have been poison. I should know what kind sometime this afternoon."

"Oh, my God," Greta gasped. "You were right, Tori."

"My cats," I groaned. "They're home alone."

The three of us rushed outside. "We're going to throw out any apple dishes that show up," I said. "No more taste-testing."

"And I'm going to lock the doors from now on!" Greta said.

Back home, we hurried into the kitchen. The cats were sleeping on the counter and appeared to be all right. I used to laugh at them for being finicky eaters and only liking Tasty Tabby Treats. Now I was grateful that they were so picky.

As Greta mopped up the mess on the floor, I looked around the room at the dozens of apple recipe entries left untouched. "I wonder whose pie it was and why Bear chose that particular one to eat?"

Garnet shook his head disbelievingly. "Maybe it was a mistake—the poison might have gotten into the pie by accident."

"Really, Garnet! No one keeps poison lying around their kitchen to accidentally fall into the food. That pie was deliberately poisoned and left here for me—maybe all three of us—to eat."

"I guess you're right," he agreed reluctantly. "I'll check around outside. See if anything looks suspicious."

He left, and I collapsed on a chair. Greta came over and put a hand on my shoulder. "Thanks, Tori," she said. "You helped save Bear's life."

I covered her hand with mine. She seemed to have forgiven me. Or at least declared a truce.

Chapter 16

Sunday Morning

GARNET'S APPEARANCE WORRIED ME. THIS morning, as we sat at the breakfast table, his eyes were rimmed with dark circles and his usually healthy-looking tan had faded to yellow. I feared he was driving himself too hard, and I couldn't help feeling partly responsible. I was coming to believe that his decision to leave the force was a good one. He couldn't keep up this pace forever. He'd been gone all night, again.

"Your hunch about the airport was right," he said. "We found marijuana and lysergic acid diethylamide there—two hangars full—enough of both to saturate the East Coast."

"LSD, too!" Greta groaned. "It's getting worse by the minute."

"The pot wasn't even well hidden. Just stacked up behind the hay stored in the hangars for winter food drops."

"Why do you suppose they didn't get rid of it after the farm was discovered?" I asked.

"They couldn't exactly burn it—the smell would

be too obvious. And they weren't willing to take the risk of flying it out. Not with the State Police around. So they've been trucking it out of town, using the logging trucks we're all so accustomed to seeing that we didn't pay any attention."

"Chaz Montrose owns a logging company, if I recall correctly," I said.

Garnet nodded. "And the airport. I did wonder at the time he built it why he was putting an airport in Lickin Creek right when the town was suffering a severe recession, but then I assumed that either he was an optimist or a really bad businessman."

"So he was the brains behind the operation?"

Garnet nodded again. "Indeed he was. According to Reverend LeRoi, who was more than willing to talk last night in exchange for a plea bargain, it was Chaz who came to him with the idea of growing marijuana on his father's land in the Hollow. He knew the Reverend could supply him with the workers he'd need."

"Is Chaz in jail now?" I knew I'd feel a lot safer if he were.

"For the time being. The judge set the bail so high, even Chaz will have trouble raising it."

A thought came to mind, which I didn't voice because I knew Garnet was not impressed with my murder investigation. If Chaz was making a fortune from illegal drug sales, then he really didn't need to murder his father for his money.

When the phone rang, Garnet answered, listened for a minute, then gave a "thumbs up" sign. Bear was almost back to normal and could come home Monday. "Jennifer received a toxicology report from the lab," Garnet told us. "The contents of Bear's stomach and the apple pie ingredients were identical: apples, ricotta cheese, a tiny bit of orange peel—and arsenic."

"Now I know why Bear chose that particular pie to eat," Greta said. "He's always been crazy about ricotta. I think he must be part Italian."

Suddenly I gasped. "Oh, no. That sounds like Alice-Ann's pie."

They stared at me.

"She described a pie she'd dropped off yesterday morning. The ingredients sounded really weird: ricotta cheese, apples, orange peel, and raisins, and there's sherry in the crust."

Greta made a face. "Sherry in the crust? Sounds gross."

"So maybe Alice-Ann's trying to poison you. Maybe she's getting even with you for stealing a boyfriend from her in college." Garnet chuckled as though he'd said something amusing.

"Very funny. I never stole one of her boyfriends. I never even liked any of them. It does make me wonder, though, why the killer would pick her pie."

"I wouldn't wonder too hard," Garnet said, gulping the last of his coffee. "It was probably the first one the poisoner saw. I doubt that the wanna-be murderer was deliberately trying to break up a longtime friendship. Hate to eat and run," he said, "but I have to go into the office. Will you be okay?" he asked me.

"I'll keep an eye on her, little brother," Greta said. "You go find the guy who tried to kill our Bear."

After Garnet left, Greta "redd up" the kitchen while I made sure the cats had fresh Tasty Tabby Treats and water.

"Tori, there's a good farm auction today. Do you feel up to it?" She was extending the olive branch, which I seized.

"That sounds nice," I said. I'd been to an auction once at Sotheby's and had enjoyed it; it would be fun to see what a country auction was like. Also, it would be a refreshing change from worrying about murder and poisoned pies, especially since there wasn't much I could do about either on Sunday with no car.

After double-checking to make sure all the windows were closed and the doors were locked, we drove out of town in Greta's big black truck. She chatted amiably with me, leading me to believe that she really had forgiven me.

After half an hour, she made a left turn onto Crooked Creek Road, which brought us to a small white farmhouse located in the middle of a recently harvested field. Cars and trucks lined both sides of the road, and some had even parked in the fields.

Greta glanced at her watch. "We've got about ten minutes. That'll give us time to look around. Make sure everything they advertised is in good condition."

"Anything particular you're looking for?" I asked as we hurried across the road toward the house.

She nodded. "Bottles. Elbert was a well-known collector."

"What happened to him?"

"Died a few weeks ago. His wife's auctioning everything off today, including the house, so she can move to Florida."

An enormous yellow-and-white-striped tent had been set up in the yard. In front stood a long table, where we signed a book and picked up cards with big black numbers on them. I looked inside and saw rows of folding lawn chairs on the grass, facing the auctioneer's raised platform.

"Shouldn't we grab a seat?" I asked.

"And risk being torn apart by an angry mob? If you want to sit at a farm auction you have to bring your own chair. Let's go take a look at what's being sold." Greta led the way into the house.

"In here," she said, pointing to the dining room, where six men were placing small items on trays and lining them up on long folding tables. "There they are," Greta said, pointing. "Won't they look beautiful in the kitchen windows?"

I saw several trays of small, bright-colored bottles.

"Look here," Greta exclaimed. "Elbert's hand-tied fly collection. I think I'll try to get some of these for Garnet." She was examining a pile of fur, feathers, and bits of colored string. "Elbert used to collect roadkill to get the material to make these. Never went anywhere without a shovel and plastic sack. See, this one's made from pheasant feathers. Garnet will just love them."

I wandered from room to room, admiring the beautiful furniture, the pieces of cut crystal, and the old Haviland china.

A set of twelve sterling silver iced-tea spoons caught my eye. I recognized the beautiful old Towle design from my pre-poverty days. The spoons brought back memories of afternoon tea parties at the embassy: my mother, smelling good, wearing a flowery dress; me, quiet and smiling a lot, plump and awkward in a dress ordered from a catalogue; ladies, chattering in a dozen languages, elegantly gowned in the costumes of their native lands.

"My mother had this pattern," I said.

"What'd you say?" Greta asked.

"Nothing important."

The auctioneer called out, "Time, folks. Time."

We entered the tent and stood in the back. "Best spot," Greta said. "This way we can keep an eye on the bidders. See if we're up against a dealer. I can always outbid them because they have to resell everything at a profit."

Greta seemed happy with the price she paid for the entire fly-fishing collection, including a bamboo fishing rod. The auctioneer rapped on his stand for our attention. "Here's a nice box of old bottles, folks."

Greta got the box for only twenty dollars. Next came the spoons I'd admired.

"Twelve teaspoons here," the auctioneer called. "Good condition. Need cleaned. Sell by the piece. Do I hear twenty-five?"

"Twenty-five dollars apiece," I whispered to Greta. "They've got to be worth at least fifty."

"I've got twenty-five. Do I hear fifty? Fifty cents a piece for some real pretty spoons."

"Fifty!" I yelled.

Greta stared at me and began to laugh. I defended myself. "Fifty cents apiece, Greta! Fifty cents. I can't let that go."

"I've got fifty, do I hear a dollar?"

A woman in the front row raised her card.

Ten minutes later, my face flushed with victory, I owned twelve iced-tea spoons, even though I had to borrow the twenty-four dollars from Greta to pay for them.

Back at the house, Greta wasted no time in placing

her newly purchased bottles with the others on the ledge of the window over the sink. She stepped back to admire the way they looked. They really were beautiful, I thought, with the late-afternoon sun shining through them.

"Shouldn't you wash them out first?" I asked. "Some of the bottles still have stuff inside."

"Of course not. They're more valuable with the original contents. If you want to clean up your silver, there's some polish under the sink, Tori. Help yourself. I need to get changed—got an important meeting tonight. There's a stuffed beef heart and pickled beets in the fridge if you're hungry." She left the room, and I heard her footsteps going up the stairs.

I went to the sink to examine Greta's bottle collection up close. The smallest bottle was only about an inch high, cobalt blue with a tiny skull and crossbones near the top over the words POISON, TINCT OF IODINE.

Next to the iodine was an emerald-green bottle with grooves down the front and the legend NOT TO BE TAKEN inscribed on the side. Another cobalt-blue bottle, this one three-sided, read POISON and TRILOIDS. Another had a cross-hatch design and POISON written down one side.

Some bottles had no lettering or symbols, only grooves or bumps on the surface. Others had flaking paper labels. One, full of liquid, had a label that read CYANIDE. I couldn't decide which was oddest, the skull-shaped bottle or the one that looked like a miniature coffin.

A dusty bottle, almost hidden behind the new ones, caught my eye and I picked it up. In flowing script someone had written "Arsenicum" on the yellowed paper label. It was half full of white powder!

And I'd said nobody would have poison lying around a kitchen!

My knees grew wobbly as my mind reeled with the implications of what I'd seen. The better I'd gotten to know Greta, the less I believed she could kill anyone. And I still couldn't imagine her endangering Bear's life—but right here in my hand was a bottle of arsenic that belonged to Greta.

A hand reached over my left shoulder and took the bottle away from me. My heart nearly stopped.

The hair on my neck bristled. I was afraid to turn around and face her.

"Tori, you still don't believe me, do you?" Greta's voice was frighteningly cold.

"I don't know," I managed to squeak. "I thought I did, but now I'm not so sure."

"I think it's time we hash this out. I want you to come with me."

"Where?" I managed to squeak.

"Just get in the car." She had a frown on her face that reminded me of the fourth-grade teacher I'd had in Prague. I never argued with her either.

She took side streets out of town, avoiding the square and the bright streetlights there. She drove without saying a word. I was in a state of near-panic, not knowing where we were going or why. At a lonely crossroads, Greta turned her truck into the parking lot of a small, freestanding bank building, where four other cars were parked. A convenience store/gas station combination across the highway was the only other building in sight.

"Come on," she ordered. I got out of the truck and preceded her down a flight of stairs along the side of the building, which led to a basement entrance. I was less afraid now, figuring if I was about to be murdered, a bank basement seemed an unlikely place to commit the deed. Up until this moment, it hadn't occurred to me that she'd have co-conspirators, but now it seemed reasonable. After all, she wasn't the only anti-dump fanatic in town.

The room we entered had yellow concrete-block walls and a green vinyl floor and smelled faintly of mildew and strongly of cigarette smoke. Ten women were sitting on metal folding chairs around a long table. When they saw us come in, they got up and clustered around us, hugging Greta and shaking her hand.

"Sit down, Tori," Greta said. I did as I was told. "I told you I had an alibi, but you didn't believe me. So, even though it's not really any of your business where I go or what I do, I decided it was time to put an end to all your suspicions and show you were I've been spending my time."

The woman at the head of the table rapped on it with a gavel. "Welcome, everyone, to the Sunday night women's open meeting. We have a nice way of introducing ourselves, starting on my right."

"Hi, everyone, I'm Greta, and I'm an alcoholic."

"Hi, Greta."

I wanted to crawl under the table, but it was my turn. "Hi, everybody, I'm Tori, and I'm . . ." I looked at Greta. "And I'm sorry."

"Hi, Tori," they chorused. They continued around the table with introductions.

Greta raised her hand, and the women waited politely for her to speak. "Friends, Tori needs to know where I've been every afternoon and evening this week. Don't worry about blowing my anonymity."

Everyone chuckled, and everyone vouched for her having been there every day and evening.

"I'm Letty, and I'm a drug addict and an alcoholic," said a gray-haired woman in a nurse's uniform. "Congratulations, Greta. You've done more than your ninety in ninety." This drew a smattering of polite applause.

I looked questioningly at Greta. "That means I've been to more than ninety meetings in ninety days," she said. "It's recommended for the early stages of recovery."

Greta insisted I stay until the end of the meeting, when we stood in a circle, holding hands, and said the Lord's Prayer together. The women hugged me and told me to "keep coming back."

After noisy good-byes in the moon-washed parking lot, Greta gestured to the concrete plinth that served as a base for the drive-through MAC machine. "Have a seat."

I sat and leaned against the MAC, while Greta used the metal column that supported the roof as a backrest.

"After Lucky died, I began drinking heavily," she began. "When I realized I had a problem, I tried to stop and couldn't. I was so ashamed of myself. I hid from everyone."

"Including Garnet?"

"Especially Garnet. I'd always been the strong, big sister. How could I tell him? Then, about three months ago, one of my friends on the CANLICK committee guessed what was happening to me and suggested I try AA. The new friends I met in the rooms convinced me to move in with Garnet, so I wouldn't be tempted to drink alone."

"And you don't think Garnet knows?"

"Women can become very good at hiding their alcoholism, you know, especially when they live alone. Now, though, I feel ready to tell him."

"I'm glad you shared this with me, Greta. I want you to know I never really suspected you."

She laughed. "Come off it, Tori."

"I really jumped to the wrong conclusion—especially when I saw the arsenic. I'm sorry, Greta. You've got good reason to be upset with me," I said. "By the way, don't you think it's dangerous to keep full bottles of poison in the kitchen?"

"I never thought about it until now," she said with a smile. "I'll flush it as soon as we get home." She patted my nonbroken arm soothingly. "That's enough *mea culpa*, Tori. You're forgiven. I figure narrowly escaping two murder attempts has affected your analytical abilities."

"So you agree with me that Percy was murdered?"

"I do now. But it took Bear's poisoning to convince me."

"Do you have any ideas?" I asked.

"I certainly do. Lickin Creek has a certified resident lunatic, Crazy Ralph."

"Ralph? What motive would he have? He barely knows what century he lives in."

"He's got a history of violent behavior—you've seen him shooting at 'cloud-seeding' planes. He could have justified killing Percy by telling himself he was saving Lickin Creek from nuclear disaster."

I shook my head. "I just don't think so. Violent people don't use slow-acting poisons. They attack immediately on provocation. Bludgeoning or shooting I can see, but not poison."

"So who do you think killed him?"

"It's a fact that the greatest number of murders in America are not committed by strangers but by close friends or family members."

"Chaz, of course! I never did like him, even when we were kids," Greta said. "He was always running to the teacher to tattle on someone. Usually me."

She appeared to be thinking. "You know, Tori, there's any number of people out there who could have profited, directly or indirectly, from Percy's death. The people who've been laid off would get jobs at the dump; there'd be more money coming in and some of the closed businesses could reopen; the dump would give money to the borough for support of its services." She stretched her long body and said, "Why, if the dump gets located here, Garnet will even have the money to set up a decent-sized police department."

I couldn't help laughing. "Are you suggesting I replace your name on my list of suspects with Garnet's?"

"I think my brain cells are scrambled," she said, standing. "Let's go home and get some rest."

Chapter 17

Monday Morning

This was supposed to be the first day of Garnet's vacation, but today he was working at putting together his case against Chaz Montrose. Just as well, I thought. I had a lot to do myself, now that I had wheels again.

Maggie's car had been retrieved from the turnpike and returned to her, unharmed, thank goodness. Despite my track record of having wrecked one vehicle and abandoned another, Greta insisted I take the loaner car, which had been delivered early in the morning by Garnet and Greta's cousin, the Ford dealer, and ordered by the insurance agent, who was their uncle. Rather incestuous, but typical of the complex relationships I'd discovered in Lickin Creek.

As I dressed, I substituted a Liz Claiborne scarf for my unattractive blue hospital sling. It was silly, I knew, but it made me feel less like a patient and more like a human being.

Alice-Ann called to ask how Bear was doing. "Merry said it was arsenic poisoning. How could Bear have gotten into arsenic?"

"He'll be home today. And it happened because someone sprinkled it on the pie you left here. It seems Bear just loves ricotta cheese."

I heard her catch her breath. "No! My pie?" I could hear her sniffling.

I tried to console her. "Don't take it personally."

"I don't know what's happening around here," she moaned. "Apple Butter Fest is supposed to be a happy time. This year, everything's going wrong."

I promised to stop by the fairground later to see her and hung up. My first stop of the day was at the library, where I apologized to Maggie for the delay in getting her car back.

"The only thing I'm upset about is nobody stole it. I'd love to have the insurance company buy me a new one." She changed the subject. "Found another mention of your Hypatia. Her obituary—it's very strange. I made a copy so you can take it along."

The photocopy she handed me gave the usual data found in an obituary. Hypatia Hardcastle was born in 1790 and died in 1853. She had lived all her life on the family farm in Burnt Stump Hollow, and owned property in the borough of Lickin Creek. She was survived by three children. The strange part came at the end. " 'Thus closes the life of a woman who had experienced the vicissitudes of the world, a woman of sorrow and acquainted with grief.' What do you suppose that meant?"

Maggie shrugged. "Haven't the faintest idea, but I'll keep looking. I heard about poor Bear. How is he doing?"

"Should be home sometime today. How can I ever thank you, Maggie. For your car. For doing all this research."

She brushed away my compliments with a wave of her hand. "You can buy me lunch someday."

"You're on."

The outside air was still smoke-scented from the courthouse fire. As I walked back to the parking lot to retrieve the car, I decided I'd quiz Haggie Aggie one more time. She had the answer I needed, and this time I was going to get it from her.

But I changed my plans when I saw Avory Jenkins getting out of his car. I called out a greeting and he responded with a nod and a smile. His pipe, as usual, was clenched between his teeth. A canvas bag was slung over one shoulder, and he had a can of bug spray tucked under one arm.

"How's that new little one?" I asked.

His grin could have lit New York for a week. "She's the most beautiful baby in the state. Maybe the whole world. They're coming home today."

He opened a meter and dropped a handful of nickels into his bag. "Luvinia and I can't thank you enough, Tori. I don't know what would have happened if you hadn't been there."

He moved on to the next meter. "Too bad about Bear," he said. "I've been telling the Oberholsers for years not to put rat poison in their yard. Someday a kid's going to get in it."

"It wasn't rat poison, Avory. It was arsenic. And it was in a pie someone left in our kitchen."

"Imagine that," he said, scratching his head. "Why on earth would someone do that?" He puffed on his pipe until he wore a blue halo.

"Avory, I think it has something to do with my investigation of Percy's death. He was poisoned, too, you know."

"You don't really think old Percy was murdered, do you? This is a small, quiet town, Tori, not New York. Things like that don't happen here."

"Murder can happen anywhere, Avory. And speaking of Percy, I understand you and he were partners in a corporation that owns the land the dump company is looking at." Subtlety is not my métier.

"Yeah. So?" He sprayed bug killer on a juniper. "Damn bees," he muttered.

"Isn't that a conflict of interest on your part?"

He bit down on his pipe stem. "Don't see why."

"It could raise questions about whether you want the dump to be built for the benefit of the community, or because you stand to make a bundle on the sale of your land."

He glared at me. "I don't need to 'make a bundle,' Tori. And before you jump to any wrong conclusions, let me tell you I had plenty of money of my own before I married Luvinia. I happen to believe Lickin Creek's survival depends on that dump."

"And Percy had decided he didn't want to sell. How was your partnership going to work that out?"

"I don't know why I'm talking to you. I've got work to do."

"Who are the other partners, Avory? Was there someone else besides Aldine Schlotterbeck? Did you know he died on Friday?"

He spun around and strode hastily away from me, leaving behind the faint, sweet aroma of rum-and-maple tobacco mixed with bug spray.

Guess this means I'm not going to be invited to be the baby's godmother, I thought. Avory hadn't been very pleasant, but I was beginning to think he really didn't have a strong enough motive for murder. He didn't need the money he'd get from the land sale, and hardly anyone is altruistic enough to commit murder out of concern for his hometown's economic future. He'd moved himself down to the bottom of my list—maybe even right off it.

Burnt Stump Hollow, here I come, I thought. *And Haggie Aggie, this time you're going to answer my questions.*

As usual, it was raining and foggy on the mountainside. By the time I reached the village of Grandview, my good hand was so numb from clutching the wheel I could barely pry open my fingers. I stopped in front of the country church, having already made the decision to ask Father Buck if he'd go with me to Aggie's. Perhaps a man of the cloth would be more effective in persuading Aggie to talk than a short, round reporter with her arm in a cast.

When I stepped out of the car, all was unnaturally quiet. I heard none of the usual country sounds; even the roar of a passing truck was muffled. The cold, damp air pressed through my light clothes and made me wish I'd brought a sweater. I headed around the side to the graveyard; there was a muted screech as I swung the gate open. I could barely see the outline of the tombstones through the vapors of mist that curled skyward like smoke. I thought of a dozen Dracula movies I'd seen on late-night TV—what a great setting this would make for one of them! I moved cautiously around the monuments and knocked on the door of Buck's "vicarage."

He appeared very surprised to see me standing there.

"Hi," I said. "Thought I'd take you up on your

promise to help me out. I could use an hour of your time, if you're free."

He moved back without saying anything, and I stepped inside. The small room was stripped bare. On the floor, where the leather chair had once stood, was a set of matched leather suitcases.

"I don't understand," I said.

"I've been called to a new church. Guess I'm not as much of a pariah as I thought. It's the most affluent church in the Richmond area—and right near home. My mother's delirious with happiness."

"How fortunate for you," I said, smiling cheerfully on the outside. He'd promised to be there for me, and now he was leaving. And apparently he'd planned to do so without even saying good-bye.

"It happened rather suddenly, didn't it?" I said. You'd think by now I'd have learned not to put my trust in a man simply because he was knock-'em-dead good looking.

"Yes, it did," he said, not noticing my disappointment. "I had a call from by bishop on Wednesday, saying they needed me within the week. I could hardly believe it at first. It's a dream come true for me."

"Did you get a chance to do any genealogical research?"

"Oh, you mean about those graves you discovered. I did mention it to a few people I know in town, but I haven't had time to follow up. Sorry. How is your arm? I'd hoped to get down to see you, but with the packing and all, you know how it is."

"Yes," I said. "I do know how it is."

As I continued, alone, toward the Hollow, I analyzed my feelings, and I realized my frustration was misdirected. It wasn't because a near-stranger had made a meaningless promise, then didn't keep it. What was really bothering me was Garnet's leaving. Even though I'd made the decision not to go with him, at least not right away, I still felt abandoned. Intellectually, I knew it was a leftover emotion from my rootless Foreign Service childhood, and I was going to have to learn to deal with it.

I parked near Ralph's school bus home. I tried to tiptoe quietly toward the trail, but from the bus came the sound of frantic barking. The side door popped open, and Ralph appeared on the top step. Thankfully, I saw that he carried no gun.

"Hey, little lady. Where you headed?"

"Haggie Aggie's," I said curtly. He could make all the incorrect assumptions he wanted about my reason for visiting her.

"I'm on my way over to see her, myself. Need to put up some more apple butter. Come on, Toto."

Dry leaves crunched under our feet as we pushed through the underbrush. I smelled the spicy apple butter before we reached the clearing. We'd had some with breakfast this morning, and it had been the best I'd ever tasted.

I spotted Aggie, once again in white slacks, bending over the enormous copper kettle. I opened my mouth to call out a greeting, but my hello turned to a scream of horror as I realized that her head and shoulders were submerged in the apple butter.

"My God! We've got to get her out!"

Ralph and I grabbed her by the waist and tugged. For a minute, nothing happened. Then, with a disgusting sucking noise, the thick brown apple butter released its captive.

Aggie's slacks were lightly splattered with preserves, but her face and her upper body were unrecognizable under the congealed brown pulp. I pulled off my Liz Claiborne sling and handed it to Ralph. "Wipe her off. Please. She might still be alive."

Ralph shook his head but used the scarf to remove some of the goo from her face. I closed my eyes, but not before I saw that the apple butter must have been at a rolling boil when she fell in.

Tears formed in Ralph's eyes and dripped slowly down his grizzled cheek to disappear into his beard. I was crying, too. "I'll call the police," I said. "Will you be all right waiting here with her?"

He wiped his nose on his flannel sleeve and shook his head. "I don't want to be alone. Toto can watch her."

The door to the trailer was unlocked and creaked when I opened it. I crossed the doorstep hesitantly, feeling like an intruder, and called Garnet's office.

"Sit tight and wait for me," he said when I told him what had happened. "I'll call the State Police—the Hollow's their jurisdiction."

I sat beside Ralph on the sofa to wait for the police. "She—Aggie—and me, we was good friends." Silence. "It weren't no accident," he said. "She's made apple butter that way for twenty years. She must a been pushed."

I agreed with him. Damn, I was beginning to feel like my name should be Typhoid Tori. This was the third person I'd come across in a week.

Poor Aggie, I thought. All she'd wanted was a little house in town, and it had brought her death. I didn't doubt for a minute that Aggie's attempt at blackmail had backfired on her.

A long time, perhaps an hour, passed before I heard the wail of sirens announcing the impending arrival of the State Police. Another ten minutes passed, time for them to hike in on the trail, then someone pounded on the door. I opened it.

Troopers were pacing around the kettle and Aggie's body, measuring and photographing the scene. Two policemen in brown uniforms and ranger-style hats entered, and suddenly the tiny living room was unbearably crowded and noisy.

The older of the two men turned to me and, without even identifying himself, began snapping questions: When had we found the body? How long had I known Aggie? Why was Ralph there? Had we seen anyone? Did either of us have any reason to want Aggie dead?

Ralph's reaction was to stare vacantly at the wall. Instead of responding to the cop's barrage, I pulled out my notebook and asked the overbearing gentleman his name and badge number. Trooper Saul Zimmerman suddenly became a lot more courteous.

When the door opened again, it was Garnet, accompanied by his loyal if incompetent assistant, Luscious Miller. He ignored the others in the room, wrapped his muscular arms around me, and squeezed me until my nose was smashed against his badge.

When I was able to speak, I asked, "Did you see her?"

He shuddered. "I did."

Trooper Zimmerman interrupted. "This is in my jurisdiction, Garnet. What are you doing here?"

"Personals reasons, Saul. Tori is a friend."

Luscious brought two chairs from the kitchen area into the living room for Garnet and me. The two troopers flanked Ralph on the couch, while Luscious sat on the flowered velour recliner.

Everyone turned to me, so I explained that I had come to Burnt Stump Hollow to question Aggie again about what she knew. I told them I suspected she had been blackmailing the murderer and that was the reason for her death. Garnet held my hand while I talked.

Zimmerman interrupted me and turned to Garnet. "Montrose murdered? I thought he died from Rocky Mountain spotted fever."

Garnet shook his head. "He got over that long time ago. It was aplastic anemia. But the rumor's going 'round that he was poisoned."

I looked sharply at Garnet. Was he, again, going to scoff at my insistence that Percy had been murdered?

"Well, was he or wasn't he?" Zimmerman asked impatiently.

"Enough has happened since he died to make me think he was murdered. Twice, Tori's been the victim of attempted murder. So, even though the autopsy report stated there was no poison in Percy's system, I tend to think something was overlooked."

"An undetectable poison," I added. "You hear about them all the time." I squeezed Garnet's hand, grateful that he had stood up for me and my theory.

Trooper Zimmerman sneered. "Sure you do. On those crazy TV shows, written by crazy New Yorkers who don't know the first thing about police work. Now where did you say you came from, miss?"

A rap on the door kept me from strangling him. Doc Jones came in, carrying a black bag. "Tori," he said when he saw me. "You poor thing. What a dreadful experience, finding two bodies in a week."

"Three bodies," I said, thinking of Aldine

Schlotterbeck. Well, I hadn't actually found his body, but it had been close, time-wise.

"What are you doing here?" I asked as he hugged me.

"I'm the Caven County coroner," he said. "The police have to call me when there's a death and no family to tell us the victim's medical history."

"Did you already examine her body?" Garnet asked. "What do you estimate was the time of death?"

Trooper Zimmerman glared at him. "Let's get this straight right now, Gochenauer. I'm in charge of this investigation."

Garnet grinned.

Doc ignored the exchange between the two policemen. "It's impossible to tell because of the condition of the body, but I'd guess she was in the pot overnight. Her watch stopped at ten-oh-six. It's three-fifteen now. She couldn't have been killed this morning because the fire's gone out and the apple butter's had plenty of time to cool. I'd guess seventeen hours. I'll know more after the autopsy."

"Be sure and have them check for drugs," I said. "She wasn't very big, but she would have struggled if she could."

Zimmerman snapped his notebook shut. "Thank you very much for your help. Don't know if I'd ever have thought of that myself. You can go now; I know where to find you if I have more questions." He leered knowingly at me and then Garnet.

Luscious drove the rental car so I could ride home with Garnet. In the car, Garnet turned to me. "Every time I let you out of my sight you get into big-time trouble. I don't want you to get hurt. Please be careful."

I leaned over and planted a kiss on his cheek. "I never had anyone who cared enough to worry about me. It takes some getting used to."

A perturbing thought entered my mind. "Garnet, did Aggie have a family? Someone who'll be responsible for arranging her funeral?"

"I don't think there's anyone left."

"Then I want to do it for her," I said. "I want her to be buried in town."

"Not on the mountain where she lived all her life?" Garnet asked, surprised.

"Definitely *not* on the mountain, Garnet."

Greta was waiting for us at the front door. "I heard on the scanner about Aggie's having an accident. What happened?"

Garnet's shoulder sagged. "She fell into her apple butter."

Greta gasped. "Is she dead?"

"It was boiling. She never had a chance."

"My God! Poor Aggie." She dabbed at her eyes with the peach silk scarf that was knotted at her neck. "Come in the kitchen. I've got hot water on for cocoa. You both look like you could use a cup. I know I could."

"I'd prefer something stronger," I said.

"Good idea," Garnet said. Suddenly a great black shape planted two huge feet on my shoulders and covered my face with enthusiastic wet kisses. "Bear. Oh, Bear, I'm so glad to see you." I buried my nose in the tan ruff around his neck.

Garnet laughed, grabbed Bear's collar, and hauled him off. "Out you go, boy," he said, dragging him to the back door. "I'm not quite as nutty about Bear as you are about those two silly cats, but it would have hurt to lose him."

He laid his hand on my shoulder, and I covered it with mine. His blue eyes studied me tenderly, and I thought: You're lucky, Tori, you've finally found a real jewel.

"Now, how about that drink?" Garnet said.

He lit a fire in the den, and the three of us sat before it, discussing today's terrible event. Bear had been allowed back in and lay before the fire. Fred was on my lap, and I let my fingers wander through his soft fur.

A milk-glass platter of applesauce-oatmeal cookies sat on the coffee table. "They're okay," Greta said, seeing my questioning look. "I was here when Mrs. Mattress brought them by about an hour ago. I've already eaten half a dozen."

I took one and nibbled on it and was surprised to find I was hungry.

"So Doc thinks she died last night?" Greta said. "First Percy, now Aggie. Nothing like this has ever happened in Lickin Creek before."

I thought of the summer's murders but didn't mention them. I knew what she meant: that Lickin Creek was supposed to be the kind of charming little place that people say is great for bringing up children in; it was not supposed to be the murder capital of rural Pennsylvania.

"Who could be responsible?" she mused.

"At least we know it wasn't Chaz Montrose," I said. "Since he was in jail last night."

Garnet shook his head. "No, he wasn't. He posted bail late yesterday afternoon."

"Then he's still a suspect," I pointed out. "Whom else do you suspect?"

He looked very tired as he answered, "I don't have any idea, Tori. I've known everyone in this town all my life. It was very difficult for me to come to the belief that Percy was indeed murdered. It's even harder for me to concede that his killer is most likely a friend of mine."

"Garnet," I said gently, "if your liking a person is all it took to make someone a good guy, there'd be no crime at all in this town."

CHAPTER 18

Tuesday Morning

I FILLED THE CATS' DISHES AND PLACED THEM ON top of the refrigerator to protect them from Bear, poured fresh water for the dog, helped myself to a mug of coffee, and sat down to think. I had to do something to stop this. Two people had been murdered. Three, if you counted Aldine Schlotterbeck, and I was inclined to do so. And two attempts had been made to kill me. If the killer wasn't stopped soon, there'd be nobody left in town—me included.

I was sure Garnet would investigate, but I didn't feel that was enough. First, he was so darn overworked that I couldn't see how he'd have time to fit anything else into his days. And second, I believed his friendship with everyone in town could influence his interpretation of the facts.

I thought over the people I'd suspected. Two, Haggie Aggie and Aldine Schlotterbeck, were off my list because they were dead. Chaz Montrose had been released from jail before Aggie was murdered so he was still a possibility. Avory Jenkins had no apparent motive that I could see: Garnet confirmed what Avory had told me about being well-off—in fact, he was just about the richest man in town, having inherited a bundle that he'd invested prudently. Greta had a solid alibi for all the times in question, including having been with me all day Sunday.

Crazy Ralph had been so obviously distressed by Aggie's death I couldn't believe he'd killed her, and I still couldn't imagine him poisoning anyone. That left Mrs. Foor; Riley Roark, the strike leader; and his lover, Helen Montrose. I still planned to check them out, but I had the feeling I would discover they had rock-solid alibis. Somehow, I needed to dig deeper into the community to find the killer.

I thought of Maggie, who was fine-tuned into the Lickin Creek Grapevine; perhaps she'd heard something I could use. I called her and invited her to meet me at noon for the lunch I'd promised her.

Shortly after speaking to Maggie, an idea began to form. It occurred to me that I might be able to use the Lickin Creek Grapevine to uncover the murderer. But I needed to talk it over with someone to work out the details. Not Garnet: he'd never go for it, and as a cop, he couldn't. Greta? She'd tell Garnet before I had a chance to get moving. Who else but my best friend in the entire world, Alice-Ann?

"Tell me—tell me—tell me. I'm all goose-bumpy." Alice-Ann was sitting on her living room floor, her enviably long, jean-clad legs stretched out under the three-legged cobbler's-bench coffee table. She popped another doughnut hole into her mouth and brushed the powdered sugar fallout off the front of her Penn State sweatshirt. I'd picked up a box of holes on my way over;

they'd been our favorite snack food back in college. "The suspense is killing me, Tori. What's your idea?"

I adjusted a gingham cushion behind my back and tried to find a less painful position on the oak church pew she called a couch. Alice-Ann's home could have been featured in the pages of any country decorating magazine; she did charming things with barn implements and old canning jars I never would have thought of. Everything looked extremely cozy; the only problem was there was nothing comfortable to sit on.

I presented my plan to utilize the infamous Grapevine to set a trap for the murderer.

"But how?" she asked.

"When Aggie told me she was thinking of blackmailing someone, she said she had positive proof to back up her demands. Whatever it was, we can assume she hid it in a safe place. I figure the killer has to locate it before someone else does and puts two and two together. We're going to spread the word that I know what Aggie had and where it's hidden. And then I'll let it slip out that I plan to go up to the Hollow to get it on Wednesday morning. With any luck, the killer will follow me there."

"I don't know, Tori. It sounds dangerous. Will you have the police waiting to grab him?"

"Someone, yes—but not the police. I'm afraid Garnet would lock me up in jail before he'd let me do something this risky."

We discussed possibilities for a few minutes. "I wonder if I can get Maggie Roy's fiancé to help out," I said. "Do you know if the reenactors are still camping out behind the Holiday Inn?"

Mouth full of doughnut, she nodded. "Whufkinnahdo?"

I laughed. "If you're asking what you can do, I'd say wait for me to call you with a made-up story, then tell it to as many people as you can think of. Whatever you do, though, don't tell anyone about our real plan."

She crossed her heart and hoped to die. I hoped I wasn't the one who was going to die.

"Do you really think it's going to work? That you're really going to trap the killer this way?"

I shrugged. "It's all I can think of. And you've been here long enough to know that when the Lickin Creek Grapevine shoots out an alert, the gossip spreads through town like wildfire."

" 'Oh, what a tangled web we weave, when first we practice to deceive!' More holes?" she asked.

"No thanks. I could barely zip my jeans this morning. I've got to get back on my diet."

"Didn't you know that even the air in Pennsylvania is fattening?"

As I drove through the square, I noticed that not even the riots, pickets, or the courthouse fire had prevented the downtown merchants from decorating for the Apple Butter Fest. In addition to papier-mâché apples suspended from the lamp poles, banners the colors of Red and Golden Delicious apples waved from flagpoles before each store, and nearly every shop window displayed great stacks of apples. It was a Norman Rockwell scene, if one ignored the black hole where the courthouse had been.

I spotted Avory Jenkins sweeping discarded picket signs, paper cups, and assorted trash off the street. From the scowl on his face, I guessed he was not terribly fond of this part of his work. I waved, and although I was sure he saw me, he pretended he didn't.

The square was quiet. Marchers and picketers hadn't yet arrived. Standing at attention, guarding the fountain, was Garnet's deputy, Luscious Miller. The only other person in sight was Ralph McDougal, who was sitting on a park bench with Toto at his side. Luscious waved at me, but Ralph appeared to be on another planet.

Behind the Holiday Inn, smoke from a hundred campfires spiraled into the sky, mingled with the appetizing aromas of sizzling bacon and sausage, and hung low over the battlefield. I parked next to a van suffering from a terminal illness and went in search of Maggie's fiancé, Bill Cromwell.

The general was in his tent, shaving with a straight razor. "Be with you in a minute," he said when he noticed me peering in. "Help yourself to coffee." He waved toward a blue-and-white-enamel pot hanging over the fire.

I sat, low to the ground, on a folding chair constructed of wooden slats, and scalded my lip on the blistering-hot edge of the tin coffee mug. When Bill stepped out of his tent, buttoning his blue jacket, I smiled up at him.

"Glad you came by," Bill said, pouring coffee. "I've got good news. I talked to a friend at the Historical and Museum Commission in Harrisburg. She's very interested in preserving the cemetery. She says our best bet is to enlist the help of lots of interested groups: veterans' organizations, the NAACP, the Rainbow Coalition, county historical societies, churches. Says we've got to move fast on this."

"Sounds like a job for Garnet's sister. I'll see if I can't get her started immediately."

"Great. Have her call the commission and ask for Buffy Petrovitch."

I dropped my voice to a whisper. "I desperately need your help, Bill."

"Anything, ma'am." Suddenly he was John Wayne.

As I outlined my plan, his face registered doubt, skepticism, and disbelief. "If you're right, and this killer follows you into the Hollow, you'll be in grave danger. He'll be so desperate, he'll think nothing of killing you."

"That's why I need you and some of your armed men to go up there early and hide in the woods surrounding Aggie's house—to protect me. When the killer shows up, you stay quiet until I've confronted him—if I feel in any danger at all, I'll call and you can come out with your guns."

"I'll be there, with a dozen of my most trustworthy men," he promised. "But I'm really concerned about this. Are you sure it's a good idea?"

"Don't worry about me," I quipped, trying to ease his fears—and mine. "Anybody who's made it for ten years in Hell's Kitchen is a survivor."

"What if the murderer turns out to be a woman? I don't know if I could point my gun at a lady."

"Believe me, this is no lady—or gentleman."

He walked with me to my car, where a woman stopped loading her suitcases into the back of a minivan to stare at him with open-mouthed curiosity. A gentleman in a Union Army uniform is not what one expects to meet up with in a motel parking lot. Bill graciously tipped his plumed hat to her. "Mr. Lincoln sends his regards to the folks back home in Wisconsin." She nodded, mouth still open.

Once I was in my car, he leaned through the window. "Don't fret about a thing," he assured me. "My men will be there for you."

He saluted and, after a brief struggle, opened the door of the disreputable van parked next to me. Suddenly, I no longer saw the brave, in-charge military officer, but only an extremely young man in a silly-looking costume.

I wanted to call him back. Tell him we weren't playing games this time. But he only waved and backed out of the parking space, spewing forth a billowing cloud of blue smoke, and emitting a roar that told of a hole in the muffler.

I was committed now. Others were involved. There could be no turning back. I drove slowly, wondering if—no, hoping—I'd done the right thing.

The drugstore, where I was to meet Maggie for lunch, had a turn-of-the-century ambiance that had not been conceived by a decorator but was all original. This was one of the few businesses in town that hadn't changed since it was built. It still had wood-plank floors, a pressed-tin ceiling with a few cobwebs in the corners, and a ceiling fan stirring the air, which was thick with cigarette smoke and the smell of home cooking.

Glass cases packed with dusty merchandise lined the front room. The restaurant was in the back. A long counter curved around a central area where the lone waitress, in a pink polyester pantsuit, was rushing around trying to wait on a dozen men wearing the Lickin Creek uniform—the plaid flannel shirt.

The drugstore was the unofficial "smoke-filled room" of Lickin Creek, where most of the town business took place. The "regulars" paused in their conversations for a moment when I walked in but quickly resumed their normal routines.

Maggie was already seated at one of the four booths on the right side of the room. The holes in the yellow plastic seat covers had been recently repaired with silver duct tape.

"I ordered for you," she said cheerfully as I slid in across from her. "La spécialité de la maison—tuna sandwich and Cherry Coke. Didn't know if you preferred potato chips or french fries, so I asked for both."

After our food was served, she asked, "Are you still interested in Hypatia Hardcastle?"

I unwrapped my flatware and laid the paper napkin on my lap. "Of course," I said. I still thought she'd make a fascinating subject for a book, but at the moment I had a murderer to find.

"Reason I asked," she said, "is I've been asking all the library patrons if they've ever heard of her family. Yesterday, one of them came back in and said his great-grandmother knew the Hardcastles. I've got her name and address if you want it."

"That's wonderful, Maggie. I'll call her soon." I took the scrap of paper she handed me and stuck it between the pages of my notebook.

"Don't wait too long, Tori," Maggie said with a little laugh. "I understand the woman's in her nineties."

Lunch was nearly over; it was time to activate the Grapevine. I leaned forward and lowered my voice. Was it my imagination, or did the room suddenly become quiet? "Maggie," I said, "the most extraordinary thing happened. You must promise not to tell a soul."

Her eyes grew wide. "You know I won't," she said solemnly.

"I received a letter this morning from Aggie Haggard."

"But she's dead!"

"Yes, but it was postmarked Thursday, so she sent it before she died. In it, she said she'd tried to call me, but of course that was right after I broke my arm and wasn't taking calls, so she wrote me."

Maggie was practically drooling. "And . . . ?"

"She wrote that if anything happened to her . . ."

Maggie gasped. "Precognition!"

"Uh—right. She told me about a special hiding place she had, and if something happened to her, I should look there and I'd know who had done it."

"Really?"

"Last week, she told me that she knew who had killed Percy Montrose and that she was going to use what she knew to blackmail his killer. I tried to talk her out of it, but now I'm afraid she went ahead with the blackmail and that's why she was murdered. I imagine what she's hidden is something that would document her demands. I'm going up to her trailer tomorrow morning to get it."

"That's great." She paused with a confused look on her face. "Why wait till tomorrow?"

I'd figured someone would ask me that. The reason I wanted to do it tomorrow was to give the Lickin Creek gossips time to do their work. I said, "It's the rental car. It keeps stalling. I'm taking it to the shop right after I leave here. They've promised to have it ready by eight tomorrow morning."

Before returning home, I stopped at the Giant-Bigmart and bought a small, voice-activated tape recorder. I intended to coerce a confession out of the murderer and get it on tape. I crossed my fingers when the clerk ran my credit card through the machine, but by some miracle, the charge was accepted.

I rushed into the house and was delighted to find I had it all to myself. It was time to get started. I made my first call. "Okay, Alice-Ann—here's the story I want you to spread . . ."

I dialed another number. "Good morning, Mrs. Butterbaugh. This is Tori Miracle. I just wanted to let you know I've received two hundred and twenty-six entries in the apple recipe contest. Yes, I should be able to make a decision soon. No, not tomorrow; you see, I got the most fascinating letter today . . ."

I was smiling as I dialed the next number. "Jennifer? Hi, I wanted you to know that Bear's doing really well. Let me tell you about the amazing letter I received . . ."

I paused and waited for her exclamation of astonishment, then finished and called the next person on my list.

"Hello, P.J., this is Tori. I'm really looking forward to starting work at the *Chronicle*. Can we get together soon and talk about it? No, not tomorrow. I have to go up to the Hollow in the morning, and I might not be back by noon. You see, this morning I received the most unusual letter . . ."

I called everyone I'd ever met in Lickin Creek. When I finished my phone calls, I was satisfied I had done everything I could. I'd set my trap, and I was the bait. Now all I had to do was wait until tomorrow morning and see if the killer would fall for it.

CHAPTER 19

Tuesday Afternoon

I COULD PICTURE THE SCENES TAKING PLACE around town simultaneously. Dental hygienists were hovering over their captive patients; women were pushing shopping carts at the Giant-Bigmart; CANLICK picketers were raising their skull masks to mop their brows; teachers were on break in faculty lounges; the regulars were sipping coffee at the drugstore. And they were all saying, "Did you hear about Tori Miracle's letter . . . ?"

If this didn't work . . . well, I'd think of something else, but I was sure it would. Whoever the killer was, it was someone who was well aware of what I'd been doing—enough to try to stop me by poisoning the pie and to kill Aggie and Aldine before I had a chance to speak with them. There was no doubt in my mind that the murderer already knew I would be at Aggie's trailer tomorrow morning.

I took a couple of aspirins to dull the pain in my arm and paced the floor until the ache subsided. It was going to be a long afternoon and night unless I found something to do to kill time, so I decided to call the elderly woman Maggie had told me about, who claimed to have known the Hardcastle family a long time ago. A pleasant female voice told me that Mrs. Cavender could not speak on the phone because of hearing problems but dearly loved to have visitors.

I made sure all the doors to the house were locked and drove toward her downtown address. Maneuvering through Main Street was an ordeal; every business had set up special "Apple Butter Sale" stalls on the sidewalk, and the street was full of shoppers. Someone tooted "shave-and-a-haircut" at me. Doc grinned and waved at me from his shiny black sport-utility vehicle.

At the end of the street, where it changed from business to residential, I saw an adorable, narrow white-brick town house with geranium-filled window boxes on either side of the front door. That was it.

A stunning young African-American woman invited me into the hallway. She was the woman I'd spoken to on the telephone. She smiled shyly at me. "I loved your book," she said. "Would you mind autographing it for me?"

"Mind? Gracious, no!" Running into a fan was a rare treat for me. So rare, in fact, I felt as if I should ask for her autograph. Her name was Daynah—I was glad I asked how to spell it before I started writing.

"Mrs. Cavender is my great-great-aunt. At least, I think that's what she is. She was my father's grandma's sister, I think . . . oh, never mind. The point is, the other day my dad came home from the library with a story about you searching for information about the Hardcastle family—he asked Auntie if she knew any of them and she said she did. She'll be delighted to talk to you—she gets awfully bored sitting here alone with nobody to talk to but me. She often tells me the same stories, over and over."

I wondered how bored Daynah got. Staying with an old woman all day didn't seem like much of a life for an attractive woman in her late teens or early twenties.

As if she knew what I was thinking, Daynah said, "I like listening to her. I'm putting our family tree on the computer."

She ushered me into the tiny living room. A very small woman sat in a wheelchair near the window. She was wrapped in a fuzzy pink crocheted afghan so that all I could really see of her was her face and a cloud of soft white hair.

"Auntie, this is Tori Miracle. The lady who wants to know about the Hardcastles." A frail hand appeared from the pink folds. I shook it gently, fearful my heavy touch might shatter it. When she spoke, her voice was remarkably deep and strong. She ordered Daynah to bring us tea, and while we waited she asked a great number of questions about what had brought me to Lickin Creek.

"I always did like that Gochenauer boy," she said with a slight smile. "He was our paperboy one year. I went to school with his grandmother . . . or was it his great-grandmother . . . ?" She seemed to slip away for a moment. Into the past, no doubt, possibly remembering when she was young and pretty like Daynah. "Did he ever get his teeth straightened?"

Over bone-china teacups, I told them how I'd stumbled over the small graveyard in the Hollow. "Really stumbled," I added, describing how I'd sprained my ankle on a tombstone.

"Do you want to find the family because you think it's a way to prevent the nuclear waste dump from being built up there?" Daynah asked.

"At first that was my reason. But now I realize it would only slow things down a little. In talking to legal experts, it appears the graves can be moved, with or without family permission."

"Then what is your interest?" asked Mrs. Cavender.

"When I was in the library reading the old newspaper clippings about Hypatia Hardcastle, I almost could see her. That's the first step for me in writing a book—when the subject matter becomes real. I want to write about Hypatia: her life in the Hollow, her family, the people who knew her."

Mrs. Cavender nodded approval. "I like that idea," she said. "Let me think on it a minute."

I took out my notebook, sipped my tea, and looked out the window where the golden and red leaves of one lone tree danced in the pale afternoon sun.

"I remember the Hardcastles. They were the richest family in town. Sat in a pew right up front in church. I was in school with Edith. Nice girl. Kind of spoiled. Guess it was all that money. Once I remember my father thought he was going to get rich . . ."

"The Hardcastles, Auntie." Daynah gently brought her back to the present.

"Did I say I went to school with Edith? She ran off to the big city after graduation. Never saw her again."

Was that it? I'd written only a few lines of notes.

"She had a little sister. I think her name was Daisy. No, it was Dulcie. And a little brother, too—it's all coming back to me now. Their father was Abe Pomeroy, who owned Pomeroy's Dry Goods. And their mother would have been Hypatia's granddaughter. Reason I know is because they used to talk about her a lot—it was Hypatia who made the family so rich—bought up all that land in the center of town back when it was cheap."

"What happened to the family?" I asked. It seemed to me if they were from such a rich, prominent family, some of them would still be around Lickin Creek.

Her mouth twisted into a sad little smile. "The little boy had something wrong with his head. It got all funny-shaped, then he died. After Dulcie's father died, Dulcie inherited the family fortune. She went out west and got married there. I heard she died in childbirth . . . God works in mysterious ways."

"Do you remember if her baby survived?" I asked. Hope for finding any of Hypatia's descendants was fading fast.

"I hope not."

"Auntie! What a terrible thing to say."

"I know, but I mean it. The reason Dulcie left town was to keep her ancestry a secret. She never should have gotten in the family way."

I was astounded and outraged. "You mean Dulcie Pomeroy, Hypatia's granddaughter, was so ashamed of her black heritage that she left town in order to get married? What kind of town was this, that made a woman feel she had to hide her background? And how can you say such a dreadful thing—that you 'hope' her baby died?"

Daynah and Mrs. Cavender were momentarily taken aback at my outburst. There was absolute quiet for about thirty seconds, then, much to my surprise, the older woman began to chuckle. "Whatever gave you the idea that the Hardcastle family was black?"

"I just assumed . . . the other graves around her . . . black Civil War soldiers . . . was I wrong?"

"You couldn't be any more wrong, young lady. The Hardcastles owned a big farm up in the Hollow. Lots of farmhands at one time—those veterans probably worked for her family."

"What, then, was this secret Dulcie Pomeroy tried to hide by leaving town?"

"Everybody in town knew—nobody would have married her—that's why she left. She wanted to have a family. You see, Hypatia and her father—they—oh, dear, how can I say this? They committed the ultimate sin."

Daynah interrupted gently. "Are you trying to say Dulcie's grandmother was born as the result of incest between Hypatia and her father?"

Mrs. Cavender nodded. "That's not the worst of it, though."

"Good grief," I exclaimed. "What could be worse?" Now I understood the line in Hypatia's obituary about her being "a woman of sorrow and acquainted with grief."

"It didn't end there," Mrs. Cavender went on. "The real tragedy was that Hypatia's son and daughter carried on the family tradition."

"Dulcie's grandparents were brother and sister?" I was totally shaken.

"That's what everybody said. Dulcie's mother should never have married. She should never have had children."

I'd certainly been way off track in my thinking.

Two incestuous generations! And a baby who'd died of a skull deformity that could have been genetic. If any Hardcastle descendants were alive today, it was no wonder they hadn't come forward.

"You said the Hardcastles owned a big farm. I saw no sign of one in the Hollow. What happened to it?"

"It burned a few years after the Civil War. My mother told me it was 'the will of God,' but the rumor was that the townspeople were so offended by the family that they did it."

I doubted that I'd ever find any of Hypatia's descendants, but I felt I owed it to the residents of that little graveyard to keep trying. "Do you recall Dulcie's married name?" I asked.

"Can't say I do."

"Do you remember where Dulcie Pomeroy moved to when she went out west?"

"Dulcie Pomeroy? Why, she was Edith's little sister. Did I tell you I went to school with Edith?"

I said my thank-yous and good-byes. What I'd learned would probably not help me locate Hypatia's descendants, if indeed any were left; I hadn't run across any Pomeroys in Lickin Creek—or anyplace else for that matter. But I knew I had the foundation for writing an absorbing family saga, using some tragic facts and a lot of imagination.

"Hi there, Tori!" someone called.

I looked up to see Helen Montrose on the other side of the street, with far more clothes on than the last time I'd seen her. "Why, Tori, what a surprise seeing you here! Wait up, I want to talk to you." She looked both ways for traffic then ran across.

She clutched a large paper bag to her chest.

"Cider," she explained. "I'm on the LCNB board of directors. We're giving out free cider samples because of the Apple Butter Fest."

The LCNB was the Lickin Creek National Bank, which was on the square at least six blocks north of where we were standing. I could see no reason for Helen to park here and carry her heavy sack of cider six blocks unless she was waiting there for me to come out of the Cavender house.

I smiled at her and waited to hear what she had to say.

"Tori, I'm so ashamed of what my husband has done. I wanted to tell you how sorry I am about what they did to you. When I spoke to Chaz about it, he swore he had nothing to do with running you off the road. That it was all something hatched up by Reverend LeRoi's punks."

"That certainly makes me feel better," I said. I hoped she caught the sarcasm.

"I'm divorcing Chaz," Helen announced.

"Sounds like a good move," I said. "I'm sorry, but I really have to go."

She continued as if she hadn't heard me. "Sunday, after Garnet picked Chaz up, I thought, That's the last straw, Helen. I packed my things and went right over to Riley's house. We talked all night, and we've decided we're going to get married—just as soon as my divorce is final."

"You and Riley Roark?" I couldn't picture it.

"With Riley, I'm a princess. He may look rough, but he'd never lay a hand on me. Not like Chaz. My mother always said, 'First time for love, second time for money.' I did it backwards."

What does Emily Post recommend one say to a

woman who announces her engagement while her present husband is in jail? I stuck with the tried-and-true "I wish you much happiness," and departed.

If I were to believe what Helen said, then she and Riley Roark were together at his house at the time of Aggie's murder. On the other hand, she could have concocted the whole story to cover up the truth. I'd know for sure tomorrow morning.

Chapter 20

Tuesday Evening

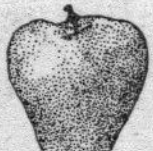

The sky was darkening when I unlocked the front door and entered the hallway of Garnet's house. I flicked the light switch, expecting the Tiffany chandelier to spring to life, but nothing happened. I'd have to remind Garnet to change the bulb.

"Hi," I called; the house was still. But in the front parlor, a fire had been lit, and the dancing flames cast a warm glow on the antique furniture. I walked back toward the kitchen. No sign of anyone there. I called Greta's name several times. No answer. Maybe she'd gone to her room.

Another large fire was blazing away in the fireplace in the den. Noel and Bear were asleep on the couch and could hardly spare a glance in my direction. I reached down and scratched Noel's ears. "Hi, pretty girl. Where's Fred?" In my high-pitched cat-calling voice, I called, "Come on, boy. Mommy's home."

I went into the kitchen and poured iced tea from the pressed-glass pitcher in the refrigerator. "Here, kitty," I called, rattling the Tasty Tabby Treats bag. It brought Noel and Bear but not Fred. I was beginning to be alarmed; Fred never missed a chance to eat. Had he accidentally been shut up somewhere? I was used to looking inside closets and dresser drawers before I closed them, but I doubted that non–cat owners, like Garnet and Greta, would think of that.

Noel, tail quivering erect, stalked back into the den. She looked at me over her left shoulder as if asking me to follow, which I did.

"What is it, Noel? What are you trying to show me?" She meowed and crossed to the fireplace. Between the inglenook and the corner of the room was a narrow wooden door with leather hinges I'd always thought hid the firewood storage area. Now, it stood slightly open.

I peered in and saw it was the entrance to a stairwell. Noel rubbed between my calves, meowing with excitement. From above, I heard an answering meow.

"Fred. Bad boy. What are you doing up there? Come on down." When he didn't, I tried a sweeter, more wheedling tone, which elicited more faint meows but still no cat.

I reached into the stairwell and groped around for a light switch. Apparently there was none, so I looked by the back door for the flashlight I thought I'd noticed there before.

"Stay here," I told Noel. "I don't need to chase you around, too." She wouldn't listen, so I pushed her out of the stairwell and closed the door behind me.

The narrow spiral staircase wouldn't accommodate the width of my shoulders, and I had to edge my way up sideways. I continued climbing, knowing I must have passed the second-floor level already. Cobwebs clung to my face, and God only knew what I was going to find crawling around in my hair. "Fred, when I find you, I'm gonna kill you for this!"

The round yellow dot cast by the flashlight revealed another door at the top of the stairs, open just wide enough for a fat cat to slip through. I pushed on the door and was struck by the heavy odor of smoke. There must be a hole in the chimney, I thought, and made a mental note to add that to the list of jobs Garnet needed to take care of around the old house.

Except for the small circle of light from my flashlight, it was pitch-black. "Kitty?" I called, and was grateful to hear Fred's answering cry from nearby. I swung the beam of light around slowly and saw that I was in an immense, windowless attic room. Eventually, the light revealed a shadowy opening in a wall. It was from the murky depths of this next room that Fred's plaintive wails were coming.

I knew he had to be caught in something, probably a mousetrap. I prayed he wasn't badly hurt and cautiously stuck my head through the doorway. If possible, this room was even darker than the rest of the attic, and the smoke was so thick I could hardly breathe.

A scratching noise near the floor startled me. I pointed the light down and swept it from side to side until I saw Fred's light-blue cat carrier against the opposite wall, which was only about four feet away.

"What the . . . ?" I took three long steps toward it and dropped to my knees. Fred's round golden eyes glowed at me through the grille. He recoiled from the light and covered his eyes with one paw.

"Poor baby," I said. "How did you get in there?"

Behind me, the door slammed shut. Before I could

get to my feet, I heard the harsh sound of metal scraping against metal. I flung myself at the door, but it was too late. It had been bolted from the outside.

I pounded on the door with my fist. "Let me out!" I screamed. "You can't get away with this!" I began to choke, and I realized smoke was rapidly replacing the air in the tiny space.

It dawned on me that I was in the attic meat-smoking chamber Garnet had told me about. Someone must have switched the flues in the downstairs fireplaces so the smoke would fill this small area instead of going out the chimney.

I placed my ear against the door and listened but could hear nothing. That's when I discovered the door was covered with sheet iron. And so, I learned when I sank down next to Fred's carrier, was the floor.

The air was cleaner down there. Fred cried pitifully, and I would have done the same if I hadn't needed to put all my energy into finding a way out of our predicament.

The wall behind me was curved. The smoke chamber must be round. I ran my fingers along the wall and discerned it was plastered—if it were lath and plaster construction, I might be able to knock a hole through it.

I braced my back against one wall and kicked at the other. Nothing gave. I tapped at the plaster gently with the back of the flashlight, and a little fell away. But the light flickered ominously, and I stopped.

I looked around frantically for something I could use as a tool and saw several wrought-iron meat hooks suspended from a beam over my head. I pulled one down and used it to attack the wall. Soon, large hunks of plaster were dropping to the floor.

I stuck my fingers in the hole I'd made to find out what was underneath the plaster. Brick. No little strips of wood held together with plaster. Nothing but solid brick. I was trapped in the attic like an idiot heroine in a Gothic novel. I fell back, ready now to give in to the tears that were very near the surface.

The murderer had won, after all. Fred and I were going to suffocate in the smoke chamber, and when we were found, smoked like a couple of country hams, everyone would assume it had been an accident. I could almost hear them tut-tutting about the stupidity of someone who'd wander into a dark room in search of a stupid old cat.

I'd have cried, if I wasn't coughing so hard. It suddenly occurred to me I was inside one of the domed towers that rose from the corners of Garnet's house. If I remembered correctly, the domes were covered with wooden fish-scale shingles. My only hope of escape was through the roof. I aimed my flickering flashlight toward the ceiling, but the upper reaches of the room were invisible in the smoky haze. If I could get up there on the beam, above the brick walls, I might be able to break through.

I stood on my toes and stretched for the beam. I could touch it, barely; its closeness tantalized me with the promise of escape.

Meowww? Fred's weak cry filled me with anguish. I bent over to offer him some comfort. "Poor baby, you didn't do anything to deserve this."

The cat carrier! If I stood on it, I'd have the extra inches I needed to pull myself onto the beam. Relief and hope flooded my body.

But I still wasn't tall enough to hoist myself up. If it weren't for the broken arm, I might have jumped and swung up. I cursed the genes that had made me disadvantaged in stature.

Maybe if I turned the carrier on end . . . I did, and heard Fred plop to the bottom. "Sorry, baby. Extra Treats later, I promise." Now, the beam was within easy reach. I threw my upper body onto it, hung on with my good left arm, and swung one leg up and over. I'm not usually athletic enough to accomplish such a maneuver, but desperation is an excellent motivator.

I pulled up to a sitting position, and then, very gingerly, with the meat hook clutched in my good hand, I stood up on the beam, swaying from side to side in the dark like a drunken gymnast. Don't look down, I told myself, just concentrate on keeping your balance and getting the hell out of here. I raised the iron hook over my head and swung with all my might at the ceiling. The rebound nearly knocked me off my feet. As wood chips and plaster rained down upon me, I struggled to stay upright. Hallelujah—no brick!

Over and over, I struck with the metal hook, until at last I was rewarded with a small hole through which I could see the beautiful star-studded sky. "We're going to be okay," I called to Fred. "Hang in there, baby." He squeaked an encouraging reply.

I continued with my frenzied hacking, jerking, pulling, and pounding to enlarge the opening. As it grew bigger, the dark cloud of smoke swirled up and surrounded me, as if as anxious to escape the tower as I was. Every thirty seconds or so, I had to stop and put my face to the gap to gasp a breath of fresh air.

The hook grew heavier, and I knew I couldn't continue much longer. Then, one last whack, and the hole was finally big enough for me to squeeze through.

"I did it, Fred. We're saved." The silence below was terrifying. I didn't know if poor Fred was dead or alive, but if he were going to have any chance of surviving I'd have to get him into the fresh air immediately.

Lying facedown on the beam, I stretched as far down as I could with a meat hook but couldn't reach the carrier. Finally, I made a chain of three hooks and snagged the handle. Ignoring the pulsing pain in my right arm, I used both hands to haul the heavy carrier onto the beam. There was no sound from inside.

I inched my way over to the hole I'd made and looked out. I was at least six feet above the steeply pitched, slate-covered roof and about forty or fifty feet above the ground. A wave of vertigo hit me, and I had to clutch the splintered wall to keep from falling. I closed my eyes until my equilibrium returned and dropped one leg outside, so I was straddling the damaged section of the dome. With my back braced against the jagged edge, I was able to reach inside with my unbroken arm and retrieve the cat carrier.

Fred was lying motionless in the bottom. I reached inside and shook him. "Wake up, boy, please wake up." He didn't react.

I tilted my head back and screamed.

"Yoo-hoo, yoo-hoo, dear . . . down here."

I stopped in mid-scream and peered over the edge of the roof. Garnet's next-door neighbor was miles below me, waving a flashlight to attract my attention. No angel of mercy had ever looked as good as that short, plump, purple-haired matron.

"Is something wrong?" she called out, winning the award for the most inane question of the year.

A cloud of smoke billowed out of the hole and surrounded me. "Fire!" she screamed. "Help—fire!"

When the smoke cleared, and I could see again, she was gone.

Within minutes, I heard the wails of sirens as a dozen fire engines and ambulances rushed toward the house. I watched with disbelief as the men below argued over which volunteer company should put up their ladder.

"Use the front door! Come up the back stairs!" I screamed, but no one could hear me through the din.

Dispute settled, one of the trucks drove onto the lawn, and the ladder began to rise. Two men in yellow slickers scampered onto the roof.

I refused assistance until they lowered Fred, in his cage, to the ground. I held my breath as one of the firemen removed his limp orange-and-white body and rushed him to an ambulance, where a medic covered Fred's whole head with an oxygen mask.

"Please, please, please . . . ," I whispered.

Two firemen sandwiched me between them and talked me down the ladder with reassuring phrases, like, "Don't look down. One step at a time. Careful. Atta girl." The ladder wobbled nearly as badly as my legs.

My last backward step took me right into Garnet's arms. I clutched at him as though I were still in danger of falling, and the tears I'd been struggling to hold back for the last hour burst through.

"Fred," I sobbed. "He's dead." It was as though my world had caved in on me. Sure, cats die, but they should die of old age, not be murdered. "I've always taken such good care of him—never let him outside where he could get hurt—made sure he had all his shots—fed him only healthy food. He didn't deserve this. It isn't fair!"

Garnet held me tighter and rubbed my back.

"Ma'am . . . ma'am."

"Go away," I mumbled into Garnet's shirt. "Leave me alone."

"Your cat, ma'am, do you want us to take him to the vet, or do you want to do it?"

"I'd rather bury him here."

"Don't think he'd care for that, ma'am."

The medic placed Fred in my arms, and he forgave me with his big yellow eyes.

"Looks like the old boy's going to be just fine, ma'am."

The curious spectators who had gathered on the lawn cheered.

"Let's go inside," Garnet said. "I think I'd better call Doc to take a look at you. I'll call Jennifer, too, and ask her to come over to check out Fred."

"Since when do vets and doctors make house calls?" I asked, feeling a hundred percent better now that I knew Fred was all right.

"When they're also good friends." He yelled over his shoulder to his assistant. "Luscious, see if you can't get everyone to go home. Tell them we're extremely grateful for all they've done."

"Yes, sir, boss."

I lay on the sofa in the den, covered with another multicolored afghan, and waited while Garnet checked the damage upstairs. He squeezed his broad shoulders out of the stairwell and brushed the cobwebs from his hair. "I can't figure out how that bolt could have slid shut like that," he said.

"It didn't slide shut by itself," I said. "Someone lured me up there by putting Fred in the smoke room, then locked me inside."

"Oh, Tori, when are you going to stop thinking there are murderers in every corner?"

"Just listen to me, Garnet. When I came home, fires were going in both fireplaces, the flues had been switched, and Fred was upstairs in the smoke chamber in his carrying cage—the bait in the trap."

Greta came bounding into the room, stripping off her jacket. "Garnet, what's happened? The lawn's all chewed up, and the southeast tower looks like it's been hit by a meteor." Doc and the vet were close behind her, so Garnet described the ordeal to all three.

While Garnet talked, Doc peered into my eyes and listened to my lungs with a stethoscope he'd taken out of an old-fashioned black doctor's bag.

"I thought those bags went out with the horse and buggy," I joked.

Doc held my wrist and looked at his watch. "I'll stop carrying it when my patients stop using horse and buggies," he said with a smile. "Your lungs sound good, pulse and temperature are normal. I probably should change your cast—this one's filthy. I could put you in the clinic overnight for observation, but I don't think it's necessary."

I shook my head. "No hospitals, please. Except for a scratchy throat, I feel fine. How about if I come in tomorrow for the new cast?"

"Fine with me." He repacked his bag.

Jennifer, who had been conducting the veterinary equivalent of Doc's examination on Fred, patted him on the head and put her instruments back into her satchel. "I do think Fred should spend the night with me. Purely precautionary," she added, seeing the worry in my eyes.

After Jennifer left with Fred, Doc said, "It's beyond my comprehension that someone would deliberately lure Tori to the tower, lock her in, and attempt to smoke her to death. How could someone have gotten in? Don't tell me that after all that's gone on, you people still don't lock the doors?"

"The doors were locked, Doc," I said. "I checked them myself before I left."

"And I suppose the key's still under the mat?"

By the guilty look that flashed across Greta's face, I knew it was.

Doc continued, "In my mind there's the big question: Why would someone want to harm you?"

"Because I know too much about Percy's death. Or at least his murderer thinks I do."

Greta spoke up. "Why does everyone assume Tori was the intended victim? I've probably got more enemies than anyone in Lickin Creek. Why not me?"

"Because Fred was the bait," I told her. "Whoever did this knew I'd be worried when I didn't find him right away and would immediately start looking for him. You wouldn't even have noticed he wasn't around."

"No, I suppose I wouldn't."

Right at that minute, I could think of nothing I wanted more than to be back in my own Hell's Kitchen apartment, watching a science fiction movie and sharing a pizza with Murray. But I was going to stay and catch a murderer—tomorrow—even if it killed me.

CHAPTER 21

Wednesday Morning

"I REALLY WISH YOU WOULDN'T DO THIS," GRETA whispered as she tiptoed with me through the front hall.

I'd taken her into my confidence, making her swear not to tell Garnet. "It's perfectly safe," I whispered back, wishing I felt as positive as I sounded.

Outside, the predawn sky was silver-gray, and graceful wisps of white mist drifted upward from the grass.

"Be careful, please," Greta pleaded.

"Don't worry," I reassured her.

She hugged me, and I dashed down the steps to where I'd left the car last night, facing the street, perfectly positioned for a quick get-away. I released the emergency brake and coasted quietly down the driveway.

This early, there was no traffic, and it was only a short time before I was out of the borough and winding my way up the Deer Tick Ridge Road. The higher I went, the thicker the fog grew. There were times when I could not even make out the white guideline on the side of the road. I drove cautiously, not wanting to take another plunge off the side of the mountain.

My stomach was full of lead, a reminder that what I was doing was both foolhardy and dangerous. Okay, I told myself, maybe this isn't the brightest idea I've ever had, but it was the only one I could come up with. Had the Grapevine worked? I wondered. Who, if anybody, would I meet today in Burnt Stump Hollow? Would it be a stranger—or someone I knew?

As I approached a treacherous hairpin turn, an enormous fog cloud shrouded the car, blinding me for a moment. It rolled across the road and was gone as quickly as it had appeared. When it cleared I saw the metal guardrail on the roadside ripped apart where someone had crashed through. Perhaps this was the very place where I'd been forced over the cliff. I shivered and slowed to an even more cautious pace.

According to the clock on the dash I was still on schedule. It was only a little past seven, and I'd told everyone I couldn't leave town until I picked up Greta's car at the garage at eight. That meant I wouldn't be expected to arrive in the Hollow before nine.

My army of uniformed protectors, led by Bill Cromwell, would already be hidden in the bushes surrounding the clearing where Aggie's trailer stood. Nothing could go wrong—I hoped.

I parked on the road, within sight of Ralph's bus. Would it be Ralph who fell into my trap? I hoped not. I liked the old man. God, this was crazy, I thought. There's nobody I don't like. I don't want anyone I know to be a murderer. But someone was, I reminded myself. A dangerous, three-time killer.

I purposely left the car where it could easily be

seen by anyone driving by and walked into the woods with all the enthusiasm of a falsely accused man marching toward a firing squad. This is going to work, I told myself. It's got to.

My footsteps were muffled by the ghostly early-morning fog. For this, I was thankful. No birdsongs, no animal cries broke the eerie silence. Once, I thought I heard something rustle in a nearby vine-draped bush. I stood absolutely still and waited, but it didn't repeat. A rabbit, I assured myself. Or even better, one of General Bill Cromwell's soldiers on guard duty.

From behind the thick trunk of a hemlock, I looked out at the clearing where Aggie's lonely mobile home stood. Good: There was no sign of anyone waiting outside for me. I was early as planned. This would give me time to get inside the trailer and look around.

"Okay, guys," I said softly to my invisible comrades-in-arms. "I'm going in. Stay close." Some leaves fluttered. It was a reassuring sound.

The door was unlocked, as I'd expected it to be. Nothing had changed in the tiny living room, yet the feeling that nearly overwhelmed me was one of abandonment.

Aggie had told me she knew who'd murdered Percy, and that she could prove it. I knew the trailer had been thoroughly examined by the State Police, but there had to be something they'd overlooked. Something so ordinary that no one would notice it. At least, I hoped so.

I began by opening the drawer in the maple end table, where I found an out-of-date *TV Guide*, some toothpicks in plastic wrappers, and two rolls of Life Savers.

The antique-reproduction washstand in the corner held a plastic fern in its basin and a supply of Hershey Bars in the base. Seeing Aggie's little hoard of candy brought her death home to me in a way that not even seeing her body had done. Tears clouded my vision.

No time for this now, I thought. I wiped my eyes and went into Aggie's cramped bedroom. The dresser drawers were open—clothes were strewn across the floor. Who could have done this, I wondered, the police or the murderer? Most likely both. The bathroom and guest bedroom were in worse shape. Police would never leave a mess like this. The killer had been here, but had he found what he was looking for?

I went outside and sat on the front steps. And waited. "Come on, you murdering SOB. Come into my trap."

It wasn't long before I heard the sound of an approaching car. How long to hike through the woods? It took me ten minutes, but I have short legs. And there could be other, shorter, paths in from the road. Five minutes, maybe three. I turned on the tape recorder in my pocket and continued to wait.

In the woods, a twig cracked. Shortly thereafter, a figure stepped out of the forest and stood on the edge of the clearing, facing me. A rifle was clutched in his right hand, and Avory Jenkins's pipe, as usual, was securely clamped between his teeth.

"Mornin', Tori," he said.

I nodded casually and stood up. "Hello, Avory."

The gun came up as though raised by an invisible string. "You was so good to Luvinia," he said, looking sad. His glasses were askew and strands of gray hair drooped across his forehead. "She truly believes you saved our baby's life by getting her to the hospital so fast. I really hate to do this, Tori. Why couldn't you have minded your own business?"

"Why'd you kill Aggie, Avory? Was she trying to get money out of you?"

The gun barrel wavered and dropped a little. Good, I thought, he's distracted.

"Money? I've got plenty of that. But I was afraid she'd take the money, then tell anyway."

"Tell what, Avory?" Keep him talking. Get it on tape. You'll be okay. Bill's men are hidden in those trees. One word from me and they'll be on top of him. I moved a step closer. I had to make sure I got his confession recorded.

"She called me Sunday afternoon—actually had the nerve to congratulate me on the baby. Said she was expecting me that night, and I'd better bring cash—lots of it—or she'd tell everyone."

I moved a little closer to him. He didn't seem to notice. "Did you come here with the intention of killing her?"

His eyes narrowed behind the thick glasses. "I had to. I couldn't let her tell. It would have been the end of everything for me. Luvinia. Our little girl. I love them more than anything in the world. I couldn't lose them!"

He sounded pitiful, but I couldn't feel sorry for him. Not when I thought of all the people he'd killed. Aggie, Percy, and Aldine would never have the chance to love anyone, ever again.

"Tell everyone what? What are you trying to hide?"

He didn't answer, and the gun barrel came up ever so slightly. I quickly asked another question. "How did you manage to get Aggie into the kettle?" I was only a few feet away from him. Please let the recorder be working, I prayed. "Why didn't she put up a fight?"

"I asked her for some of that lousy herb tea. Dropped in a handful of Luvinia's sleeping pills when she wasn't looking. She didn't suspect a thing—guess she thought I was too much of a wimp to try and stop her. Then it was easy to drag her outside and push her headfirst into the apple butter. I thought it'd look like she had an accident. She never felt a thing, Tori. She was sound asleep."

"That's the most horrible thing I've ever heard of."

"I had to do it. Luvinia would have left me."

"A lot of wives stick with their husbands, even if they go to jail. Luvinia loves you. Don't you realize she would stand by you—no matter what?"

"Jail?" His eyes were watery behind the glasses. "I don't understand you. Why would I go to jail?"

Was I talking to an idiot? I spoke to him in a voice I usually used for conversations with children. "For murder, Avory. People go to jail for murder."

Tears splashed down his cheeks. "I had no choice, Tori. You see, I thought I was safe until I met Luvinia; I was almost fifty and never dreamed I'd fall in love. We got married, then she asked me to give her a baby. I shouldn't have done it. I knew it was wrong, but I wanted to make her happy."

"What on earth are you talking about?"

"It was all your fault—you stirred everything up by finding the Hardcastle graveyard—then running all over town asking questions about my great-great-great-grandmother. It made Aggie remember the stories she'd heard about my family when she was a kid. Said she'd tell Luvinia if I didn't give her money."

Mrs. Cavender's story about the incestuous Hardcastles came back to me with a rush. Suddenly I knew what Avory's grave secret was. "Avory, your mother was Dulcie Pomeroy, wasn't she?"

He wiped tears from his face with his free hand. "You know? Oh, my God—if you know, then everybody in town's bound to. Luvinia will never understand—the baby—my God—at first I was scared to even look at her . . . all I could think of was what if she had the same condition that killed my mother's brother?"

He was crying so hard I could barely understand him. "My father found out by going through my mother's papers after she died. He said I was an abomination in the eyes of God. He hated me for being born. Until Luvinia, nobody ever cared for me."

I was nearly within touching distance of him now. He seemed to have forgotten the gun. It dangled loosely from his hand, pointing at the ground. Now was the time for Bill and his men to rush out of the woods and take him.

"Okay, guys. Get him!" I yelled.

So where was my army of guardian angels in blue? When no one responded to my cry, I realized something had gone terribly wrong.

The gun jerked up and pointed directly at me. "What's going on?" he demanded.

"The clearing is surrounded," I said. "Drop your gun."

Avory was no longer the confused, sobbing man he'd been a moment ago. Now his eyes glistened coldly, and he greeted my bluff with a scornful laugh. "Some trap," he scoffed.

The fact that he hadn't already blown my head off

gave me slight hope. I might be able to grab the gun and turn it on him, but given that I'm a foot shorter, a hundred pounds lighter, and had one arm in a cast, I thought again.

I needed to keep him talking—distract him. "What did you poison Percy Montrose with?"

He opened his mouth to answer, but before he could speak something crashed out of the underbrush and launched itself at him. A snarling jumble of brown hair and gnashing white teeth sailed through the air and attached itself to Avory's leg. Toto!

It was all the diversion I needed. I took a giant step forward, raised my right arm, and swung at Avory's head with all my might. My cast connected with his skull with a noise like a crack of thunder. He went down without uttering a sound.

Pain screeched through me like a fire engine, and a wine-dark curtain dropped over my eyes. But I stayed upright, grabbed the gun, and pointed it at the motionless man on the ground.

Toto watched me with bright eyes and wagged his stumpy tail. "Good boy," I said. I swear he smiled at me.

Avory groaned and stirred. Fearing he'd regain consciousness and escape, or, even worse, come after me again, before I could call the police, I grabbed his gun and ran to the edge of the woods, where I gathered an armful of vines. I wrapped them around Avory's wrists and ankles before he began to moan again. They didn't look too secure, so I pulled off my Liz Claiborne sling and secured his wrists.

I heard footsteps crunching through the dry mulch on the forest floor. "Bill? Is that you?" I cried.

Doc Jones shoved his way through the low-hanging

tree branches. "Tori, thank God you're okay," he exclaimed. He stared at the man on the ground. "My God, tell me that's not Avory Jenkins!"

"What are you doing here?" I stammered.

"Alice-Ann told me about your cockeyed plan to trap the killer. I came up to protect you. Good thing, too. Bill Cromwell's old van went off the road. He was taken to the Hagerstown Hospital by his men."

The realization that I'd been all alone with a killer hit me so hard I began to shake violently. Doc wrapped his arms around me and hugged me tightly. "Alice-Ann would never forgive me if something happened to you, Tori."

Avory grunted and began to struggle against his bonds.

I'd placed Avory's gun on the ground while I tied him up. Doc picked it up and pointed it at Avory. "Go call the police," he said. "I'll watch him."

I raced to the trailer and called Garnet. "Garnet, thank goodness . . ." I quickly filled him in, ignoring his irritated splutters when he learned what I had done. "I'll be there as soon as—" The end of his sentence was cut short by a loud noise coming from outside the trailer. I knew immediately it was a gunshot.

"Hurry, please. I think someone's been shot."

Doc entered the room, his clothes awry and speckled with dry leaves. "Is that Garnet?" He reached for the phone as I nodded.

"Garnet, this is Doc. Avory Jenkins is dead."

I ran outside. Avory was on the ground, his arms flung out to each side, with my scarf still tied to one wrist. The vines I'd hoped would restrain him were undone, lying in torn heaps around his body.

There was an enormous black stain on the front

of his golf shirt. I had to turn away from the hole in his chest.

Doc joined me and put a hand on my shoulder. "He got loose and grabbed my legs. Pulled me down and tried to wrestle the gun away from me. It went off . . ." He began to sob. "God knows I didn't mean to kill him . . ."

CHAPTER 22

Thursday Noon

"HOW 'BOUT SOME SHOO-FLY PIE, HON?" THE waitress asked me.

"Just coffee, thanks."

Earlier, Garnet had taken me to the clinic where Doc made sure I hadn't rebroken my arm on Avory's skull, then changed the cast. He also painted all my red, itchy, exposed body parts with an opaque white lotion. "Next time you tie someone up with vines, try to make sure there's no poison ivy mixed in."

Garnet and I then drove over to the Log Cabin, where we met Greta for a celebratory lunch. While we waited for the waitress to bring our food, he lectured me about the foolishness of getting into dangerous situations.

"It wouldn't have been dangerous if Bill had been there with his men," I said. "Have either of you heard how he is?"

My dashing protector, Bill Cromwell, driving up the mountain in his scruffy van, had lost control and gone over the edge. The men who were supposed to stand guard at Aggie's trailer had been following behind him in two cars. Naturally, they'd stopped to help him and drove him to the Maryland Trauma Center, where he was still a patient.

"Serious but stable condition," Greta said. "I talked with Maggie this morning. She said the first thing he wanted to know when he came to was if you were all right."

"Poor guy," I said. I was thinking this was another example of the lesson I should have learned a long time ago—if you depend only on yourself, you don't get let down.

I had little appetite and could eat only a few bites of food. When Greta had finished her hog maw, she stood, tapped her water glass with a fork, and called for attention. Heads swiveled to face us.

"I want you'uns to drink a toast to Tori Miracle." She raised her glass. "To you, Tori. Thanks for catching the killer."

The room rang with applause. My cheeks burned with embarrassment. "Sit down, please," I whispered to her.

"Speech . . . speech!"

Garnet gave me a little shove, and I reluctantly got to my feet. "Thank you. It was nothing, really."

"Nothing?" Greta spluttered when I sat down. "Capturing a cold-blooded murderer is nothing?"

"I'm not feeling very pleased with myself. I wanted to catch him, not kill him. Now that little baby girl is going to grow up without a daddy. She's the one who's going to suffer for his actions."

Garnet nodded. "The saddest thing of all is that Luvinia knew all about Avory's family, and she still loved him enough to marry him."

"She did?"

"Absolutely. When I went over there last night to

tell her, she told me her father had paid for a thorough investigation of his background when they announced their engagement. Rich people do things like that, I guess. She even knew about the disorder that had killed his uncle. From the description, her family doctor thought it must have been craniosynostosis, an abnormal fusing of the skull that limits the growth of the brain. She never told Avory that she knew, though."

"And she didn't care?"

"Not a bit. She said she loved him and nothing else mattered." He tasted his coffee and added cream. "But she realized it was a secret best kept quiet for the baby's sake, and when she learned you were trying to trace Hypatia's descendants, she did her best to keep you from finding out. Even went so far as to have her father pull strings to get Father Buck transferred out of the state when she discovered he was asking questions in town."

I shook my head, feeling even more depressed. "She should have known that could only postpone the inevitable. Once the townspeople started discussing it, it would be only a matter of time before someone would remember. If Avory had only talked to her about his worries, she would have told him she already knew about it, and none of this would have happened."

Greta dropped her napkin on the table. "Guess he was afraid to take that chance."

Garnet nodded. "His mother died when he was born, you know. He was raised by his father, who hated him. He impressed upon him that he should never marry."

"That's what he told me," I said. "Then Luvinia came along, and even though Avory believed that having a baby with her was wrong, he took a chance. I'm really surprised that Luvinia wasn't concerned about having a child, knowing about the family background and all."

"She was," Garnet said, "but she said her family doctor told her that often the cause of craniosynostosis is unknown. There was the possibility that it did not have a genetic origin. And, like Avory, she was thinking with her heart, not her head."

"I'm confused about something," I said. "I could have sworn Avory was a native of Lickin Creek, from his accent and because of his position in town, but I thought his father's family was from out west somewhere. Where Dulcie went to find a husband who wouldn't know about her background."

"All true," Garnet said. "But there was a family trust, leaving everything to Avory on his mother's death. The father was in control of it until Avory's twenty-first birthday, so he moved back here to keep an eye on it. According to Luvinia, the father had no qualms about living quite extravagantly on the Hardcastle fortune. Evidently Avory's father didn't consider the Hardcastle fortune as tainted as the Hardcastle blood."

I felt deep sorrow for the tragic Hardcastle family, starting with Hypatia, who, more than a hundred years ago, had been a victim, not an evil person. And her children, isolated in the Hollow, who'd repeated the only lifestyle they knew. And their children and grandchildren, who'd been the true casualties.

Guilt was weighing heavily on my heart. I thought of how miserable Avory's childhood must have been as he grew up with a father who despised him, through no fault of his own. And I knew what it had been like for him, although my own family didn't turn away from me until I was thirteen. "It really was my fault, then. If I hadn't gotten interested in that old graveyard . . . if I hadn't asked P.J. to write an article about Hypatia Hardcastle . . . Aggie would probably never have thought of blackmailing Avory."

"Don't blame yourself, Tori," Greta said. "After all, even before he killed Aggie there was Percy's murder."

Something wasn't right. Why had Avory killed Percy?

"And he firebombed the courthouse," Garnet went on, not noticing my distress. "To destroy the records. I found the empty gas cans in his shed. He only looked like a Caspar Milquetoast. Under that drab exterior lurked a ruthless killer."

I jumped to my feet, bumping the table so hard that water splashed on the table.

"Tori, what's wrong?" Garnet's eyes expressed alarm.

"I'm not sure . . . I need to think . . . Garnet, why, do you suppose, did Avory kill Percy Montrose?"

"Why? The land deal . . . Tori, what's the matter?"

"I don't feel very well. Could you please take me home?"

Ralph's yellow school bus home glimmered like a candle flame in the mist. I rapped on the door. "Ralph? Are you home?"

Toto came running toward me from the bushes, his tail making little circles in the air. I dropped to my knees and gave him a one-armed hug. "You are a good boy, yes, you are. You saved my life yesterday."

"Glad he could help, miss." Ralph stood in the open doorway of his bus.

"Hello, Ralph," I said. "I have some questions I'd like to ask you."

He took a soiled handkerchief from his pocket and dusted off one of the two bus seats that faced each other like couches. "Have a sit down," he offered. "Want a cup of tea? Got some Aggie mixed up special for me." I nodded and sat down. Toto stretched out at my feet and rested his chin on my shoe.

Ralph poured water from a plastic jug into a kettle, which he placed on a small kerosene stove, and struck a match. While he spooned herbs into two mugs, I looked around his bus home.

There was no full-size stove; neither was there a refrigerator or a sink. From the pile of blankets, pillows, and sheets on the backseat, I assumed that it was Ralph's bed.

Along one side of the bus, boards supported by piles of bricks held his possessions: two aluminum pots, a cast-iron skillet, a few chipped dishes and mugs, two neatly folded plaid shirts, two pairs of jeans, and a short stack of nearly white undershorts. On the bottom shelf were canned foods and two fifty-pound sacks of kibbled dog food. His gun stood in a corner beside a well-worn rod-and-reel.

Ralph handed me the mug with the fewest chips in the rim and sat down across from me. "Like my house?" he asked.

How to answer that? I settled for "It's—unique. I've never seen any place quite like it."

My answer seemed to please him, because he directed a gap-toothed grin at me. But his smile faded immediately, and he said, "Hollow used to be a nice, peaceful place to live in. Don't know if I'm gonna like it here without Aggie. She and me was best friends." His face twisted with anguish, and he began to blow on his tea to hide his sorrow from me.

I waited until he regained control of his emotions. Then I reached out to him and touched his hand. "I'm sorry," I said.

He wiped a tear from his eye. "Thanks, miss. You're the first one what said that to me."

"It's because of Aggie that I'm here, Ralph," I said gently. "I think you can help me."

He appeared confused. "Don't know nothing but what I heard on the radio. Avory Jenkins done killed her, then got killed himself."

"Yes, that's true. But Aggie told me she knew about someone in town who'd done a bad thing—I think she was going to . . ." I couldn't think of a nice word for blackmail.

Ralph had no qualms about using it. "She was blackmailing Avory, right?"

"Yes. Do you know if she was blackmailing anyone else?"

He shook his head.

"She must have had evidence to back up her demands. She wouldn't have kept it in the trailer—it would have been too easy for someone to find it there. She'd have wanted to hide it in a really safe place. Do you know where that place is?"

Again, he shook his head.

I was growing frustrated. "You told me she was your best friend. Best friends share things. Are you sure she didn't tell you anything about what she was doing?"

"She gave me something to hold for her. Told me not to tell anyone."

Was that the "Hallelujah Chorus" I heard playing in the background?

"Why don't you give it to me, Ralph? She wouldn't mind."

He went to the back of the bus, where he lay face-down on the floor and groped under his bed with one arm. He stretched, he grunted, and he uttered a few mild obscenities. I was beginning to fear whatever he was hunting for was gone. But after a minute, he said, "Aaaah," and sat up. In his hand was a small, crumpled brown paper bag.

Chapter 23

Friday Evening

Greta was dressed for a special occasion in an Indonesian batik skirt, dangling dragon earrings, jingling bangle bracelets, and knee-high cowboy boots, and she appeared to be in the middle of a major panic attack. She stopped her frantic pacing when she noticed I'd come into the kitchen. "The recipe, Tori—which one did you pick to be the winner? We've got to get over there right now for the ceremony."

"Is that tonight?" I hung my sweater on the hall tree.

She groaned. "Just tell me what you liked best, and I'll try and remember who fixed it."

"In a minute. I need to talk to Garnet," I said.

"He's already at the fairground. You can catch up with him there. Now hurry, please."

"This is really important. I'll call the office and have the secretary beep him."

"She won't be there. Everybody in town is at the Apple Butter Fest but us. This is Awards Night." I could hear the capital letters as she spoke the words.

I tried Garnet's number anyway. While the phone

rang, I said, "I don't really care who wins. How about that apple-sausage pizza?"

Greta made a bad-taste face. A machine answered at the police station/garage, and I hung up.

Greta waited impatiently with my sweater in her hands. I realized the faster I picked a winner, the faster we'd get to the fairgrounds. "Cookies, then. I liked the ones we had Monday."

Greta smiled, and I knew I'd chosen well. "Okay. Martina Mattress is the winner. Now, let's go," she urged.

At the fairground, Greta rushed me directly to the Cider Barrel Stage, where Bathsheba and Salome greeted me with cries of "We thought you'uns weren't coming!"

"See if you can find Garnet," I called over my shoulder to Greta. "Tell him I've got new information about—"

I was shoved up the steps to the stage by Bathsheba, who was a lot stronger than she looked. The audience greeted my arrival with enthusiastic clapping, stomping, and a few wolf whistles. *I've done it,* I thought. *I've been accepted.*

Bathsheba took a few minutes to tell of the hard work she and sister Salome had put into the Apple Butter Fest. Never once mentioning Alice-Ann's name, I noticed. "And now I'm real proud to present Lickin Creek's own well-known author, Victoria Miracle, who will present the trophy to this year's winner of the apple recipe contest." I was so thrilled to be called "Lickin Creek's own," I didn't even correct her about my name.

Mrs. Martina Mattress came forward tearfully to

accept a silver loving cup that made the Heisman Trophy look cheap. She thanked her husband for his support, her children for sampling her cookies, God for having blessed her, and me for having honored her.

"That's all, folks," Bathsheba announced. "For you'uns what wants some good eats, the Apple Princess is passing out free apple muffin samples over to the corner of Ox Roast Junction and Candied Apple Lane." I'd never seen a place clear out so fast.

"Nice job," Bathsheba offered. "Though I was surprised Mrs. Featherstone's pie didn't win, seeing as how she's one of the town's leading citizens."

I excused myself and left the stage. Where were Garnet and Greta?

"Tori, over here." Alice-Ann, arm in arm with Doc, waved at me. "We're going over to the maze. Want to come?"

"I'll be there in a minute, after I find Garnet," I called. They smiled and left.

I wandered through the happy crowd, hoping to spot Garnet or Greta. The atmosphere was carnival-like with many games of chance, pony rides, demonstrations of various country crafts, and dozens of tiny food stands filling the air with mouthwatering smells. Overhead, on the lighted Ferris wheel, kids were screaming with fearful delight. The carousel calliope provided cheerful background music for the festive scene. I envied the happy people I saw having fun; how I wished I could be enjoying the festival with them.

At last, I came upon Greta at a shooting gallery where she was popping off little ducks with a rifle. "Did you find Garnet?" I asked.

"Shhh. You'll spoil my concentration." She mowed down the last of the lineup. "I'll take the teddy bear," she told the young man behind the counter.

"No, I didn't see him," she said, admiring the ratty stuffed animal that looked as though it had reached the end of its shelf life. "But I did find Luscious, and I told him you were looking for Garnet, and he said he'd . . . Oh, hello, Zachariah."

Zachariah Mellot, the county commissioner, ignored her pleasant greeting and glared at her. Beside him, his wife, who'd once accused me of devil worship, stood with feet apart and arms akimbo as if aching for a fight.

"I suppose you're real happy now, aren't you, Greta?" he said with obvious sarcasm.

What did he mean? I turned to Greta, questioningly. She gave a "haven't got a clue" shrug and studied him with amazement. "What the hell are you talking about, Zachariah?"

"Radioactive waste. The low-level, radioactive waste dump that is *not* coming into Caven County. The one that *won't* be bringing us jobs, and money and prosperity. The dump you've been fighting against for this past year. That's what I'm talking about."

"You'd better explain," Greta said. "What's happened?"

"Bunch of know-it-alls came up from Harrisburg today. Called a special meeting of the commissioners and the council, like they own the county. Had the nerve to say the geologists did borehole drilling up there and found carbonate rock formations. They've gone and disqualified us."

"Carbonate rock can be limestone or dolomite," Greta explained to me. "They dissolve in water—then fractures open up that allow water to flow underground. That's why Lickin Creek is undermined with caves." She began to jump up and down. "We won! We're saved!" She triumphantly waved one fist in the air. "NEVER in my backyard!"

Around us, the throng began to chant, "NIMBY—NEVER—NIMBY—NEVER—NIMBY," as the Mellots slunk off.

"I'll be waiting for you—and Garnet—at the straw maze," I said, wondering if she could hear me over the clamor. I, too, was grateful the valley wouldn't be changed by the dump, but I also couldn't help wondering what would have happened to the quality of life here in Lickin Creek if it had come in. Whether the changes would have been for better or worse—we'd never know.

Bales of straw had been placed outside the maze so folks would have a place to sit while waiting to go in. Only a few people were there when I arrived, so I assumed the other fairgoers were either getting free "eats" or celebrating with Greta. I was relieved to see Garnet, who was chatting with Alice-Ann and Doc. All three were eating curious-looking loops of fried dough dusted with powdered sugar.

Garnet jumped to his feet when he saw me. "Come sit down," he said. "I looked everywhere for you and finally decided to stay still and wait for you to find me. I saved you a funnel cake." He made room for me beside him and handed me a paper plate covered with a greasy dough coil.

"Have you ever seen so many people?" Alice-Ann said happily as I sat down across from her. "This has to be the best Apple Butter Festival ever."

"Did you hear what the geologists' report said about the dump?" Garnet asked.

I nodded and forced a smile, although my lips felt leaden.

Alice-Ann hadn't heard, so Garnet told her the story. She grinned and clapped her hands. "That's wonderful news!" Her expression suddenly turned sorrowful. "Except it means Avory killed Percy for nothing."

I swallowed hard. "Avory didn't kill Percy," I said.

Greta spoke so close behind me that I jumped. "So it turns out that old Percy wasn't murdered, after all." She was standing on one foot, balancing herself by clutching Buchanan McCleary's arm. She plopped down on a bale of straw, pulled her right boot off, and began to massage her foot. "Twisted my ankle dancing," she explained.

"Want me to take a look?" Doc asked.

"You mean now you think you were wrong about Percy? That maybe his death was natural, after all?" Garnet asked me.

"It *was* a natural death," Doc said. He was kneeling before Greta, holding her ankle between his two hands. "I've been telling you that all along." He opened his ever-present black doctor's bag and said to Greta, "I'll wrap it with an elastic bandage. Should be fine."

I interrupted them. "What I said was Avory didn't kill him. But someone else did."

Garnet's face showed concern. "What are you saying, Tori? What is it that you know?"

"I'm saying Percy was murdered, just as I originally thought. And it doesn't matter who had an alibi for the night he died, because that's not when he was poisoned."

"But he couldn't have been poisoned," Doc said. "The autopsy would have found traces of something."

"Not if it wasn't a poisonous substance that killed him."

Doc rolled his eyes, and he and Garnet shared one of those "just between us men" looks that mean "humor the little woman."

"Don't tell me that now you don't think Avory killed Aggie, either? He *did* confess, didn't he?" Greta asked, putting her boot back on. "Thanks, Doc," she said with a smile.

"Oh, he did do that." I got to my feet. The time had come. "I think I'll check out your maze, Alice-Ann."

"But you said you hate mazes," she said.

I stood at the maze entrance. "I know who killed Percy and how," I said, and stepped into the black opening.

"Tori, don't . . ." Garnet's protest and the others' astonished exclamations faded away into the distance.

The baled straw towered high above me on either side, creating a narrow tunnel, through which I ran. Several times I bounced against a wall, and my broken arm pounded painfully. The sensation of claustrophobia was worse than I'd ever dreamed it could be. On the verge of near-panic, I shook from fright and from the dread of knowing what could happen. I could only hope I was doing the right thing.

I couldn't get lost, I assured myself, if I alternated right turns with left turns. Then the second right ended in a dead end. I backtracked. Now, should I turn right or left? Would I remember what I'd done coming back?

I touched the tape recorder in my pocket with my sweaty fingers. There was a brand-new tape inside.

"Tori," someone called softly.

"I'm right here," I answered. Blood rushed through my ears as my heart pounded frantically. Slowly, my eyes adjusted to the dark; the sliver of new moon above cast a faint, cold light into the maze. I leaned back against the straw and waited. My heart ached, for I knew the next few minutes were going to be some of the worst of my life.

I heard footsteps approaching. Not children, I knew. Children would be laughing, screaming, shoving each other, like the ones who were ahead of me in the maze. No, these were footsteps of a killer. I felt a cold chill of terror seize my spine.

"Hi, Tori. Alice-Ann sent me in to keep you company. She said you're frightened by mazes."

I tried to keep my tone of voice casual. "Hi, Doc. I was waiting for you."

"Me? What on earth for?"

"Don't play games, Doc. It's too late for that." I hoped I sounded confident.

He leaned back against the straw wall and studied me. "You think I killed Percy?"

"I know you did, Doc. Aggie said she had proof, and she did."

"What are you talking about?"

"An ordinary therapeutic vitamin bottle with Percy's name on it. She had Crazy Ralph hide it for her so you wouldn't be able to find it. He gave it to me yesterday afternoon."

"So what's your point? I prescribed the vitamins for Percy's anemia."

"The point is it looked like any ordinary bottle of

therapeutic vitamins. But I took it to the drugstore on the way home to have the capsules identified. You see, I've never heard of any multivitamins that you're supposed to take four times a day like the label said. The label's from the Lickin Creek Medical Clinic."

"And what did the druggist tell you?"

"The capsules were unmarked, which he thought was odd. He had to take them to a lab to have them identified. About an hour ago, he told me that they contained a prescription broad-spectrum antibiotic called chloramphenicol. The drug always comes in a very distinctive-looking capsule—so obviously it had been transferred to the unmarked capsules to disguise it."

Doc slapped his hand against his head. "Percy always was careless that way. He must have put his medicine in—"

"Drop it, Doc." I looked at his hand, covered with calamine lotion as both of mine were. "The druggist showed me his *PDR*. It said chloramphenicol should be used only for serious infections where other, potentially less dangerous drugs wouldn't be as effective. One of the illnesses it mentioned was Rocky Mountain spotted fever."

"That's right. That's what I prescribed for him when he fell terribly ill."

"The pharmacist said one of the side effects of chloramphenicol is that it can cause blood changes that may be fatal. One of them is aplastic anemia—Percy's fatal illness. You couldn't have known that would happen to him, since according to the book it doesn't occur in every case."

Doc studied me for a moment. I'd trapped him in a corner, and he knew it. "It was serendipity," he finally said. "I simply took advantage of the situation when he came down with the anemia. If I had stopped the medication he might have recovered, but if he continued taking it he was very likely to die."

"Why did you put the medicine in a vitamin jar?"

"If the medication is stopped early and the damage to the bone marrow is not great enough, the patient can recover on his own. I wanted Percy to continue taking the medicine—long enough to make sure he wouldn't get better. I filled gelatin capsules with the drug and told him the vitamins would cure his anemia. It was the perfect murder method."

"It probably would have been if only you'd destroyed the evidence."

"Where is the bottle now, Tori?"

I smiled. "Like I'd tell you."

"My plan was simple. The best ones always are. I knew that when Percy died I'd be called in as the family doctor. Then I'd be able to remove the bottle without anyone noticing. Even if someone saw it, they'd think nothing of it. It was classic—hidden like Poe's 'Purloined Letter' right under everybody's noses. How was I to know that damned old mountain crone would get her hands on it?"

Tape recorder, don't fail me now. "She was blackmailing you?"

"The woman called me and made me come out to that abominable place she called home. She called me a murderer, then demanded money from me. I pretended I didn't know what she was talking about. She told me Percy had begged her to help him when he continued feeling sick. First thing she did was ask to see his meds. Aggie was no fool, despite that mountain redneck exterior, and she knew what he showed her were not vitamin capsules. When she returned to warn him, it was too late; she found him dying. She took the pill bottle away with her, figuring even if she couldn't save Percy's life, she could still put it to good use."

"Why'd you do it? Was it the land after all? Were you one of the partners?"

"Percy double-crossed me. He fast-talked me into investing in his ski-vacation property. It was like a dream—I, Meredith Jones, the son and grandson of poor Welsh coal miners, was going to get rich and own a glamorous resort. I assumed he'd have made sure the property was approved for development before he bought it.

"After I put everything I could scrape up into it, we learned there wasn't enough water to support our planned community. It was a nightmare—worthless land we couldn't see—and it was costing us a fortune in taxes.

"I had to get some money. I had loans to pay off—the clinic hasn't even broken even, much less made a profit. And I'd borrowed on the building to get the money to invest in the ski resort. If I had to close the clinic, it would have left Lickin Creek without any medical care. I couldn't do that to the town."

The town needed him! How altruistic.

"And then there was Alice-Ann to think of—all those debts her late husband left her with. She was going to have to sell her home to pay his creditors off. How could I ask her to marry me when I couldn't support her any better than he did?"

How dare he bring Alice-Ann's name into this?

"When the dump company began looking at our land as a possible site, I thought that was the solution to my problem. They were offering us far more than we'd put into it. Then Percy turned into a tree-hugger, and he persuaded Aldine to vote against selling it. We had an agreement written in our partnership saying all decisions about the property had to be unanimous. Percy and Aldine were both rich. They didn't need the money. I was desperate."

"How did you kill Aldine? The nurses said he had no visitors the day he died." I wanted to keep him talking—get it all on tape.

"Easy. I left the clinic right after Luvinia's baby was delivered and drove to Harrisburg. Walked right into the hospital wearing a white coat with a stethoscope dangling from my pocket. Doctors aren't considered visitors. He was sleeping and already had an IV tube in; it only took a second to inject a toxin into the bag. I was gone before it reached his system."

"And then you shot Avory, so I'd believe he'd killed Percy as well as Aggie?"

"Serendipity, again. I was hiding in the bushes waiting to see if Aggie's murderer would show up. I planned to kill both of you and make it look like he'd done it. I waited to hear what Avory had to say, just in case he knew where the vitamin bottle was hidden. Fortunately, you knocked him out before he could tell you he hadn't killed Percy. Then it occurred to me if I shot him, then untied him, while you were inside, there'd be no need to kill you. You'd already heard his confession."

I nodded. "That's when you got the poison ivy on your hands, isn't it?"

He glanced down with a surprised look as if he'd forgotten that. "I never wanted to hurt you, Tori. You mean too much to Alice-Ann. Even the poisoned pie was only meant to scare you—there wasn't enough arsenic in it to kill you, only make you sick."

"How can you say you never meant to hurt me? How about those aspirins you gave me before I drove to Harrisburg? They were sleeping pills, weren't they? I could have been killed on the highway?"

"You weren't." He smiled smugly.

"And then you attempted to smoke me to death."

"I only planned to have you find the dead cat. I knew that would send you home to New York. But you came back earlier than I expected, before the cat died, so I decided to lock you in with it.

"Why are you talking to me like this, Tori?" he asked. "Why didn't you tell Garnet what you knew?"

"Because I wanted you to have the opportunity to break the news to Alice-Ann before I told him." As soon as I said it, I realized I'd made a huge mistake.

Moonlight glinted on his teeth as he smiled. "That was a fatal error of judgment on your part, Tori, not telling anyone."

I suddenly knew the meaning of fear. "Let's go," I said, trying to regain control of the situation. "Garnet will be looking for us."

"No." He reached into his pocket. For a gun, I feared, but what he pulled out was a cigarette lighter. He flicked the wheel, and fire appeared to shoot from his fingertips. "I'm not giving myself up," he said.

The tiny orange light went out, and he stepped

close to the dry straw wall of the maze. "It'll be fast," he said. I heard the awful clicking sound again, and a new flame leaped to life.

Dear God, the man was going to burn us both to death. "No!" I gasped. I couldn't scream for my mouth was dry. "You can't do that," I croaked.

"Just watch me. I can't face Alice-Ann. It's better to go this way." The lighter was only inches away from the wall.

"Doc, there are children in this maze. They won't be able to get out." His hand stopped moving, and he looked at me.

"Think about the children, Doc. You probably delivered most of them. You've saved their lives, set their bones, comforted them. Do you want them to die in here?" I was counting on Doc's years as Lickin Creek's only healer to take over—to pull him back from the madness that had taken him over.

As if to emphasize my words, children's laughter drifted back toward us. Doc dropped the lighter and sank to the ground, knees drawn up to his chest, his head buried in his arms.

I took a deep breath and grabbed the lighter with my shaking hand. Everything was going to be all right.

"Tell Alice-Ann I loved her," he whispered, so softly I could barely hear him.

"I'll be right back," I told him and went to find Garnet. Left turn, right turn, dead end. I had to get out. Had to find Garnet. Another dead end. The walls were closing in on me. Utterly frustrated, totally lost, facing another wall of straw, I screamed. I only stopped when Garnet's reassuring arms wrapped around me.

We rushed back into the heart of the maze, losing our way over and over again, until we finally came upon Doc, still bent over in a fetal position with his head resting on his knees. At first I thought he hadn't moved at all, but when Garnet touched his shoulder he slowly toppled over sideways.

His black bag lay open on the ground next to him, an empty hypodermic needle beside it.

CHAPTER 24

Wednesday Morning

CASSIE KRINER WAS P. J. MULLIN'S EFFICIENT part-time secretary and gofer. Today she was attempting to teach me all about the workings of the *Chronicle* in a few short hours. Yesterday, P.J.'s condition had turned much worse and she'd been taken to Baltimore for immediate surgery. I had been thinking about turning down her offer of the temporary editor's job and accompanying Garnet to Costa Rica, but this changed everything. I couldn't let P.J. down when she needed me so desperately.

Garnet came in and tossed his hat on the brass hall tree. He nodded hello to Cassie and crossed the room to kiss me.

"I'll make a pot of coffee for us," Cassie said, tactfully leaving us alone.

"Whatever you do, don't drink it," Garnet warned me with a grin. "I've heard *Guinness* is creating a new category just for her: world's worst coffee maker."

It was good to laugh with him once again. There had been no reason for laughter during the past four days since we'd rushed Doc to the closest hospital, in Maryland, where he'd died without ever regaining consciousness. Alice-Ann was inconsolable and had left yesterday, with her son, to stay with her mother in Seattle. I knew it would be a long time before she got over this. Having it happen so soon after her husband's murder made it doubly hard on her. And Garnet, who had considered Doc his best friend, was so depressed he could barely talk.

"The autopsy results came in today," Garnet said. "Doc injected himself with a neuromuscular blocking agent, curare, that's normally used to promote muscle relaxation during surgery. Fast acting. Caused respiratory failure. Probably painless." His voice faded.

"It doesn't sound like the kind of thing he'd carry around routinely in that little black bag of his," I said.

"He must have known he'd be found out, eventually. He was prepared for the worst."

How very strange it was, I thought, that this quiet little town had harbored two murderers, linked together by a pathetic woman who had tried blackmail as the way to escape poverty and had lost her life as a result.

"Hey there, cheer up." Garnet was smiling at me. "Not everything's bad. The dump company has moved on to search for greener pastures; Greta and Buchanan are working with the historical people from Harrisburg to preserve the graveyard; Luvinia's taken her baby back to Virginia to live, far away from Lickin Creek gossip; and Maggie's fiancé, Bill, is recovering nicely from his accident.

"You've got the *Chronicle* under control." He glanced around at the stacks of papers piled everywhere. "Or soon will have. And we've got ten days before I leave. Let's make the best of them."

"I'd like that," I said. "Very much."

Applesauce-Oatmeal Cookies

The Prizewinning Recipe by Mrs. Martina Mattress

1¾ cups all-purpose flour
½ teaspoon baking soda
½ teaspoon baking powder
½ teaspoon salt
1 teaspoon cinnamon
½ teaspoon cloves
½ teaspoon nutmeg
¾ cup raisins
1 cup quick oatmeal
½ cup butter
1 cup sugar
1 egg
1 cup unsweetened applesauce
½ cup chopped walnuts

Preheat oven to 350 degrees. Sift flour with baking soda, baking powder, salt, and spices. Stir in raisins and oatmeal. In a separate bowl, cream together butter and sugar; add egg and beat until fluffy. Add dry ingredients alternately with applesauce to the creamed mixture. Stir in nuts. Drop by teaspoonfuls onto greased cookie sheet. Bake at 350 degrees for 15 minutes.

Makes about 3½ dozen cookies.